Fool Me Fool You

Russell Campbell

Chapter 1

Ever fancied becoming a crook but been too scared? Everyone's thought about it at some point or other because if we're being honest, *life is all about incentives*. Don't we all ultimately become bored with our assumed characters, almost incarcerated within our own existence, and desperate to do something?

To lie and cheat?

I was probably better primed than the average person because I worked for Scottish Chartered Bank. "Bank"—a dirty, four letter word. I know, I'm sorry. And what's worse, I was something of a spin doctor as I ran a foundation that manipulated events to make the bank look like a great corporate citizen.

After the slash and burn tactics had shaped the bank into a much leaner organisation, it meant that there was more work on my plate, tedious management without much reward. Feelings of emotional rescue for having avoided the chop quickly subsided and I resumed the fear of the career flat-line. Where was the challenge? Or the money, for that matter? Contentment is a transitory phenomenon, and I could feel the incentives seeping away just as winter steals the warmth.

Wouldn't I have been better off just being sacked? At least that would have provided the catalyst for doing *something*. Travelling the world. Buying a bar. Playing the market when stock values were volatile. But no, I'd dropped into a secure safety net, and the inertia proved to be a huge disincentive for doing anything other than going through the corporate motions. Turning up at work at 8.00 a.m., yes sir no sir, a million bags full sir (none mine), hurried lunch, post lunch corporate bullshit, yes sir, no sir, three bags un-emptied, kissing the ass of a capricious boss and finishing at 7.00 p.m., rush hour, and then more after hours work to ensure that things didn't implode. Life was becoming one big excuse for a Prozac fix.

Until, by chance, I encountered the inspiration for my crime.

When I first met Doug Fox, he appeared something of an enigma. The odd, purple designer glasses coupled with an attitude of slight superiority triggered my curiosity. An inch or two shorter than me, with slightly unkempt curly brown hair, he generated the impression that he was a subtle catalyst when it came to making something meteoric happen. Like a poacher in a football match, almost stationary for the first 89 minutes, but he then toes in a last minute winner to the rousing acclaim of the crowd. Someone who seemed naturally lucky.

Doug had appeared at a charity function where Scottish Chartered had sponsored a table. The function was being held in the Caledonian Hotel, less than a mile from the bank's headquarters. Doug had sat across from me during dinner in the seat my girlfriend, Mandy, had been due to occupy. Mandy's laryngitis had been my apparent gain, as Doug, who explained that he had been working for one of our competitors on an IT consultancy job at the time, had literally turned up for a five minute chat with another banker which resulted in his being cajoled into taking the spare place. The fact that he'd appeared out of context showed a certain networking confidence—determination even—that I couldn't help but admire. During an increasingly drunken conversation, I discovered that behind his public persona lay another individual equally pissed off with life; someone hungry for a project that would bring personal returns.

This mutual dissatisfaction with life morphed into a pint a couple of weeks later. When Doug called and made the suggestion, Mandy had encouraged me to go out, hinting that I needed more of a life outside work. She instructed me to hit the town with another "loser" before no one at all would spend the time of day with me. This was characteristic of Mandy, stated in apparent jest but delivered with more than a hint of criticism.

I'd been seeing Mandy for about six months. She was distinctly different from girls I'd dated previously—a confident, 29 year-old who knew what she wanted, including a high octane career. A Czech national, she'd lived in London until recently but had relocated to Edinburgh to pursue a new opportunity. Her shoulder length auburn hair and striking jade eyes often elicited stares from other guys as I looked on, and although I sometimes revelled in the reflected kudos, such occurrences sometimes verified my own sense of insecurity. She shared a luxury pad with a friend in Murrayfield Avenue, an upmarket district of Edinburgh. It outshone my own flat in Stockbridge, though I'd been attempting—unsuccessfully—to get her to move in with me and simultaneously dump her flat mate.

Doug and I met at the Elle Bar, a trendy place on a prominent corner on George Street. This was a former bank branch, ironically, replete with large wrought iron window-bars. Seemingly, the name and demeanour of the pub were supposed to attract beautiful women, yet they were strangely absent that night. Doug ordered two pints of Carling lager and immediately started asking lots of questions.

In market research there is a principle that those undertaking an in depth interview initially ask more generic questions, and only once a respondent becomes more comfortable, do more penetrating or personal questions arise. Human beings often need to be coaxed into a sense of assurance, and will only volunteer how much they earn or how often they change their underwear once they're more relaxed. In a similar manner, Doug's questions slowly evolved to enquire about my finances and aspirations, not something I'd normally discuss with a new acquaintance.

In my own case, the conversation increasingly focused on career disappointment. Wasn't it all so unjust? Wasn't life expensive? Weren't we due a bigger share? What would we be willing to do about it? Doug ventured an old adage about dissatisfaction—how in a given situation we had three choices; live with it, leave it or change it. I said I was currently living with it, and then I'd probably leave it. *Pathetic*, he said. And then he casually dropped in a telling question.

'How honest would you say you are, Ally?' He looked me straight in the eye.

I thought about his question for a moment, scratching my nose. 'Pretty honest. As honest as the next guy.'

'You just scratched your nose, a sure sign of a lie. Discomfort with what you were about to say. And you also *hesitated* before answering. A split, noticeable, second. And you're saying that you think the next guy—Joe Average—might not actually be any less honest?' He was measuring me up.

'Everyone's dishonest sometimes, Doug. I read an article in *The Times* a few months ago that quoted research on honesty, with the average person telling something like two thousand lies per annum, depending on the definition of a lie.'

He raised his eyebrows. 'I bet you got that statistic wrong. Or made it up. But it doesn't matter, does it? Minor lie? Sure it wasn't on Google or the *Wall Street Journal*? What matters when you lie is whether there's *something in it for you*.'

I said that he was being cynical, that white lies were probably harmless.

'How about stealing, then?'

Again I hesitated, engendering a crooked, raised eyebrow from Doug. Even though we were more than half way through our beers, he winked at me then motioned to a waitress for service. The waitress, with a bright pink badge boasting the name 'Suzie', appeared and smiled pleasantly.

'Hey Suzie, there's something up with the beer,' Doug said. 'I didn't want to make any fuss at first,' he continued, 'in case it was the meal I had earlier on, but after half a pint, I'm sure I was right. Can I have something else?'

'Oh, I'm sorry about that,' Suzie said, picking up the two glasses. 'What would you like?'

'Oh…something different—something premium.'

Suzie returned a couple of minutes later with an apology from the management, two new pints of Peroni on the house, together with snacks. When she moved away Doug assumed a smug, satisfied air.

'Did we just steal something there or not, Ally?'

'I note the insertion of the first person plural.'

'Well buddy, you were complicit because you said nothing, even though you knew it was a lie. You sat on your butt and accepted a full new pint, an apology for no wrong doing and some nibbles. An accessory before, during and after the fact. It even delayed your round, so you benefitted more than me. Guilty?'

'As charged.' I sat back, happy to be corrected, a pint up.

The conversation drifted to football and women, as it often does with blokes, whether they know each other well or not. When we eventually left the Elle Bar, Doug leaned forward in a more conspiratorial manner. 'Just think, Ally. What if that little free pint transaction had been worth a seven figure sum?'

Scottish Chartered's tinted glass dome and sandstone-effect frontage alluded to its current status as a modern, progressive bank. *A new building for a new millennium*, the slogan had declared when the company decided to create a city centre new build after demutualisation. It stood amongst a blend of old and new architecture near the Edinburgh International Conference Centre, the tinted windows perhaps a sign of the opaque nature of the business. Inmates in the building called it the *Dosh Dome*, including, apparently, the board of directors, though after the banking crisis the phrase had acquired a certain hollow resonance. I parked and entered the building, negotiating the tight security entry system that the company insisted upon despite the fact that financial crime and other such threats were now principally electronic.

I enjoyed a second floor corner office with a partial view of Edinburgh's famous landmark castle, though also one of the city's notoriously congested traffic on the street below. The constant flow of buses and cars often provided a counter to those on the other side of the glass walls of my office.

As I logged on the company's intranet I spotted Kostas on the other side of the internal glass partition. Kostas could be described as humorous yet sincere; a colleague who possessed a doctorate in mathematics, and appeared capable of cracking the most complex IT conundrum whilst simultaneously telling a sick joke his kids had brought home from school. A short, dark Athenian, he'd been in Edinburgh since his student days and had acquired a lilting Scottish-Greek inflection. He'd initially been accepted into medical school in Greece when he was seventeen, achieving the best technical test scores of all applicants, though he'd declined an opportunity to enter the profession because of a bizarre dispute with his own doctor at the time. I'd formed the impression that he'd never gotten over that decision.

Kostas's dark eyes darted to the side, prompting a covert message with one finger: *your boss is coming.*

It was often said in the office that you smelled Leslie Weir before you saw him. The plentiful cologne—perhaps the product of Christmas and birthday gifts to a man devoid of a genuine personality—remained in a given space long after his departure, which usually couldn't come too soon. Perhaps he had a body odour problem; like the rest of the office I suspected this made sense but I feared proof of such a revelation first hand. Ignorance can indeed be bliss. I avoided too much time in his company for his nebulous actions, dismissive command of those he condescendingly (and often erroneously) considered beneath him and his perfection of smugness. I toiled under the leadership of Attila the Pedant.

As Weir entered my office, strong aftershave immediately penetrated the limited air space. He was only one step off director, enjoying a senior link role in management, where he floated between PR, Marketing, Finance and the foundation, pulling rank whenever the opportunity arose. He was also on the board of trustees for the foundation, thus directly influencing charitable spending decisions.

'Need a report on this charity foundation stuff,' he grunted, surveying the view outside.

Abrasion was his style. "Hello", "how are you?" etcetera, were rarely used except in grunt form. Associated small talk about family or football was totally absent from his repertoire.

'Nice of you to come down Leslie,' I said. 'What sort of report can I do for you?'

'Justification. Are you aware the whole foundation costs more than twenty million per annum. That's way too expensive.'

I felt a strange twang in my stomach.. This was the first time he had made such a complaint. The foundation was pretty fairly efficient, and the cost of reaching our target audience was very low. The efficacy of the project in reaching key corporate and political *decision makers* was even better. We made contacts in industry, show biz and politics that were difficult to generate in other ways—engaging the kind of opinion leaders from whom every successful business needs endorsements. Hell, the foundation was tax efficient as Inland Revenue rules permitted charitable donations to be tax deductible providing that certain criteria were met.

'Justification?' I asked, cautiously.

'Justification,' he replied, curtly.

I cleared my throat. 'I'm surprised you say that, Leslie. The global cost, as you know, is cheap compared to alternatives. Someone's got to get the exposure for the bank.'

'Yes, but you waste money here. Things could be outsourced.'

I gritted my teeth. *He* drifted around wasting money. He got involved with senior staff in any junkets—playing Santa Claus with other people's money—enhancing his claim for the 'brown envelopes' with share options and bonuses that arrived annually on the desks of certain members of senior staff.

'Leslie, you said at the outset that it was essential we ran all this from the *inside*.' I clearly remembered the day he had said it.

'Not true. Certainly, I did engineer the corporate strategy for the whole process, which allowed this to happen. But you have the responsibility of delivering and justifying *your* costs.'

Lying bastard. This intrusion was infuriating, but then I needed my job. I didn't fancy breaking the news to Mandy that I'd been fired for making a fatal error over trivia—an idiot unable to construct a report justifying his position. She'd really love that.

I said, 'The CEO seemed happy with everything as far as I was aware.'

'He's abroad, and not likely to be back.' The CEO had suffered a family tragedy and was being treated for depression.

I sighed, just loudly enough for Weir to hear. 'What exactly is it that you need from me?'

'A plan to save money. I'm not asking - I'm *telling*.'

'Okay...I'll speak to someone on the board directly to get further clarification.' I suggested this to tie him down.

'No you will not. Don't raise this with anyone else—senior or junior—understand? You need to report to me in absolute confidence.'

'But what if I need to ask other staff for information?' I asked.

He wandered over to the door, suddenly turning. 'Don't. Undertake some independent research. And keep this report focused. Outline how you could cut costs downstairs. You could even get a bonus. Have something for me inside a week.' He then marched out of my office without another word.

I had a strange sensation of being hit by the carrot as well as the stick. A *week*—just like that. Who did he think he was? Alan fucking Sugar?

The phone rang. Mandy.

'Hey, how's it going?' Her voice sounded a little husky, as if she'd just delivered a full blown blues song, although the Eastern European inflection often conveyed such.

'Pretty shit, actually. That clown Weir has just torpedoed my morning,' I explained.

'Making you work for a change?' she asked.

Where was I going to start? Mandy was the sort of person who saw tenacity as a necessity in life, and she often treated obstacles as opportunities. She sometimes alluded to a determined streak gifted by her father, who apparently had her on the tennis court at three years of age, primed never to give up. *She* wouldn't let Weir's bluster faze her.

'Just been told to slice though the foundation and fire people. A quiet morning at the office,' I said.

'I take it you're up for the challenge.'

'I've still got you if I get the sack.'

'Ally, don't sound so negative.'

'It just came from left field, as the Yanks say. Oddly enough, that guy Doug I was out with for a pint was saying how unrewarded we all are at work—you know—how the fat cats get all the cream—and now *this* happens.'

'Maybe you'll get a rise out of it,' Mandy suggested.

'Weir's parting shot was along the same lines. But what about those who might get the boot?'

'Not your problem. Oh, by the way, tonight's going to be out, so I'll see you tomorrow. Fix your work problems. And remember one other thing.'

'What's that?'

'I don't date losers.'

Chapter 2

The next morning, I put my messages on hold for an hour and ventured outside my office. I'd been brought up in the West Highlands and still harboured an intermittent desire to move back one day, for a little fresh air, among other things. But even city air would suffice right now. I avoided the team in the basement—I often popped in even when not required, just to show a little presence, but at this juncture I did not want to face that particular group. As the cool late morning air kissed my cheeks I felt minor relief at having exited the Dosh Dome. I navigated the rear car park, which was nearly full and coincidentally passed my own, old Audi estate. This was something of a tank that I'd promised Mandy I'd ditch, but nostalgia had displaced rationality on the babe-car axis. Parked adjacent to it was something she'd actually respect—a Mercedes SL 500 Sport, with a metallic charcoal finish and a new plate. I hesitated and briefly looked in as I passed. It even smelled new from the outside. As I veered left towards the street, a voice echoed from the car park behind.

'Casing the joint to nick my wheels?' Doug stood with his hands on his hips, sporting a broad grin and a maroon scarf.

'That's two clichés in one sentence. But as you're asking, I could use some more hard cash. This yours?' I asked, already realising the answer.

'Yip.'

'Nice mover. You must be doing all right. The depreciation on that machine must dwarf my last bonus,' I said, with not a little envy.

'Thought you didn't get bonuses anymore?'

'Thanks for reminding me, Doug.' I changed the subject. 'What brings you here? You didn't say you'd be visiting the other night.'

'Hadn't intended to. Just popping in for a bit of this and a bit of that. Picking some underpaid brains, you could say.' He suddenly appeared more serious. 'Listen, bud—got time for a coffee?'

'Sure.'

'Hey, watch this, mate,' Doug said. He flipped the remote and the electro-hydraulic roof mechanism engaged automatically, personifying German engineering.

We headed round the corner to a small Italian cafe on Grove Street that I sometimes visited. They made fresh biscotti and the seductive aroma of exotic coffees from round the globe provided the perfect counter to any hectic morning. When we entered the cafe, Doug unravelled the scarf and sat across from me at a window table.

'Look at this place.' I motioned to the bustling staff. 'It's always busy. If you think about it, it's all about basics, isn't it? People have to eat and drink. I can see why folk like bankers often want to escape and run cafes or hotels—to do something tangible, something real,' I suggested.

'Nothing's real, mate. And this is all too labour-intensive for me. Too many staff bumping into each other. If someone's off sick the next person has to run about twice as hard while pissing off the customers for being slow. Machines break, business rates and VAT never go away. Sure, I'm all for *other* people doing leg work, but I wouldn't want to employ them personally.'

'I've realised that you are a tad cynical. But hey—getting others to do the graft while not employing them sounds fair enough to me.' I watched Doug's reaction, an almost imperceptible smile appearing.

'Glad you're coming over to my way of thinking, mate. So why were you clearing the building? Avoiding the bureaucracy? Or has that considerate boss sent you out to buy the cookies?' he asked, casually.

'Bit of both,' I replied.

'So there's a hole at the centre of Scottish Chartered's business? Next they'll be paying you in Polo Mints in lieu of a salary.' Although Doug was clearly fishing, I felt like a moan—what harm could it do?

'You've got a point. Don't get me wrong, the balance sheet is fine in that company. They've restructured and are way ahead of some of these other basket cases we had in the industry. That's not the problem. The crux is that they can never save enough in terms of costs.'

'Facing the squeeze?'

'Possibly. But that's confidential so you'll get a kick in the nuts if you tell anyone.'

'My nuts will remain intact. Hey, what if I tell you something else that's also confidential?' He eyed me carefully, reducing the tone to below the ambient bustle of the cafe. Perhaps there was equity in trading secrets.

I sat back in my seat. No doubt there would be a lecture on why entrepreneurs never work for others, or how we could get a free cake or some shit out of Luigi, the cafe owner. Luigi would wonder what the hell I was doing if I suddenly started to complain about cold coffee or some other fake grievance. Doug cleared his throat, as if initiating an important sermon.

'Ally, what you do works for the bank. I know that. You didn't need to explain it to me at the charity bash. I've seen the evidence splashed all over the business media. Christ, your company has even appeared in product placement in movies. But that's not the point. From what you've said yourself, the management at the bank doesn't appear to genuinely appreciate it—or you—one iota. You're just an unwanted cost, right? I've been giving your foundation some thought since the night we spoke.'

'And what's that?' I asked. He'd gained my attention.

'You should run this thing more for *your* benefit and a little less for someone else's,' Doug said, pointing his empty coffee cup directly at me.

'Easier said than done,' I replied. 'It's kind of odd that we're having this conversation, though. My boss seems to think I can pull a magic rabbit out of the hat, cutting costs and increasing the media impact in one fell swoop,' I explained.

'There you are. But what if there was a method of saving the bank a packet, and *simultaneously* generating money for *you* at the same time?' The enthusiasm seeped through. 'Aren't you going to buy me another coffee for the free consultancy?'

I ordered two more lattes, my interest kindled. Doug leant forward in a conspiratorial manner. It seemed as if other customers were suddenly interested—maybe the pensioner to my right was a plant for the board? Doug had begun to whisper.

'Look Ally, I'm deadly serious. You're sitting on a marvellous opportunity but you can't see it because you're too close to the action. What's that old business saying about working *on* your business instead of *in* your business? In your case you should be working for *yourself* rather than on someone else's business.'

'Doug, you're talking in riddles, and why the sudden interest in me?'

'Because I have a plan.' An articulated bus passed the cafe, sloshing the contents of a large puddle over those still waiting at an adjacent bus stop.

'Want to stay in the slow lane like these fuckwits out there?' he asked.

'No.' I was being honest. 'But I wish you'd spit out your plan.'

'At last, some guts showing through. Good. Now, listen. This stays with us—all right?' He extended a hand which I duly shook, curious as to what was coming next.

'Everyone loves to *look* like they are giving to charity. No one likes to look like they are *avoiding* giving to charity. And if they give, they would prefer that it's someone else's money, or better still, that it's actually a tiny amount because at heart they're all miserable bastards. Are you with me so far?'

'You're a cynic.'

'I'm a realist.' He sat forward, toying with an empty biscotti wrapper. 'Ignoring the bank's current account holders, who are more difficult to tap, you have something like nine million web-based deposit account holders here and overseas, seven million pension plan holders, and how many mortgagees—four or five million? Even if some have multiple financial products you have more than twenty million, let's say…*opportunities*?'

'I suppose that's about right. You've been doing some homework,' I said, before Doug leaned in closer, eyes fixed, fingers poised in a revolver shape.

'I've done a lot of homework.'

'Like what?' I asked.

'Hear me out. You could restructure your whole foundation. Instead of the bank paying for the PR, the *customers* should be paying. These millions of customers simply need to be asked for a web-based donation. It even works on the phone. Look, three American academics called Goldstein, Martin and Cialdini conducted a study about charitable donations for the American Cancer Society. Once the researchers had introduced themselves they politely asked if respondents were "willing to give a small donation." For half the sample, the question ended there, and for the remaining group, the researchers added "*every penny would help*". The results were that while 28 percent of people donated to the first request, 50 percent responded to the second. In fact, for every hundred prospects, they got $72 from those hearing the 'every penny' line and just $44 from the rest. And all that was via blind, unsolicited requests from people that the respondents had never met. In fact, these were people with whom they had no prior relationship, whereas your bank's customers already have existing relationships with the bank, some for decades. And they wouldn't miss a small amount. In fact, it would make them *feel better* about their pathetic lives. And you don't ask them to opt in—you only vaguely offer them the opportunity to opt *out*. The wording has to be legal, but it can easily be done.' Doug may have looked like someone half way through a hard sell, but he was beginning to soften me up.

'Okay Doug. Let me extrapolate. You're suggesting that I ask the bank's customers for a small amount each, say one pound for each financial product they have with us, in lieu of twenty million or so the bank currently puts into the foundation? Is that it?'

Doug nodded, but hidden behind the affirmation was a more sinister glint in his eye. A toddler knocked over a cup at another table causing a minor commotion. I hesitated, momentarily distracted as I digested Doug's plan, though I knew by now that there was clearly more to it.

'Go on. I suspect that the really confidential part is still to come, right?'

'Correct. I know for a fact that your bank does not currently request online charitable donations directly from customers, so this would be a first ask. But given that the majority of accounts you run are web-based savings accounts, this is actually the easiest forum in which to elicit low value donations. This has been confirmed by research here and in the States,' Doug said.

'And what about my team? Would they still be utilised in the same way?'

'Nope. Unwanted cost.'

'What? The staff would have to go?'

'Fuck the staff. Chuck them in with those marketing wankers. Fire them. Who cares? It's dog-eat-dog in the real world and if you don't fight a little harder, you'll be next, pal.'

'That's a bit rash,' I said. 'These people have mortgages to pay, Doug.'

'So do you, I assume, but do *they* care about *you*?' Doug replied, shaking his head. 'But never mind that. You won't need all the staff, but you will need some kind of organisation to do the work. A cheaper organisation. How much does your team cost in salaries at the moment? Between one and two million, I guess?'

'How do you know that?' I was surprised, but then perhaps I shouldn't have been.

'A guess. Come on, you told me how many were in your team, add in all the usual extra costs in the PR game—anyone can do the arithmetic.'

'So what are you suggesting?'

'You need to outsource it. Simple as that.'

'I'm trying to avoid taking this approach with my boss, Doug. You say we should outsource? Bangalore?' I asked, facetiously.

'Don't knock Bangalore. Look, you can still attend events to squeeze palms. But in order to receive the donations, you insist on the charities you donate to making the spin *for you*...think about *their* motivation here. They're lazy bastards, these guys. It should be no spin from them, no money from the bank. You could even let your boss choose all the charities. He could indulge his ego while bolstering the bottom line.'

I cleared my throat. 'Doug, there are two other big questions from my perspective.'

'Let me guess,' Doug replied. 'In reverse order. Number two: will it work if you don't control it?'

'Well, yes.'

'How can you *really* measure the exact impact of what you do right now?' he asked. 'It's not *that* scientific. How do you know for a fact it might not work another way? You could still use your media contacts, albeit through a different, cheaper conduit,' he said. 'Bribe some of the more dodgy ones in the media to get some space and favourable comment. It happens all the time. You *know* that. And don't tell me you're beyond devising a little spin yourself—getting the message to Scottish Chartered's management that there's a marvellous job being done? And your second question? I bet I can guess that too.'

'Go on.' I was curious about this one.

'Ally, you're wondering what's in it for *you*.'

'Are you some sort of mind reader?' I asked.

'Just being logical. With the money you'll be earning out of this, you won't care if you've a job in the bank in three or four years.'

As a consequence of my confusion, he was suddenly looking ultra smug.

'Why's that?'

'Ally, you'd be raking in rewards because you'd *control* the company to which you'd outsourced the work, a shell company that essentially sends out donations under instruction. For a very lucrative professional reward.'

I shook my head but he simply nodded in response. 'Doug, this is *unethical*. You must know that. Even if I could persuade them to run with it, there would be a huge conflict of interest. How could I tell my boss that I'm scamming a big slice of charitable donations on the fly, that X Ltd is actually Ally Ltd in disguise?'

'You won't be telling him anything of the sort. This is where I come in.'

Then the penny finally dropped.

'You mean that *you'd* be running the outside company. Well, me…and *you*?'

'Bingo. At last we get there! Your *name* would be nowhere in sight. Don't you see how cool this idea is? Under a corporate guise, I rig alternative quotes from other fictitious organisational agencies, and the lowest one also happens to be the *best* in terms of a plan we set out—to suit *us*. They'll buy it because it suits the bottom line.'

'But what about the ethics of all this?' I asked.

'Look, Ally, the customers would get a cheap feel-good fix – they donate loose change. *They* support the charity work. The company saves a packet. The PR still gets done. But the icing on the banking cake is that you get a decent slice for once in your life. There are no losers here.'

'I could lose my job.'

'Not if this is done discreetly. And there's something else. I already have part of the mechanism in place for something like this set up, including an offshore incorporation. This baby would be ready to go as quick as you can redeploy or fire the staff. I've already done a large chunk of the administration work because I saw the potential opportunities for an idea like this in financial services a while back. Forward planning for another venture, if you like, but that's another story. When I met you I thought, *bingo*. This would fit. But if you don't bite, someone else will, and instead of you, *they'll* be sitting on a yacht with the cocktails in two or three years.'

Doug stood up, and swung the scarf round his neck. He was the consummate salesman and there was a post-pitch confidence about him that I couldn't help but admire.

'I'll need to go, bud. Have a think about it. Have another coffee. No pressure. If you want to remain a serf, fair enough.' He smiled. 'But give me a ring either way. And keep this to yourself.'

And with that he departed. I sat in the cafe for another five minutes, contemplating his proposal.

I didn't see Mandy until forty-eight hours later when we met for dinner after work. She wore a sleek black dress that barely reached mid thigh, and matching high heels. We'd chosen the *Fire Dragon*, an intimate little Thai restaurant on Castle Street in the city centre. I was going to leave the whole charity debacle and Doug's concept aside for the moment, until I gathered my thoughts. We ordered a bottle of Pouilly-Fume, that smooth, crisp white from the Loire valley that always seems to complement Thai spices, whatever the dish. Mandy was actually quite quiet, contemplative even, so I asked her how her day had been.

'Actually, pretty damn good.'

'Oh right,' I said, surprised but pleased that at least one of us was making some sort of professional progress. I asked her what had gone well.

'Sometimes you just feel that you've made a breakthrough. Sure, we have opened a couple of new accounts, but it's not that. Do you know what I mean? I'm in a good mood and I don't exactly know why, but underneath there's bound to be a reason beyond complex biorhythms.' Her command of English had always impressed me.

We engaged in the usual trivia in which couples who have become fairly familiar with each other specialise. What was her flat mate up to? Why didn't the girl have a boyfriend? Was she a lesbian? Mandy said that I must have a fantasy of a threesome, and that she'd only consider it when I made my second million. I replied that maybe she'd had an easier time than me recently.

'Every silver lining has a cloud,' I offered, sceptically. Given the general feel-good introduction to the night I realised that this was an error approximately two seconds too late as Mandy raised her eyebrows in a disapproving manner.

'Thanks. Be positive, why don't you? You're about to moan about your work, aren't you? But the reality is that work—or life—is what *you* make of it.'

'Hold on,' I interrupted, suddenly defensive. 'It's not every day that the product you nurtured gets the once over, despite its resounding success to date. I thought you'd be a little more empathetic.'

'Unfortunately, even if you have a point, other people usually see things from their own perspectives. You're complaining, but in lots of jobs—especially with clients like I've worked with, you're only as good as your *current* move.'

I was about to reply when a waitress arrived to take our order, and sensing the awkward moment she offered to give us more time, though we declined. We both ordered dishes with an appended motif of three little red flames. Do people eat as they feel, or did we naively anticipate that the wine would temper the chilli spices?

'Do you really think that I'll be fired if I don't move on this?' I asked.

'If things are going to get shaken up, you should be doing the shaking. You should be delighted that the boss hasn't just fired you first. *You've* been asked to look at options. Well, devise a plan. Go further than he would expect. Impress the guy, even if you don't like him. Be creative. You might even make some money out of it.'

I sat back in silence and peered into my red Thai curry, certain that I could see a devil's face framed by tiny snippets of chilli. Maybe it was me. Perhaps there lurked a naked Thai emperor at a table behind me, with an assembled laughing chorus. Mandy had a point. She was usually consistent in her approach to life, but I hadn't been sure whether to spill the beans to her about Doug's proposal. This might seem strange, but because it was unethical I figured that I'd be associated with the moral low ground. But shit, she was my girlfriend, and she was telling me to get the finger out....and my hand in....so I outlined the conversation I had in the cafe earlier on.

Mandy sat in silence as I explained the key details, but a subtle change in her demeanour became evident, particularly as I outlined the money that might be involved. She was impressed.

'You actually sat on this proposal all day yesterday *and* today and didn't tell me about it? You should definitely think about it.'

'I don't know.'

'For God's sake, Ally,' she said.

'What do you mean?'

'Be open minded to change, that's all?' Mandy held her glass up, raising her eyebrows.

'It's just that it could be a disaster if I was discovered,' I responded, on seemingly new, less confident ground.

'Life's one big risk. Right now you're risking nothing. Do you think I didn't take a major risk setting up the stuff I do? I could have gone for a safe corporate job, become an average suit. Get real.'

'So you think I'm just an average suit?'

'I did not say that. But you have been laying off about the bank, how you're unappreciated, and then when a new concept comes along you instantly dismiss it?' She bumped her wine glass down with a little force, suddenly hostile.

'What if I get caught?'

Mandy flicked back her auburn hair in a kind of angular movement. ‘What’s your alternative right now? Leslie Weir’s given you, what, a week? You could be outnumbered by the board before the battle commences. Where’s your passion? You’re becoming a *wimp*. You’d better come up with some kind of plan, or…’ she said flatly, leaning in closely.

‘Or what?’

‘Or you’ll be yesterday’s man.’

Chapter 3

First thing the following morning I was summoned to Weir's office with an early phone call. The deal had been a week's grace to research an innovative new proposal for the foundation, but Weir barked snidely down the phone, telling me that he—and the *board*—now wanted an instant action plan.

I noticed Kostas leaning on the office photocopier on my way to Weir's office. He grinned, looked at his watch, and flicked his thumb, mimicking a cigarette lighter movement. This was the office code for someone being fired. I nodded and smiled back as nonchalantly as possible. Little did he know where things might lead. When I reached Weir's office, his secretary, Wendy, held out a thick arm like a traffic cop, with the clear implication of STOP! Wendy was like one of those formidable, huge women often featured in Gary Larson's cartoons.

'Wendy,' I began, resting my own hands on my hips. 'Leslie's called me in ASAP, I don't want to keep him waiting—it's strategically important.'

'His wife is in with him. *Sit*,' she snipped. I made a gesture of checking my watch but by this time Wendy was busy accessing her computer, perhaps creating her forthcoming best-selling manual for ignorant fuckers. Then the Weirs appeared.

'Ah. You're here at last.' Lucy Weir averted her eyes from her husband, and gave me an almost imperceptible gesture of empathy.

'Hi Lucy,' I smiled. 'How are you?'

'Oh, fine,' she probably lied. 'Just sorting out some arrangements for a short holiday.'

'Good for you. You deserve it, Lucy. Could do with a break myself.'

Lucy Weir viewed me sympathetically before politely exiting, and I followed Weir into his office, taking the non-power chair across from his desk. A distinct odour of cologne engulfed the room, framing one or two trappings of status, including two original Peter Howson pencil drawings from a collection the bank had commissioned. These were now worth significantly less that the purchase price; another reminder of how the banks—even relatively cautious ones such as Scottish Chartered—had indulged themselves during the good years.

Weir put his hands together in a prayer motion, his two index fingers resting together underneath his lower lip. 'Shoot'.

Despite the earlier phone call, this still caught me off-guard.

'Right…I haven't had much time to think. There was a minor crisis at the whisky event yesterday, which I had to sort out.'

'I know all about that, and you're evading the issue. What are your ideas about *restructuring*, and getting real shareholder value from the foundation?'

'I've only had a couple of days. This sort of thing takes time.'

'You had enough time to dine out last night,' he said flatly.

How the hell did he know that?

'Surely I'm allowed to eat.'

'Mmm. A couple of guys from IT saw you living it up with your girlfriend. But it would be nice if you considered the fat strategic issues here, instead of the Phat Thai. When I was in a junior position I sometimes used to work until midnight. That's how you get on. Times are less buoyant than they used to be, in case you hadn't noticed. I assume that you want a career here? I mean, there's plenty of talent out there that would love a shot at a project like this one.'

Shit.

Weir raised his head, visually endorsing how things appeared to be rapidly deteriorating for me. I was in a corner.

I swallowed. 'Well, as you know, I've worked hard here to build up the foundation, including late hours and weekends on many occasions.'

He lifted the large silver pen on his desk, a power pen if ever I had seen one and pointed it directly at me. 'Have you any ideas for the development of the foundation?' he asked.

I looked at him directly, considering the words I should employ. When he laid the pen on his desk, it pointed directly at me, almost accusingly.

'Ally, it's now the fourth of November, right?'

'Yes.' Was this important? Pre-bonfire night or something?

'And?'

'I have been thinking about, eh, restructuring.'

'Okay.'

I could see a clear image in my mind of Doug's beaming face. I grasped the nettle.

'Well, this is all, eh, preliminary, but, there could be a way to save substantial costs and still generate effective public relations benefits for the bank.'

'Oh, really? That sounds interesting. The foundation has been an excellent PR tool to date, not to mention a clear benefit for good causes we support. However, we're always looking to make things more efficient. Can you expand?'

He sounded as if he was suddenly surprised by the agenda of the meeting—that *he'd* demanded—but I hesitantly continued.

'Well, we spend in excess of twenty million per annum.'

'That has been a worthwhile investment to date.'

What was he playing at? He was the one shouting about changes. 'But you want better shareholder value? The board would welcome more efficiency, right?'

'Of course. The board is a thoroughly professional body that will review any proposed changes in the light of strategic and operational considerations.'

This was the sort of bullshit statement that poignantly illustrated Weir's style. To avoid getting into an argument, all I could do was nod.

'So can you outline this plan you've brought to me?' he said.

'It might be possible to…re-organise the foundation, and fund it through a different vehicle, reducing the bank's exposure to costs…maybe go outside to undertake the work.'

'I see. How would this operate?'

I cleared my throat. I was uncomfortable with what I was about to say, but had he just asked if I wanted a career here? I decided to start with the part that had greatest moral disrepute.

'Well, for a start, the current sum spent on the team downstairs, while very effective to date, could perhaps be, eh, more efficiently used.'

'Go on.'

'Rather than organise bespoke charity events and customising the impact through related media exposure, we could reorganise the way we deliver the PR and use the funds generated in a more direct manner.'

'So you cut out the people in the basement and write cheques to things like Save the Children?'

'Not exactly.' This wasn't far from the truth the way Doug had put it, but I could hardly admit that to Weir. He needed a little more spin to pull him in.

'It's about much more than that. We would donate—or perhaps *invest* might be a more appropriate description—the funds with very specific conditions.' Blah, blah. I continued, matching his bullshit with my bullshit.

He viewed me without comment, almost in acknowledgement that this was the exact sort of management rubbish he would use himself if he were selling this to the board. I continued.

'These charities we donate to will listen to instructions, because money talks. They are desperate for funds.'

'Okay. But who would do the administration work if we had no team?'

'We can outsource it. I believe that there are some companies—agencies—out there who do this exact work.'

'Oh. That's a departure from current circumstances. You know of such firms, eh, agencies?'

'I've begun my research.' I lied.

'And how would you guarantee the media exposure?'

'It would be a challenge. But media people can also be rewarded. Half of them are on pay freezes these days anyway and a little extra can make arbitrary exposure go a long way.'

'We bribe journalists, editors and producers?'

'I would use different language, but we could *incentivise* necessary conduits in subtle ways.'

'Interestingly put. We couldn't condone illegal behaviour, of course.' I tried not to smile at the irony of his observation. 'You said that we could save a lot more?'

'Yes. The bank currently funds the foundation to the tune of around twenty million. This is, effectively, a sum that could be added to the balance sheet if the foundation could be funded through independent means.'

'Independent means?'

'*Customers.*' I sat back. I'd deliberately left the funding part of the plan to the end, as this would be the part that would likely sell the idea to Weir and indeed the board.

Weir appeared to be warming to the idea.

'I'm listening,' he said.

I explained the remainder of the concept, carefully paraphrasing what Doug had suggested to me, whilst integrating a measure of spin into the process. I reminded myself that I would benefit financially, and I kind of enjoyed the fact that I was party to a clever scam and Weir was oblivious to the subterfuge. I outlined the facts surrounding the significant customer base, the psychology behind ordinary people being asked for just a little, or rather being given only a subtle opportunity to opt *out* during the guilt trip that is the essence of the charitable appeal. As I spoke, I could see that Weir was quietly impressed, chiefly with himself, as he began to contribute and make noises as to how the scheme could maximise income generated from this large and as yet untapped source of funds.

However, I made sure that I sold myself as being central—*crucial*—to the project's success. There was no way I was going to instigate this plan only for Weir to cut me out afterwards. I did not want to be the equivalent of an HR manager who puts the lights out after firing everyone else, so I emphasised the fact that I would be essential in liaison with any outside agency; how Weir himself was a little too 'senior' to be getting bogged down with the role I would play. This pandered to his ego. At one point he actually asked why 'he' hadn't thought of this before. This would normally have infuriated me, but in the circumstances I didn't care. If he wanted to drive the scheme forward and argue redundancies, then that would make me feel less responsible for potentially destroying the livelihood of other staff. Weir had set the ball rolling after all, hadn't he? In any case, I could hardly admit that some bloke called Doug dreamed this up in order to scam money from customers.

Weir's attitude had altered substantially during the meeting. Was *his* job on the line? Was it relief, perhaps that most under-rated emotion? Or was he simply thinking about how cool this would sound when *he* presented it to the board, and how his own bonus might rise?

'Okay. That's you off the hook for this morning,' he said flatly. 'But I need a specific plan to take this forward. I need to know how the customers will be asked to donate, where these charity agencies are, and what they charge. Remember, your job's definitely on the line.'

As I exited Weir's office, stage left, a sudden thought occurred to me: just how much I needed Doug Fox.

Chapter 4

'Thank fuck you've decided to be a winner,' Doug retorted. I could almost smell his satisfaction over the phone. 'This is a career move that you *won't* regret, Ally. We need to meet straight away. I have some quiet office space in the city centre which I keep on a retainer. Let's get this baby started.'

He gave me the details and suggested I block out the afternoon. Weir could hardly object if I said I needed to undertake research, so I cancelled the rest of my diary for the day. Needless to say, I didn't give the team downstairs any explanation for my sudden departure. Diminutive lies can often turn into monsters, so I employed good old fashioned omission.

Opening the office door, I noticed Kostas in conversation with Elise Stewart, our most recent executive hire. A subtle brunette with deep, cobalt eyes, Elise had arrived from North Carolina on a two-year contract in marketing. She favoured striking power outfits that accentuated an athletic figure, and had already drawn a number of suggestive comments from the guys in the office. Elise smiled at me politely as she answered a call on her phone and moved away.

'Cute girl,' I ventured.

'Yes, indeed. You look like a man on a mission. Another big phone call? That your broker this time?' Kostas asked.

'Afraid not. But the world of PR does have its moments,' I replied. I trusted Kostas completely, but I would have had to deceive him had the conversation evolved. He was an honest guy, and he almost certainly wouldn't have approved if I had spilled the beans, even if he was able to retain a secret. He observed me carefully, before speaking.

'As a cafe owner in Kifisia used to say when I was a kid, make sure you go to bed with the same conscience with which you woke up.'

Shit, was my plan that transparent? I smiled while preparing some kind deflective explanation. 'Like you did when you hacked into the Greek government's computer system and moved the Finance Minister's money?'

'For God's sake Ally, keep your voice down! I wish I'd never told you that. I was only a student at the time.'

'Absolutely, Kostas, and I'm now a spin-doctor. And PR, like hacking, is of course less about smoke and mirrors, and more about fire and broken glass.'

'Bar room philosophy.'

'The only kind we have in Scotland,' I replied.

'Or in Greece.'

'See you tomorrow.' I said. As I walked away I heard his parting shot.

'Make sure that you don't get lacerated by the glass or torched with the fire, my friend.'

Kostas's metaphor echoed in my mind as I left the Dosh Dome. I couldn't afford to let comments like that, however innocent, affect my confidence. I had now embarked on a specific route, and although I shouldn't prejudge the outcome, there was no room for self doubt. I knew from experience that confident people are more likely to succeed with a project, particularly when requiring approval from others; or perhaps more aptly, those lacking confidence are efficiently destroyed because decision makers can smell fear a mile away.

Doug had hired office space in Forth Street, close to the city centre. The offices were in an old Georgian sandstone building. There were the usual suspects listed on various floors—designers, surveyors, and so forth—and then this temporary office rental space towards the top of the building, complete with some secretarial support. It crossed my mind that a few plans might have been hatched here over the past, though I suspected that this was the first one of its kind in this exact category.

The office space was predictably generic, with basic furniture and a few pieces of equipment, and it produced a minor odour of mustiness. Doug was dressed in black casual clothing, but was still business-like. He quickly purloined two large mugs of coffee from the shared secretarial centre, closed the door firmly behind us and manoeuvred his laptop amongst a large pile of papers that were spread out over a conference table.

'Right, mate. It seems that we're going to have to move pretty fast on this. The good news is that, as I explained before, I have already set up a company that can facilitate the work.'

'You must have been confident,' I said.

'Not necessarily. A lot of the groundwork was done prior to this stage. You were the best match, but there were other candidates.'

'Who were they?'

'Can't say. Confidential.'

'Why?'

'Look, you wouldn't like me to give your name out to anyone, would you?'

He had a point, but I challenged further. 'You're sure these folk aren't a security risk later on?'

'If I thought that I'd never be going ahead. Besides, *you're* the one that phoned *me* back, right? I have a willing partner. Now your boss even seems to be keen, so hey presto, what's to complain about?'

He was correct of course. I'd been under no obligation to call him back, and equally, Doug owed me nothing. The term 'partner' left me slightly uncomfortable, but I guess that's what we now were. 'Doug, if we're partners, we need to be upfront with everything from now on. Okay?'

He gave me that self assured, cocky look I'd clocked the first night I'd met him, but then spoke quietly, as if suddenly under observation.

'Agreed. We both stand to win or lose in this thing, so we must be completely straight in our dealings with each other. Me, and you too. Fair enough?' He offered a hand, which I took, slightly embarrassed.

'Fair enough.'

'Okay,' he said. 'I'm glad we got that straight. Now for the plan.'

He'd set up three holding companies. Two were effectively empty vessels containing named sub-corporations that had been set up for the purposes of making fake bids for the work. He reckoned that three quotes would be enough, basically relying on the premise that millions would be saved by Scottish Chartered, so why would anyone senior contradict a recommendation to have a manageable set of three quotes? These two ghost enterprises would have their own stationery, 'official' head offices and websites, but would quote expensively and, crucially, would be unattractive as they would offer poor strategic fit. There was a minor insurance element at play here; Weir might want to select the cheapest, but he wasn't daft and would want to assess all the plans, so the cheapest would also, rationally, have to appear to be the best. It also clearly helped that I knew of the typical selection procedures that the bank employed when selecting other types of outside agencies.

The CEO and board of directors would have to approve the recommendation given by Weir. The CEO was on bereavement leave in Australia after a family tragedy, and the Finance Director was acting CEO. I could not predict his views. However, I partly understood Doug's confidence that this could be manipulated in our favour, because of the times in which we lived. Saving money counted, and because the bank had demutualised the days had gone where any residual sentiment of a member-owned organisation held sway. This thought, however, engendered within me a sudden guilt about those who would lose their jobs. I would have to keep reminding myself that Weir had pushed me into this position.

I asked Doug to clarify the names of the two shell companies.

'Gold Star Charity Liaison, and Jerusalem Saviour.'

'You must be kidding.'

'Yes, they're both deliberately crap. Both sound odd, the former in terms of credibility and the latter as religious connotations often put business people off.' He grinned, pleased with his own psychology. I understood where he was coming from, but hell, these really did sound manufactured. Doug spotted my concern.

'Should they actually undertake any *real* business, there wouldn't be a problem,' he continued. 'But of course they won't. They'd be subject to the normal rules governing company law and would be Inland Revenue compliant. However, these two will be wound up afterwards—assuming the fake bids are rejected—so that we do not encounter any type of investigation in relation to the nature of trading or payment of tax, however unlikely such a scenario would be. No loose ends. I will be a director of one these companies. You, obviously, will not be a director for security purposes.'

'But you'd need more than one director,' I added.

'Yes, I have additional directors for both.'

'So who are they, then?'

He held his hands up. 'Again, this is confidential. But before you complain, this is in your interest. The less you know, the less you have to conceal. A couple of folk owe me favours, and this is a paper exercise, remember? You don't know the people, and in any case they're from out of town. Both of these businesses will be registered in London, providing greatest anonymity. So, sleeping directors are irrelevant to you, but necessary for this project to work. They will not be involved directly.'

'Directors who don't direct?'

'Exactly.'

'And I can have your reassurance that none of these figureheads knows what all this wider scam is all about?'

'Yes. Trust me. Remember, this was all set up before we met, so you don't need to worry about the details. You're safer that way.'

This only partly assuaged my doubt, though I would have to get used to risks. We were not breaking the law directly—yet—but I would be in breach of contract and fired if we were caught plotting, and for that matter I could be black-balled in the financial services industry.

'A question, Doug.' I scratched my chin.

'Shoot.'

'If the two fake firms are lacking credibility, what's stopping Weir or the board asking us to draft in other, more credible bidders to go alongside the main firm we will be running? Couldn't this elaborate plan come to pieces if we are forced to go out to real alternative players to operate the work?'

'Several reasons it won't. Firstly, there are comparatively few of these agencies around. Most of them are based in London, which is not a deal-buster in itself, but there is another problem which we can argue has led us to eliminate these firms at the first trawl.'

'So what's that?'

'They are all too expensive. I have researched the costs of a few genuine firms, and the norm is between fifteen and twenty percent commission to undertake the kind of show we're talking about. We'll be quoting lower than that so the bank will save more money and the bottom line will benefit. In short, we want Weir and the directors to view this as a no-brainer for the bank. They came to you, after all.'

'But what if they still insist on other bids?'

'Come on, you're on the inside, for fuck's sake! This is not an open tender situation. You can engineer what you like. Suppose that one of these other firms really was asked to quote—we get to see the numbers *before* we submit our bid. Ally, this thing is a fix!' Doug sat back, perplexed at my naivety.

He was right of course. I would have to get used to thinking more like a crook. How often in life do we have inside information? How often do we act on it? However, I had further concerns so I pushed on.

'What about all the admin work that's going to pile up? The last thing I need is to be engulfed in work as I no longer have a team. We run events and I'm busy enough as it is—so who actually does the graft?'

'Have you not listened to anything I've said? For starters, you've alluded to the fact that Weir said that your foundation should become more generic and less bespoke. Am I right?'

'That's what he said, though I'm still not sure it will work,' I replied.

'He's the boss, right?'

'I suppose.'

'You've said it yourself—get the hacks and producers to do the work for you. We set aside, eh, gifts for those we need. Get the charities off their asses if they want the money. Christ, some of these organisations are on their knees—the cash they get from us would be conditional, dependent on *them* doing PR *for* the bank. This will be part of the plan. I have draft legal agreements that anyone receiving money would have to sign before they get a penny. This is hard business.'

'All right, Doug. I'm running with you, mainly. You mentioned in the cafe that there was an off-shore element?'

'Yes. This is where it gets interesting,' he said.

'I'm listening.'

'I've set up something called Lexicon Chartered.'

'Sounds more legitimate—even shares one part of its name with the bank.'

'That's a coincidence, of course, but you are correct in that I've aimed for an air of competence.'

'So what's the deal here?'

'Based overseas. It will have no employees in this country, though as a minimum requirement, a skeleton staff overseas. It will be owned by a holding company, also based overseas. We can *legitimately* avoid tax by splitting the activities involved. There is a favourable jurisdiction I have identified. Obviously, as the business will be vetted I want the venture to be legitimate in the sense that any investigation by Scottish Chartered before entering an agreement will show full compliance with international law. As with magicians, we want most of what's on show to be real and genuine, to deflect the subterfuge in the background.'

'But if you've only recently set this up, there won't be any company accounts filed or a successful track record to entice the bank to do business.' This had been a nagging doubt I'd had from our conversation at the cafe.

Doug smiled. 'You think I haven't figured this out, don't you?'

'Well, yes.' I sat back, swallowing some coffee, awaiting an explanation.

'Look, I've invested a bit of money in this, and I know what I'm talking about. If this is all pitched properly, your board will buy it. The company will pass any credit references, trust me. Do you know it's possible to borrow a stash of money for very short periods of time in some countries, giving the impression of a healthy bank balance, paying only short term credit and legally complying with tax laws? This company will look legit, and in a modest way, successful. And bent lawyers—those who can provide 'evidence' of legitimacy—are easy to find here, let alone overseas. I can drum up evidence of successful work by Lexicon Chartered, through checkable testimonials and a network of web work where any Google search will show respectable points of reference.'

'But what if the board wants the same sort of evidence from the fake companies.'

'Christ, you're hard going. You can sell this concept no problem. Ally, I've investigated every angle with this venture. Is it one hundred percent foolproof? No project ever is, mate. But I've covered all the bases I can anticipate.'

'Where's it registered, then?'

'Antigua.'

'Antigua?'

'Yes. St John's is a nice spot for a scam.'

'But that's just a front.'

'Yip. Did I mention Ireland?'

'No.'

'Lexicon will have, let's say a base in the Republic of Ireland.'

'You've lost me here.'

'Well, a little insurance, shall we say. Ireland is close to home, and trusted. The Irish do a stack of financial services work for a lot of firms in Scotland and in England. Of course, we won't have a real stack of employees, but we will have the impression of such,' he said.

'Explain.'

'I have a contact over in Dublin who runs a direct marketing company, with over fifty employees. Suffice to say he owes me a favour. He's offered to 'lend' us his staff as necessary. If Weir or anyone else for that matter wants to see bodies, they can see them over in Dublin, peppered with one or two real ones, and some bullshit with my contact. We can have someone ready to deal with calls in that office whenever necessary, at fairly minimal cost. This adds the final legitimacy to the venture, should anyone fear that the Antiguan angle on its own is too distant.' Doug shuffled through some of the papers on the conference table before us, pulling out some printouts and certificates. 'Here are some of the details.'

I briefly viewed the paperwork in front of me. There was clear evidence of his prior engagement with the project. I reflected on what he had outlined. It was shaping up, though there were still some obvious holes.

'What about the work for the pitch? For starters, we'd need to generate presentation material. I realise that we'd be covering both halves of the process—I suppose we'd be falsely acting as both vendor and client—I'd need this information plus a business plan to make the case for fund raising from customers.'

'It's virtually all covered. Obviously you'll need to give me inside information to beef up the plan. You know financial details that I don't. I understand ballpark numbers of customer groups, but I'd need more data to firm up any projections.'

'You really must have been confident that someone would bite to go to these lengths on spec.'

'Yes, actually.' He appeared suitably smug. Perhaps he felt he'd earned the right. 'Okay Doug, I admit I'm impressed. It appears too good to be true, and of course all this is all hypothetical at this stage.'

'You still don't trust me?'

'It's not that. But there's something you haven't mentioned yet.'

'Let me guess. Money?' he asked. 'Our costs in running the show, all in, are going to be around a hundred thousand per annum. I think that we should ask for a chunk of money up front from the bank.'

'Why?'

'Shore the whole operation up.'

'But that's going to look bad, Doug. If the bank's going to be sacking people, it will generate bad feeling if they're seen to simultaneously hand out cash to an external agency.'

'But we'll need some working capital.'

'Well, I'm not comfortable asking for money at the start.'

'But even if this is a skeleton operation, there are costs. We will still need resources.'

'Can't agree here, especially if I'm arguing this with Weir.'

'Let's park this for the moment.'

'Okay…' I let it go for the time being before Doug continued.

'First, the bank needs to get the donations from customers. Sure, there's compliance with the law, but that's a formality. Now, the question is: how much can they bring in and what percentage can we get?'

I considered his query. 'We have around twenty million opportunities that we previously talked about.'

'Yes, and obviously, some of these have their mortgage, saving accounts, the whole caboodle, with the bank. But even then, if this is pitched correctly, people may give duplicate donations.'

'But a bunch of people will still un-tick the donation box, won't they?'

'Some will, but this percentage is typically small. Prior research says that this can be anything between eight and twenty percent. But we know how to make the pitch properly, so averaging out the repeats saying 'no' and those who will never give in any situation, I reckon about 85 percent will comply.'

'So you think that we're talking about sixteen or seventeen million plus in overall revenue?'

'Possibly. It could go higher if we can obtain *monthly* donations from the bigger accounts such as mortgagees. I will work out the specific forecast once you give me the data. And our percentage would be approximately 12 percent—which could generate about *two million* per annum, depending on the repeat donations. Mainly profit, of course.' Doug cleared his throat, pleased. I was equally impressed.

'Wow. Two million. Though the board could still argue that this could be done in-house at this cost.'

'Yes, but you won't be making that case. You'd be arguing that this whole set-up is the most efficient way to *save* the bank more than twenty million. Everyone's outsourcing these days. Get real. I've also spent about fifteen grand of my own so far.'

'Right,' I said. He'd put his money down, then.

'I did the Antigua thing mainly on the net. Company formations aren't that expensive, even with the legal costs. The rest has been research and favours. And time, essentially.'

'So you won't need an investment from me, then?' I figured he'd hit me with a demand.

'I need few thousand. Money to cover some of the material we need to pitch, but after that we can call it quits.' He looked up as if conjuring a number from thin air. 'No more than ten grand—fair?' He observed me carefully. As the consummate salesman, I instantly knew that he'd deliberately minimised the contribution from me in relation to his own, as yet unproven investment. That way I'd be more likely to acquiesce.

'Okay.' I suddenly found myself offering a chunk of cash. 'But what about the rewards, how would we split the spoils?'

'I'm not going to quibble. We're both trained in negotiation. I've put in all the initial money and effort. There's no point in starting to haggle or bluff, so I suggest...eighty-twenty. In my favour of course,' he said flatly, without a hint of humility.

'Eighty-twenty? You consider that fair? I'll be doing just as much as you and I have much more to risk.' I could feel my temperature rising.

'Ally...I'm only joking. Fifty-fifty, my friend. Deal?'

When he offered his hand, which I shook, I realised that by making the joke about the split, he had again temporarily made the real deal seem more attractive in order to gain immediate agreement, irrespective of our differential risk. Once again, I wondered again what the hell I was getting myself into and exactly who with—but then, what option did I have?

'Hey, that's *bold.*' Mandy gave me one of her winning smiles and a full kiss on the lips. 'You kept this news from me all day?' Actually, there were good reasons for this delay. I'd decided earlier on that day—call it paranoia if you like—that I'd cut out any chance of being monitored electronically. Why set up a potential evidence trail? But right now I was safely at Mandy's place in Murrayfield. Her flatmate, Laura, was off on a business trip, so we had the place to ourselves. An *Eagles* album was playing in the background, and I was cradling a glass of champagne.

Doug was happy, Weir seemed pleased—for *him*—when I'd called in to explain the progress, and my girlfriend now appeared content that I was being more active. Everyone was in good spirits, even if it still gave me the heebie-jeebies.

Mandy looked stunning. She wore a figure-hugging electric blue dress—short—with six inch heels and chic silver jewellery I'd bought for her birthday. With the heels she looked down on me—but it was worth it. In fact, another turn on.

'So tell me, when do I get to meet this Doug guy?'

I suddenly felt a twang of possessiveness at the thought of Mandy being introduced to Doug. I'm not really the jealous type, so why would I experience such an irrational fear? Did I not trust my new business partner at all? Come to think of it, I knew relatively little about him, including his current love life. He'd implied that he was a bit of a player, juggling a girlfriend here and there.

'Oh, there'll be time enough for that. He's a bit of a chancer, Mandy. Probably not your type. Don't get me wrong, he's got some good ideas, but it might reduce potential security problems if I keep him under wraps at the moment.'

Mandy eyed me suspiciously. 'You sound as if you don't trust the guy. I mean, he's all right, isn't he?'

'A bit cocky, but fine.'

'That's a relief, because trust is all important in business.'

'I trust him.'

'Well, is it me that you don't trust?' She appeared miffed. There was no way I was going to spoil the mood, so I offered her a wide smile.

'I trust you completely. You were so more enthusiastic about me doing something to shake up my career. And you know what? You were right. I needed to get the finger out. I just don't want you to be exposed to any risks, and I'd like you to share in the rewards but you've got your own career to think about and I don't want you to get mixed up in something unethical.'

'I don't think what you're doing is unethical. It's actually quite entrepreneurial. You're not stealing anything. Rather, you're simply trying to ensure that you get a decent reward for all your work—and the bank saves money too—what's not to like about it?'

'You're right. It's just that my team will lose their jobs, and I'd lose mine if they found out who was behind it.'

'But none of us has a guaranteed career. Do you think your team would worry about you losing your job?'

'Probably not.'

'Well, there you go. QED.' She seemed to warm to me in the light of her own explanation, and moved closer to me on the sofa, touching my cheek. 'Well, handsome. Let me know if you need help, once your plan is secure. And I'm sure I can handle Doug. I deal with chancers every day of the week, and I eat them up.'

'Don't eat up Doug. I need him undigested until this gets going.'

'So you're not going to have any second thoughts. You're going for it?' She glanced at me, semi-casually, semi-seriously.

'Yes, so we get rich,' I said with a little more conviction.

'*Rich*, I like,' she replied huskily, turning towards me.

'*Rich*, I like too,' I said.

'Mmm...'

She put down her champagne glass and gave me one of those looks. If money turned Mandy on, that was fine by me. She took my hand and made me stand up, and then grabbed my tie and pulled me towards her, kissing me fully with her eyes wide open, almost as if looking straight through me.

She then pushed me back onto the sofa, just as *Peaceful Easy Feeling* kicked off on the sound system. I began to enter some kind of champagne inspired trance.

She stared directly at me, smiling. 'The richer you become, the better this will get.'

Chapter 5

By this stage I had all the motivation I needed: Mandy, Doug, Weir and my own disillusionment. I might have been missing details about Doug's past, but I had ascertained one thing at least: the man had drive and commitment.

I briefed Weir on some detail: projections, sensitivity analysis, research findings, and 'strategy'. I knew that boards loved strategy, even if many senior people were often vague about what it really meant and confused it with tactical manoeuvring or operational issues. I also asked Weir if the team could all be offered redeployment. He grunted about the cost of redundancies, and mentioned the possibility of limited redeployment to other areas.

He couldn't have cared less.

The foundation had agreed to sponsor the launch of a children's charity sports initiative in the Caledonian Hotel. The Caledonian was located near Scottish Chartered, and we often used the hotel as a venue for various initiatives as it ticked all the corporate boxes. David Moritano—one of the PR executives in the team—was running our side of the show so I'd be there purely in an observational capacity, chewing the fat and spitting out the lean, implying that it was business as usual.

When I entered the foyer of the hotel, I could hear a band playing in one of the function rooms. This would be the up and coming teen band that David had invited. When I entered the function room, a number of children were being photographed holding sports equipment and posters. Proud parents were huddled in a group behind the cameramen, delighted at the exposure their children were about to experience. A member of the Olympic sailing team had agreed to appear for nothing, and smiled genuinely with the children. Of course, the bank's signage was prominently displayed behind the kids, and even if the photographs were cropped and reduced, there was no way the bank's logo, a saltire linked to three sovereigns, could be missed. This type of thing was our bread and butter. An investment of ten thousand on a launch and, say, a hundred thousand on a subsequent programme such as buying sports equipment or funding travel, could usually generate an impact of a half a million in advertising, especially if we milked the post launch activities, tying in human interest and sporting success as part of the future story of the investment.

David Moritano caught my eye and raised his eyebrows in acknowledgement. He was a genuine hard-worker; an enthusiastic colleague of Italian origin who seemed to radiate confidence. He was grouped with the kids and the Olympic medallist, a perk of the job. I momentarily reflected on the fact he'd probably be forced to leave, as he was a PR guy—a former journalist—who might well not be easily redeployed. David motioned to his right, and I followed his lead, surprised to see Charles Henderson standing on the periphery, chatting to a sports journalists.

Charles Henderson was a non-executive director on Scottish Chartered's board. I'd no idea that he was going to show up. Normally I'd have been briefed by Weir, who would almost certainly have attended had he known, as Weir rarely missed a networking opportunity with someone who might help increase his bonus. Charles Henderson was old school, a slightly portly man in his mid-sixties with a depth of economic knowledge and an apparent lack of time to visit a barber. I sometimes wondered why some bald men left the bushy parts at the sides unattended—perhaps they just didn't care. What was that old phrase about nothing growing on a busy road, except the weeds on the verge? Charles Henderson was also an astute businessman though, and I understood that he supplied the bank with a valuable commodity: counter intuitive advice.

Curious as to his attendance, I hovered while he concluded a chat with the journalist. I knew better than to avoid Henderson—Weir would crucify me if he heard that I hadn't pressed the flesh when I had the chance. Charles Henderson lived in Bearsden near Glasgow, so he must have had his reasons for being here. Certainly, he'd spoken to me previously with a favourable view of the foundation's work. I approached cautiously, offering my hand.

He gripped strongly, and smiled genuinely. 'Super event,' he said, in an earthy, deep tone.

'Good of you to come along Mr Henderson—it's fantastic to see support from the board.'

'Charles, please. Alasdair, isn't it?'

'Officially, though everyone knows me as Ally.'

'That's right. Some of my American friends insist on calling me Chuck, but I always say it has a throw away feel about it, like vomiting across the ocean. I'm never sure whether I'm being insulted or not.' I laughed.

A twelve or thirteen-year-old girl broke free from the photography group and grinned at Charles, who ruffled her hair. 'This is my granddaughter, Ailsa. She's from Edinburgh, and she's a future Olympian I'm sure. Runs faster that a gazelle. No doubt trying to avoid the gentle folk of Edinburgh.'

'Grandpa, you can't say things like that. It's not politically correct. There's nothing wrong with Edinburgh.'

'Nothing a journey back to Glasgow wouldn't fix…only kidding my dear. But we always need to keep up the east-west banter. I love to do it at board meetings at the bank. They're even harder work than teenage super-athletes.' He winked at me, and then beamed at Ailsa, who rolled her eyes in mock indignation, before being dragged back for more photos and some freebies.

Charles turned toward me. 'This is genuinely great work, Ally. I mean, this is what it's all about. The kids get the support they need—and let me tell you that's essential the way it is with public money these days—but the bank really benefits from the action. There's no crowding here with competitors vying for coverage, no ambush marketing, and even the sports journalists are happy to write up a favourable commentary as it's a good news story for a change. Well done.'

'Thanks…I value the compliment.' Then, fleetingly, I considered my role in the scam.

He continued. 'Oh, I'm just an old-timer now. But I like what you achieve. We must make sure we keep this going. The formula works.'

This was very odd. Surely he would be aware of unfolding events? Weir had specifically told me that the board were on his back and viewed the foundation as indulgent, and *expensive.* Charles Henderson was saying nothing of the sort, yet I had always considered him as a straight guy, no bullshit.

'So you're in favour of the investment the bank puts into the foundation…you know, funding it directly….public relations effects through customised, media-friendly programmes?'

'Absolutely. If it ain't broke…'

'Yes. I understand.' I decided to push a little further.

'I know you're a busy man. You've been able to attend all the recent board meetings. The one at Gleneagles and the two at HQ?'

'Of course, haven't missed one in three years.' He replied. 'Try not to be a slacker.'

'Not at all. I was only wondering…your support for the foundation is really appreciated. It's nice to see that it's…eh, shared among the board.' I checked his expression as he pointed at his granddaughter, smiling. If he figured that I was digging, then he concealed it.

'You know, Ally—and I'm speaking candidly now—the foundation is one of the few programmes we run that causes little controversy at board meetings. There are always those who go for the short term buck, but I've never been one of them. Yes, I'd say the foundation was a long-term winner.'

I felt another twinge of guilt. Here was a successful event, running professionally, helping a good cause, and being praised by a very respectable and knowledgeable individual. People often assume that board rooms must be stuffed with ruthless suits. He was a genuinely nice guy and a man of some influence, yet he appeared to have no idea of the conversation Weir had had with me. Ailsa's mother then appeared, and they politely made an exit. I thanked him again, and wished Ailsa good luck with her Olympian career.

I didn't tell Doug about my conversation at the Hilton Hotel. There was no point in exposing him to my opinion of boardroom imponderables. Perhaps there was some sort of division within the board, and Charles Henderson was simply out of the loop on this one. It might also be possible that Weir was over-playing the desire for change. I was wary of formally going above Weir's head. I knew from past experience that leap-frogging a boss to query a decision or question advice always causes problems, so I decided to email Weir from my office.

Hi Leslie,

I met Charles Henderson at the Children's sports charity event at the Caledonian. He was extremely positive about the foundation, praising it as it currently stands, with funding and the customised PR events in which we specialise.
Just checking that you still wish me to proceed with the new proposal? I assume that there is a genuine desire for change—though CH didn't seem to reflect this last night.

Please advise accordingly.

Regards, Ally

Reasonable enough, I thought. Then a response.

My office. Now. I want to know exactly what you said. LW

It's odd how curiosity can turn on its head. I was the one with legitimate questions, but suddenly I was being summoned in order to defend myself. I felt like a school child being dragged to the headmaster for a crime of which I was innocent. But then I quickly nipped myself.

I *was* totally complicit in setting up a scam.

And I had convinced myself of its merits. Why was I being hostile to Weir right now? Did I not desire to share in the potential future revenue? I decided to approach him cautiously.

I by-passed Wendy, the sizable gatekeeper, by signalling that I'd had a phone call from the boss. She frowned at me on entry to Weir's office. Unfortunately, her eyebrows met. In Weir's office, the distinct presence of aftershave permeated the room. On the phone, he beckoned me in and shortly concluded his call.

'What did you tell him?' *Hello, it's a pleasure to see you Ally.*

'Virtually nothing.'

'You'd better have been discreet.'

'Completely.' Meet an accusation with a positive, as the PR textbooks said.

He looked at me squarely.

'So?'

'I agree entirely that we need to be discreet here, and discreet I was, Leslie. I said virtually nothing, for obvious reasons.'

'Well how the hell did it all come up in conversation? Are you sure you didn't make hints of some sort?'

I told him that I was convinced that discretion was the order of the day, and that Henderson had simply praised the foundation. I'd explained that I'd assumed from what Weir had said that the board was behind change, so therefore Charles Henderson would be fully aware of things. Weir hesitated, placing his fingers together in a prayer motion.

'And you told him nothing of any plans we...*you*...may have discussed recently?'

'Eh...*us*. Nothing.'

Weir sat back in his chair. He searched my eyes as if waiting for me to blink first, suspicious of my words.

'Just bear in mind that boardrooms are not always linear. There is plurality of viewpoints. Henderson is an old fashioned type who believes business is about relationships before the bottom line. People like that are living out of their time. Relationships are only of any value if they *aid* the bottom line. The foundation is a huge drain on our resources, and thus, the bottom line.'

'So...he knew of possible changes but politely said nothing to me for reasons of confidentiality?'

'That's an assumption. The CEO's indisposed, the acting CEO has enough operational issues on his hands, so they look to people like me and I look to people like you. They can't be experts in everything, so they fly kites.' This was the sort of management lingo shit at which Weir excelled.

'Flying kites,' I repeated, slowly, waiting for him to continue his masterly explanation.

'Yes, kites. I don't want you talking to anyone about this project, board or non-board. Understand? When you present them with our proposal, I wouldn't be surprised if members act nonchalantly, even surprised.'

'Oh, right. So it has to look like our proposal?'

'*Your* proposal, Ally.'

'Okay, I suppose I'll have to…agree with that.'

'Yes, you will.'

I had entered the room concerned, but when I made my way back out I was pissed off. What a manipulative bastard. This had all begun with Weir telling me that there was a cast-iron will for change. When I'd questioned the need for change—why we were disrupting a winning formula—he'd threatened my role. Now, having committed myself to change, and having put substantial time and work into it with Doug, I would now personally take the flak for job losses or any criticism that some charitable causes missed out.

And there was one other fact I needed to consider: I could possibly fob off Doug if this thing disintegrated before it started, but what about Mandy? Doug I owed nothing, but Mandy was different. If I was fired she'd be truly impressed. P45 man? It didn't have a ring to it, let alone an engagement ring; something I'd considered might be appropriate once the dough began rolling in. I could leave the job, but then I would be quitting a project I'd set up, and could be looking for work from a position of weakness. Quitting wasn't an option.

When I took myself back to my office Kostas appeared. 'Coffee in the canteen?' he asked.

Downstairs I picked up a tray and ordered coffees, and I made the unusual move of adding two chocolate donuts. The pressure must have been getting to me.

'The pressure must be getting to you,' Kostas observed when he noticed the donuts.

'Piss off. You don't want to know.'

'I want to know.'

'You know Kostas, if you weren't such a decent bloke, I'd say you were one nosey bastard.'

For some reason this tickled him, and he roared with laughter. I just stared at him while some others looked on, mildly curious about what was apparently so funny. One was Elise Stewart, who had appeared in the queue at the checkout and had spotted Kostas's outburst. She wandered over to our table, but remained standing. I'd kind of wanted a semi-confidential moan with Kostas, but I sensed that Elise was cool and, well, why would we turn down a good-looking and engaging new member of staff?

'Donuts?' Elise pointed distastefully at the saturated fat and sugar adorning our plates, and shook her head. Her understated Appalachian accent added to the value of her critique. 'Is this some kind of corporate plan at Scottish Chartered? Stuff the execs full of cholesterol, keep them nice and content, until they keel over with a coronary, reducing the headcount.'

'Pretty much, Elise. Though you'd have to factor in the payments to next of kin for death in service due to the provision of donuts. Another Americanism to hit Scotland?'

'It would never happen in Athens,' Kostas stated. 'The seat of human civilisation would not countenance such wickedness.' Kostas patted his sizeable stomach in a rotating gesture.

Elise raised her eyebrows. 'Yes, but Ally's right, it would happen in the States. For folks back home a muffin or a donut is a constitutional right. I mean what do they put in these?' She smiled. 'There was a study in the US based on asking people to pay into an honesty box for their morning donuts—from the lower reaches to the top brass of a corporate HQ. Guess which employees were most honest?'

'The poorest ones on the bottom floor,' Kostas said flatly.

'Ah, you've heard of that one,' Elise noted.

'Stands to reason,' I said. 'We understand the logic, though Kostas and I only steal on Fridays.' I lied, briefly contemplating the fiddle on which I was embarking.

Kostas then said, 'I bet that arse who's Ally's boss would steal the donuts *every* day, Elise.'

'Arse? So much more derogatory than *ass*, don't you think? And delivered convincingly by a Greek using a semi-Scottish accent with odd dialectic nuances.'

We both stared at her. 'Good point, Elise. Weir would be off with the entire bakery,' I replied.

'It's great to see such loyalty for one's boss. I'm going to report you both immediately,' she said, before returning to the checkout with a tray. She stopped to talk to another colleague, leaving Kostas and I alone.

He leaned forward. 'What's on your mind? You seem totally preoccupied these days.'

I didn't know what to say. Was he telepathic? Another word derived from Greek, ironically. Kostas was probably my best friend at work and yet I couldn't share any of the details of the plan. I attempted to give a neutral response, but this didn't satisfy Kostas.

'Taking the fifth, are we?'

'You could say that. All will be explained, at some point. I promise.'

'Well, I hope you're behaving yourself.'

'I'll endeavour not to become a chancer.'

'I think that you're spending too much time with Leslie Weir to avoid it.'

Chapter 6

'I need the cash now, mate,' Doug said on the phone.

'What?'

'*Money.* Remember? You agreed to invest in this venture too. There are expenses for this thing.'

'I didn't realise that you needed the money from me so soon.'

'Ten grand, mate, as agreed. But no electronic transfers—for obvious reasons. This is in your interest too. And you're not getting a receipt either. No trail. This has to work on trust.'

Yeah, trust.

'When do you need the money?'

'I've done a lot of work, including analysis of the figures you produced. These have been useful. But there is a bill for some legal work and a website—*image enhancement* shall we say—to finalise the work for Gold Star Charity Liaison and Jerusalem Saviour.'

I considered the notion, sceptical about these two stupid company names that Doug had conjured up. I realised that he had made a case for their necessary 'rejection', but I could just imagine Weir's reaction when I revealed the titles of two of our recommended bidders. And now I was to pay for their "image enhancement".

'Is that a yes?'

'It's always been my ambition to pay for PR spin for shit-sounding fake companies doomed to failure. I suppose I can get it for you tomorrow. How about your office, say six o'clock?'

'That's fine. And we need to discuss the pitch. I think that we should bring this forward.'

'Why?'

'Strike while the iron's hot.'

'But there's still a lot of work to be done. I know that Weir's expecting me to provide details, but there's still some time.'

'Look Ally, I've been working like you wouldn't believe behind the scenes. We're ready to go. You need to mug up on all the detail.'

'I've got more to lose than you.'

'Do you really think so? Doing nothing is not an option, mate. You've said so yourself.' He hung up.

The problem was, I suppose, putting down my hard earned cash without a receipt or guarantee. Such a move touched an old family nerve. Yes, my mother would have objected. And my father. And all previous antecedents. I wondered what exactly the old Highland ghosts would say to giving a few thousand to someone like Doug. But then, how on earth would they interpret the jeopardy in which I was putting my career?

I accessed online banking. I was about to move on Doug's 10K request when there was a knock at the door. I swivelled round in my chair to see David Moritano, whom I beckoned in.

'David, have a seat. What can I do for you?'

His facial expression revealed an imminent, awkward question. He was a smart dresser and had an eye for style which normally matched his manner, but right now he looked less confident than usual. What did he want? Surely he hadn't figured something out about changes to the foundation?

'Ally, been meaning to talk with you.' He watched me, nervously and cleared his throat. 'I realised that you were busy the other night, what with Charles Henderson turning up at the sports event.' There was a momentary pause as he sat back in his chair, and I began to anticipate a problem. Best to be positive: I placed my hands behind my head, and smiled.

'No time like the present, David. Shoot.'

David immediately sat forward in his chair again. 'It's about my career,

Ally. I want to be honest with you. I've been offered another job.' He looked at me almost apologetically, as if he was letting me down personally.

'That's great, David!' Then I checked myself. 'I mean, it's nice to be wanted…not that we want to lose people such as yourself. Where's the job, or don't you want to say?'

'Clydeside Bank. Same sort of role, but more money and perks. Based in Glasgow, though, which is the only problem.'

'Don't want to re-locate?'

'Kids are at school here. As you know, my wife's from Edinburgh—she doesn't want to move. And the job would involve a lot of evening events, mainly over there, so I'd have my work cut out to keep all the balls in the air.'

'Like a one-man volleyball team.'

'You could say.'

'Have you decided what to do?'

'No. I wanted to talk to you first. I mean I could earn another few thousand, but have a worse life. I wanted to know what the prospects are going to be here. We've had the re-engineering and all that, and the unit is pretty efficient. Everyone pulls their weight—in fact this is the best team I've ever been in. You shoot straight as a boss. I assume that we're on a solid footing with the success of the foundation to date, meaning that there can be career growth here.'

Shit. I'd been hoping to avoid questions like this, particularly right now. I stood up, putting on my public smile. Sometimes, when faced with difficult responses, it's best to use analogies that are ambiguous. I'd learned this trick from a former boss. It's not as irritating as answering a question with another question, but it can help give you time to think. I realised that this may seem pretty manipulative, but what choice did I have? I pointed out at the traffic on the street below.

'David, see the cars out there?'

He looked out of the window, nodding.

I continued. 'There's a constant flow of vehicles out there; people on the move from A to Z. All day, every day. Commuters, gas guzzlers, tourists, truck drivers, kids, grannies, business men, tradesmen—you name them, they're out there, all with different start points and different destinations.'

'Right,' said David, uncertainly.

'Yip,' I said, as if certain of my comparison, whatever that might be. There was a brief pause before he spoke.

'So your analogy is that I don't know where I am really heading?' He scratched his head.

'I'm saying…that you'll be going from A to Z but you don't know what Z will be like, so it's difficult to advise you on your proposed destination, so to speak.'

'Right. What about my start point then?'

'David, to some extent none of us, me included, know what this start point might be like for you, or any of us next week or next year.'

'Okay.' His voice appeared to display a hint of disappointment that I wasn't going to offer a carrot. How could I when I was burning the midnight oil to set up a proposal to ditch the whole team, David included?

'So there's no chance of a steer on where I might be if I stayed here?' He looked me directly in the eye.

'David…what I'm saying is that in a world constantly on the go, new things come up all time that alter the dynamic.' I felt embarrassed, but I was in a corner. 'So I am afraid that I'm not in a position to guarantee anything. I'm really sorry.'

'Maybe I should take the job offer, then,' he ventured, as if choices had been removed from him during our short conversation. I felt slightly guilty, so I qualified my position a little further.

'Your gut instinct will tell you what to do. It sounds like a good job, and if I were you, hell, I would probably take it. Glasgow isn't that far away, and you might find a new role builds a platform for something else later on. I wish I could offer you more money, but I know what I'd be told if I ask upstairs.' This much was true. 'I'm not advising you to do anything specific.' I felt like telling him that if he waited a month or two he might get a redundancy cheque which would smooth the whole process, but of course, such advice was out of the question.

He left my office telling me that he was going to talk it over with his wife, and that he'd come back to me. The conversation had bluntly reminded me of the morals of the position I was now occupying. I had to lie those who looked up to me, lie to my employer, and hand Doug my money.

Though PR people were different, weren't they? Able to see others as they saw themselves, and see themselves as others saw them? Really? Be a bull in order to be a bullfighter?

The following day I met Doug at six o'clock as arranged. I'd had to pay a penalty to obtain the cash so quickly and I couldn't remember ever having handed over that amount of cash with nothing, precisely, to show for it.

'Don't worry, mate. I'm not going to blow it on horses.'

I stared at him. I wished he'd stop calling me *mate.*

'Dog racing has better odds,' he then said, grinning almost as if he knew this was the moment he had me. *No way out,* as in Kevin Costner's role as a spy, lying to his colleagues day in day out…*until* he got caught. I considered the parallel, while Doug stuffed the cash in a brief case he'd planked beside him.

'Look, extra time would help before we pitch. I always thought that the key to optimising the potential of a sale was preparation. I spoke to one of our board last week…and he thought that we were doing a sterling job as it was.' I figured that I'd drop in the Charles Henderson discussion to buy some time.

'Oh really? Who was that?'

'Non-exec, Charles Henderson. Know of him?'

'Vaguely. What did he have to say? Surely you didn't bring this proposal up with him, for fuck's sake?'

'Of course not. You sound like Weir. It's just that Charles Henderson was very supportive of the work the foundation is currently doing.

'Well he must be a prick. Now Ally, you, not Weir, need to be in there at the next board meeting, leading the charge. Are you telling me that an ace sales person like you doesn't want to be in there at the kill? Let's get this baby going.'

I sat forward, rubbing my eyes intensely with my fingers. I was tired, and frustrated at the whole thing. He was right, to a point. But then he didn't have to go into the lion's den. His personal reputation was not at risk—Doug was a behind the scenes partner as far as this venture was concerned. And I had just given him ten grand.

'Okay, okay! We'll see what Weir says, but if he wants to take centre stage, that's fine by me. And remember, we need to sell him on the rest of this first.'

So Doug began to talk. I had to admit he was in command of his brief. As he expanded on the plan, I considered that Doug himself should be the one pitching. That couldn't happen, of course. Yet, if I were honest, he was a better salesman than I was and he appeared to really believe in the value of the project, that it could work, and that we could pull it off.

There were three key strands to the deal. Initially, the primary case had to be made that the foundation was now unfit for purpose as it was currently configured and funded. This brought us onto the second part. Should we succeed in convincing the board, the fake bidding process would need to follow, with the conclusion that "Lexicon Chartered" would win the contract. This might entail visits to Ireland or some kind of internal audits. Suffice to say, there would be scrutiny of some kind. Thirdly, there was the small matter of operating the PR process through Ireland and Antigua while effectively scamming customers' money while no one noticed.

A piece of cake, really…

Doug elucidated on the financial detail. The figures that I'd stolen for him included psychographic analysis on internal customer profiling, and internal projection of future loyalty patterns of customer groups and their likelihood to recommend other products to third parties. This was sensitive information, and I reflected that I would be fired should it be revealed that I had removed this information from the Dosh Dome and shared it with someone else.

It was crucial, however. Could the bank request a donation twice? Three times? Ten times? How gullible were customers? Doug had produced academic research evidence from both the USA and Europe that indicated that more than 60 percent of customers would be likely to agree to each *subsequent* donation—in effect multiple minor donations, providing the donation request was reasonable. We would pitch this detail to the board in a fairly conservative way—erring on the side of caution, and providing relevant evidence from top business schools and commercial studies in this area. All of this information was now included in the business plan I witnessed before me. It really was an admirable plan.

So why had no one thought of this before now?

I was pleased that Doug had not insisted on Lexicon Chartered having an up-front fee, as this would be likely to add complexity to the pitch, possibly raising questions about why, and potential suggestions to look for other, larger *real* agencies in this sector which would not require a fixed fee as their operations could cope without one. Doug had also firmed up the business history for Lexicon Chartered: search engine friendly results, a positive credit rating, two websites, and testimonials from people who could be contacted. I was pretty impressed. As before, he briefly alluded to confidential favours owed, and the direct marketing company in Dublin. It would be available for a potential site visit should one be needed and 'real' people would respond when enquiries were made. Obviously this was also the case with Antigua, where we would employ two people, though the Irish element was to provide both assurance and relative locality.

I feared that Weir might want to have a physical interview or presentation from all three companies. I reminded him of the protocol at corporations such as Scottish Chartered—to be seen to be above board, and achieve compliance. Sure, this wasn't the public sector with a requirement to comply with EU rules on government procurement, but the bank, as with any other recruitment or supplier exercise, might legitimately demand to see real people making a presentation. Doug, still confident that we could make Lexicon Chartered seem such a sure-fire partner, attempted to assuage me by saying that he could arrange other people to help—people who owed him a favour.

How many people owed him favours, and why? Wasn't this a security risk? This part of the deal also brought me to another concern—suppose we could convince Weir or others at the bank to reject the two fake companies before any presentation, we would still need someone— a real person—to represent Lexicon Chartered at the bank. Who was going to take on that role? It couldn't be me or Doug, and presumably we wouldn't be flying someone in from Antigua.

Then Doug said he had someone primed to do this job. I asked when he had been going to tell me this part as I'd been so busy with everything that it had slipped my mind to ask. Anyone involved in this had to be in on the scam and by implication would know about *my* criminal complicity. Doug stared at me.

'Need to know principle.'

'What? Who's this third party?' I frowned.

'Calm down, Ally. This is for your own good. If you must know it's my old friend from Dublin, which fits in with the whole justification thing.'

'How much does he know about me right now?' I stood up, annoyed.

'He only knows bits and pieces. He's on need to know too,' Doug said.

'Doug, this is not a fucking spy movie we're involved in here. We're not terrorist cells with you as the mastermind at the nerve centre. And I take it that this guy isn't another mystery partner in the venture who turns up at a later date causing problems?'

'No, he's a necessary part of the jigsaw. Mike Canavan is his name. He will deliver as he owes me.'

'Why's that? How come so many people owe you? What have you got on them?'

Doug suddenly became angry. 'Do you want to make a ton of money or not? It is impossible to run something like this without a little help. You're an intelligent person, so you should fucking well know that. I'm taking more risks than you here as I'm implicated with more people than you. But I am minimising the risk by using a couple of people I know who can vouch for us when we need it. We're trying to do this on the cheap—the ten grand you just gave me barely covers the basics I need to finish off. And before you ask, the legal work is also being done by someone else who owes me. *You* benefit from that too—capiche? We need a couple of corners cut, and the business history and credit rating for Lexicon Chartered, *et cetera*, has not been created by accident. This thing is *not* actually legit? Got it? You need to get with the programme if we're going to pull it off.' Doug stood up, hands on hips.

I held my hands up. 'Okay, okay! I've got the point. I'm just not used to all this stuff. I want to meet this Canavan guy beforehand though. I need to know who I'm dealing with. This thing works both ways.' I sat back down, as did Doug.

'Look, Ally, let's not blow the deal on trivia.'

I took a few deep breaths, and accepted the coffee which he produced as some kind of peace offering. The caffeine hit me pretty quickly and sharpened my mind. Two hours later we had chewed the detail sufficiently to move things on. I'd switched off my phone during the meeting as I needed to focus. I'd just turned it back on, and it rang instantly.

Caller ID indicated Weir. I motioned to Doug not to interrupt.

'I've been trying to get hold of you all evening.'

'Been at a friend's place.' White lie.

'There's a board meeting next Tuesday and I want you to have your plans finalised— all the strategic options for the foundation. I take it that you must have fully researched things by now? I've kept off your back, but this is too good a chance to miss.'

Shit. 'That's too soon, Leslie.'

'Why?'

'Well, I'd need to speak with you. Firm up the research material. You'll want to help communicate the proposals to the board too, I take it?'

'Oh, I don't think there'll be any need for that. I may be the senior manager here, but this is your baby, and they'll want to hear it from the executive in charge of the project. How about you firm up your plans tonight and I'll pencil you in for seven a.m. tomorrow so you can enlighten me about your ideas.' This was delivered as a statement, not a question. He hung up.

'Bastard wants me to brief him at bloody 7 o'clock tomorrow, and present at Tuesday's board meeting. Christ, he doesn't even know the whole structure or anything yet,' I said.

'It's just as well we got moving on this stuff because it sounds like they may be ready to bite. We need to get on with it.'

'Yeah, right,' I said. He walked toward the door before turning to face me.

'This is your shot at glory, buddy. You better not blow it.'

Chapter 7

There's nothing quite like the waft of overpowering cologne to turn your stomach at 7:00 a.m. in the morning, particularly when you can't stand the person drenched in it. I'd struggled to achieve two and a half hours of disturbed sleep. This was because after a brief call to Mandy I'd stayed up until four, during which time I'd interrogated the data, triple checked the assumptions made, interpreted the legalese involved in key places and streamlined the material. We were nearly there.

Initially, Weir listened carefully, pretty much with the absence of interruption. He nodded now and again, and surveyed the ceiling at some points as if searching for flaws as the board might see them. He'd heard the gist of the sanitised version before, of course, but now there was detail—three potential companies that could do the job and a "brilliant" plan based on external research to fund the charity work from an untapped source and save the bank millions of pounds per annum. He barely smiled at the mention of Jerusalem Saviour and Gold Star Charity Liaison. I'd wrongly assumed that he'd ridicule the names of these businesses. I iterated the key strengths of each, why I'd "chosen" to select these three as suggested bidders, and of course strengths of *one* particular firm. He appeared to see nothing out of the ordinary. But then, why should he?

I said that I deeply regretted the potential loss of some good people and that we should redeploy those in the foundation to the PR and Marketing departments. People such as David Moritano deserved some choices in their futures.

Suddenly Weir stood up, and pointed directly at me.

'So which of these bidders do you consider the best? I know that you must have a view on this issue.'

I swallowed before bullshitting further. 'I would recommend *Lexicon Chartered*. They seem like an excellent company, compliant with what we would need, possessing relevant experience. They have a presence not too far away in Ireland. Personally, I think that this would be the way forward.'

He reviewed the electronic copy blurb I'd produced. He appeared distant, as if contemplating an entirely different proposition.

'So, have you spoken with anyone at Lexicon Chartered?'

'Yes, as it turns out, I have spoken to the Irish representative. Very erudite, knowledgeable and experienced.' I lied again, never having even heard of Mr Canavan until the previous night. 'Sometimes you just have a gut feeling, you know? We were looking for an alternative way of running things, and here's a company with all the ready-made skills, and it is also the cheapest.'

'And there's no one else in the market that might be better?'

'No.'

'Why?'

'Because of the specialist nature of the work, and of course the fact that Lexicon Chartered is substantially cheaper. I've researched alternatives and they all charge more commission. So this is a bigger saving for the bank.'

Weir nodded, almost as if assessing me as to how convincing I would be in front of the *board* rather than in his presence. The strange bluster about justification that he'd pulled in his office the last time had dissipated and he now appeared much more convinced.

'Any idea of the potential level of support amongst the board?' I asked.

'No,' he replied bluntly.

'It's just that if I thought we had allies…'

'Treat everyone as sceptical prospects.'

'But this leaves me going in blind. Surely you know who has been pushing for change? Obviously, the CEO is still out of the picture, but have you still not spoken with Peter Lawrence?'

'I have no reason to doubt that the acting CEO will support this proposal, especially if the board approves it.'

'Won't he feel ambushed if you've not mentioned it to him?'

'I have mentioned a scheme, in principle, to save substantial sums, so he'll be pleased to hear it once the board hears it first.'

'First?'

'Yes. Time hasn't permitted me to give all the details as you've only just finished your preparation…and Peter won't be at the board meeting. He has an unavoidable appointment.'

'They're still having a board meeting without the acting CEO?'

'Yes.'

This was oddly fortuitous. 'And you've, eh, managed to squeeze this into the agenda?'

Weir remained silent, as if the question was rhetorical.

Well, I had one more non-rhetorical question. 'There shouldn't be a problem with legal compliance, I take it? With Lexicon Chartered being based overseas?' I had to ask this question. Doug would have killed me, but I wanted some kind of reassurance.

'No, not a problem with me,' Weir replied. 'Banking and overseas business go hand in hand. I'll run it by our legal team. It will be okay in principle. The bank does business via the Caribbean every day. Our compliance rules are robust, and there looks like ample justification here to do business. I mean, it's not like cronyism or anything.'

'Eh, no…I'd never heard of them until…recently.'

Weir looked at me strangely. 'You need to firm this all up by Monday. I'm going to recommend that you speak on this issue as the first item on the board's agenda. Obviously, you'd need to meet the Lexicon people soon—if they're as good as it looks, then we won't have to interview the others.' He looked directly at me, and I tried hard not to reveal a smile.

Weir continued. 'Speak to Lexicon's management today and confirm contract details. And it goes without saying that this is still absolutely confidential. Seven in the morning doesn't suit me either, but even my secretary doesn't know about any of this, so keep your mouth shut.'

And that was it. No “well done”. No “thanks mate”. No “I appreciate your hard work”. Just *keep your mouth shut.*

The weekend was hectic. I briefly met Mandy at her flat to let her know the good news, but she was so busy that more of the sexual highs we’d experienced so recently seemed to be off the cards for the present, despite that throwaway line about success being the key to the bedroom. I accepted my current fate of postponement; the ultimate reward would be worth it.

Meanwhile, Doug was in the background. Only when I insisted did he arrange a chat on the phone with Mike Canavan. This guy was vague. This was ironic of course—I was in dialogue with someone who apparently knew of only some parts of the jigsaw, when Weir had requested that I speak to the very same phantom about a possible contract. The truth was that I was worried about Canavan’s credibility. If Weir—or anyone else—wanted to interview Canavan or have him make a presentation bullshitting about detail, he’d be shot down in flames. I still felt suspicious about sharing so much about the deception with a third party who was there simply to act as a decoy. Canavan didn’t appear particularly interested, which fitted with Doug’s explanation that he was just paying back a favour. I mentioned this to Doug, but he just brushed me off.

One thing I was pleased about is that Lexicon Chartered was not going to ask for up-front fees. Sometimes when a larger client is about to embark on a project with a specialist agency the agency may request a fixed fee before work commences, but I felt that this sent the wrong message. Doug had said that we needed such a fee, but I had argued the case that it could jeopardise the project, so he had finally acquiesced.

And so, Tuesday morning arrived impatiently. In my mind I had titled it ‘D Day’—*Deception* Day. Apprehension and then raw fear gripped my entire body. I’d engaged in lots of public speaking over the years, including presentations to large groups and a few times on live television, yet this was different. Is this what crime was really like? More than the cost of replacement underwear? I wondered if it was just an urban myth that burglars (no different, even if I tried to convince myself of the superiority of white-collar crime) often shat on the premises they'd entered? Leaving their DNA for the nose-clipped cops. And shit is exactly what I did in the men's room prior to entering the corporate lair.

The boardroom exhibited a mixed design mode, with a modicum of the grandeur of the past—mainly old portraits of past chairmen dotting the oak panelled walls—spliced with modern art that was partially integrated into the fabric of the ceilings and windows. I liked the room as it smelled kind of oaky, but today I had other things on my mind. Two board members were already present, whispering in an animated manner over coffee. I'd set up my presentation material before my second comfort stop.

Rule number one: be prepared.

Rule number two: if you talk shit, make it good shit.

The board members already present were Ian Duignan and John Hopkins, both non- executive. Non-executives are supposed to be a fundamental element of any boardroom. Their raison d'être is to provide an independent critique and to distinguish the immediate operational issues from longer term strategy. They also have legal responsibility to provide specialist knowledge so that companies trade properly and conduct compliant accounting procedures. New legislation drafted after the financial crisis had launched something akin to a board MoT—so at the back of my mind I wanted to assure these guys, to keep them focused. I waved over as if they were old mates, to which they responded with 'public' smiles. I was more worried, however, about some others. Charles Henderson for one, given our recent conversation. I suspected that he would be a blocking influence.

The chairman, James Hughes, was also old style, and I was led to believe that he often absorbed the wisdom of others, as a wise steward should. He would be present today, though there would be no CEO, due to his absence in Australia. Given that his temporary stand-in—the Finance Director—was also absent, there was an odd feel to the whole affair. The Finance Director had previously chaired the audit committee at one point, and although he would not occupy that role while Finance Director, he had an interest in compliance, which was at the back of my mind given the bullshit I was about to proclaim. Other major players still to arrive for the meeting included Carole McLetchie, the Director of Compliance, Niall Kidd, Marketing Director and Liz Duncan, HR Director. Tom Knight, Director of Strategy, and Lex O'Hara, who ran the retail banking and insurance arms of the bank, were also coming. As this was not an AGM or EGM, there would not be a full quota, but I might still get blown away as Weir had kept me ignorant—deliberately or otherwise—about whom might support the move or not.

My presentation material was set up and ready to go. I exited the room and waited outside as was protocol. I'd be called shortly, assuming no glitches. The remaining board members arrived, with one notable exception: Charles Henderson. Weir appeared outside the boardroom and sat beside me. I whispered to him, enquiring about Henderson's whereabouts.

'I've just had a phone call,' he whispered in reply. 'He's going to be an hour or so late.' He looked straight ahead, slightly away from my direction and though I couldn't tell precisely, I could have sworn that he wore a subtle smirk.

'I thought he was stickler for time keeping? Did he say why?'

'Apparently he's had a burglary or something at his home in Bearsden. He's been forced to sort things out with the police before coming through. Bad luck.' This projected a different quality of light on the situation.

'Right,' I said. 'So, would he have...known in advance about...the extra item on the agenda? The plan for the foundation?'

Weir scratched his head. 'Well, as you know, this has been a last minute thing. Agendas get altered at the last minute all the time. He might not have seen the most recent agenda until this morning. But then if he does he hasn't passed on any messages.'

'I guess he's got more to worry about.'

'His place has been trashed. Or so his wife said. Must have been a silent invader during the early hours. You never know what's round the corner in life.'

'It's an ill wind.'

'Don't fuck it up, eh? *Sell* this plan.'

I nodded. There was an odd feeling to all of this, but there was no way back. Weir spoke in quiet tones again.

'Now finally, before we go in—about that fixed fee that you added in for Lexicon Chartered. That's okay with me, but given the cost, it would have helped if you'd discussed it with me first.'

'Fixed fee?' I swallowed. What the hell was this?

'Yes. The four hundred grand towards the set up? It's all here in your presentation material. I printed off extra copies for the board this morning.' He held up a hard copy of the presentation material I was about to use, opening the section concerned with the costs of running the operation.

I stared at the page. There it was in black and white. A fixed start fee of 400K! Where the hell had that come from? I'd only finalised the material last night and got a final edit back from Doug before emailing it to Weir. Doug must have sneaked this in at the last minute despite the agreement we had about this issue. The greedy bastard. He must have known that I'd no time to make any corrections—and now that Weir, as a senior manager with 'strategic liaison responsibility' was sitting two feet from me I couldn't say anything.

Weir continued. 'The strategy is clear enough with this fee, but you might need to make the case with the board, what with the up-front costs involved.' I nodded in response—what option did I have?

The door to the boardroom opened and the PA to the company secretary appeared.

'Mr Weir and Mr Forbes?'

I took a deep breath and followed Weir into the room. He sat at the side, while I made my way to the lectern and display hub. The company Secretary briefly introduced me to the chairman and other board members, and then invited me to make a presentation about the charitable foundation, saying that Weir had 'recommended' that I address the board in person with 'my' special plan. I had twenty minutes, plus questions.

Perhaps this seems strange, but after the first half minute, I actually enjoyed myself.

It was one of these situations when up until a critical point is upon us we're consumed with fear and uncertainty, yet adrenalin then kicks in and we embrace the moment and elevate our performance to a new level. Or so I pretended. I sought to integrate the strategic with the operational, the rational with the emotional—after all there were needy charitable beneficiaries involved—and remained focused on the compelling elements of the plan: let our *customers* fund the needy causes. I even—what the hell, feel the fear and do it anyway—stressed the essential need for up-front fees as I praised the merits of Lexicon Chartered as our favoured agency, and softened my tone when explaining that we would do our very best to redeploy those affected internally. Throughout there were nods and affirmations, perhaps one or two indications of ostensive surprise and brief whispers between board members, but nothing obviously negative.

'Thank you, Ally,' said James Hughes. 'That was very enlightening. 'Leslie—have you anything you to add?'

Weir cleared his throat. 'No, Mr Chairman, I think that Ally's summed up...his project...succinctly.'

'Yes, all right. Now fellow board directors, questions?'

John Hopkins was first up. He asked whether I'd produced cost-benefit analysis of the current foundation versus the new plan in relation to long-term media coverage. I'd anticipated this one, as it was a weak point so I referred him to one of the appendices. Here, I outlined the case for change. John Hopkins appeared satisfied.

The next question came from Tom Knight. He was very complimentary—a hawk, you might say. He asked if we could generate even *more* in the form of donations from the client base than I had projected, leaving more cash for the bank. Doug and I had erred on the side of realism when making the forecasts, so we could go under the radar. I thanked him and said we'd make every attempt to maximise the revenue.

Lex O'Hara then said that he had no immediate comments, but was in favour in principle. Carole McLetchie countered, however, by questioning the need for an upfront fee for Lexicon Chartered. Thanks, Doug. She wore half moon glasses and peered over the lenses as she spoke. Surely if they were such able agents, they wouldn't need extra resources to be spent on them before any credible results had been realised?

Perhaps surprisingly, Weir answered the question before me.

'This is a very good point, Dr McLetchie.' Weir was so much more sycophantic of these people than of his direct reports. 'Like you, I myself wondered about the value in such a payment. However, Ally has assured me of the validity and quality of the company, and I've passed the details before our legal team just in case. I've not met representatives of the firm yet, but Ally has, and having reviewed some of the alternatives they all charge greater commission than Lexicon would, so the break-even point is relatively early on.'

'But what about their registration in the Caribbean?' Carole McLetchie asked a legitimate question. All eyes moved to me during a moment's silence, before Tom Knight raised his hand.

'Carole, we live in an interdependent global village. As you know, despite having been born down the road, I travel all over the globe meeting people to assess our next move. Services are being off-shored all the time. And remember, some of our main shareholders—take the sovereign wealth funds—would be very interested in this kind of thing. Personally, I think that this looks like an extremely efficient manner of doing business—in fact the bank should take a greater lead from executives such as our two colleagues here.' I suspected that he was probably the main board member who had encouraged Weir to save costs in the first place. Perhaps he didn't want to look like the instigator, but he appeared a fully paid-up supporter here. Knight smiled after he spoke.

Carole McLetchie didn't smile. 'Everything is not about immediate cost, Tom. However, I'm not against off-shoring completely. I've argued in favour of bits and pieces before. I am concerned here about the control and compliance aspects. Ally, do we have your assurance that there will be full approval of this firm before engagement?'

Again, everyone looked at me, including Weir.

'Yes, I will… ensure that we—*you*—are happy with the ability and compliance of this firm before we go further.' She nodded slowly, with accompanied pursed lips. Everyone else remained quiet.

'Right,' the chairman spoke again. He exhibited a typical Edinburgh 'private school' accent which I was pretty sure could be attributable to George Watson's in the city. 'Thank you for your comments. I have a couple of questions. Ally, the first is a little personal, if you don't mind? This is a question that I'm certain Charles Henderson would be asking if he were here right now, and maybe the CEO, circumstances aside. This foundation was—is—your responsibility and you deserve much credit for setting it up. I'm happy to see advancement with the times, and I appreciate that you've made a strong endorsement for change. I also like the concept of asking our own clients to donate small amounts. However, I'm a little surprised that you're in favour of moving much of the operational control outside. Everyone here is aware of the media coverage the bank gets through the foundation. It works. So my question is: what inspired the change of heart?'

I deliberately avoided touching my nose, covering my mouth or looking down. Or unwittingly displaying Bill Clinton's infamous furrowing of the brow when asked if he'd had an affair with a White House intern. I looked him in the eye and smiled as benignly as was feasible.

'Mr Chairman, may I quote Erica Jong?' There was a muffled response around the boardroom. '*If you risk nothing, you risk everything*. A fresh set of eyes assessing the administration might create real value. Much as it pains me to reinvent, what is the real alternative?'

'And the staff members who may lose their jobs?' Liz Duncan, the HR Director, spoke for the first time. 'We're non-unionised, but we attempted to draw the line under redundancies last year with the restructuring of the whole business. Won't there be bad publicity from that? How would this be handled?'

Weir stepped in again. 'As fairly as possible, Ms Duncan, ensuring that we redeploy the best talents for other parts of the business and let others…pursue new interests.' The board members recognised this euphemism for what it was, leaving James Hughes nodding and pointing at his watch.

'All right. It's a pity that Charles has been held up. I'm sure he would have had something constructive to say. But we must push on. Can I have a show of hands in favour of this plan, in principle?'

Everyone raised a hand except Carole McLetchie, who waited until for a couple of seconds before speaking. 'I'm not voting against, Mr Chairman. But I'd like to note for the record my concern about corporate governance issues and financial compliance in relation to this foreign agent.' She sat back as the PA noted her comment in the minutes, and James Hughes duly confirmed the agreement of the board.

Game on.

Chapter 8

'I've never heard anyone complaining before about being *four hundred thousand* up! You would never have asked for it, so *quit* moaning,' Doug shouted down the phone.

I'd told him about the board's green light, but also harangued him about covertly introducing the up-front fee for Lexicon Chartered. I was out in the car park—in the rain again—paranoid about anyone overhearing the conversation in the office. I'd also witnessed Charles Henderson appearing late in the car park.

'I just don't like being surprised like that. You promised to be open and honest with me. Luckily, Weir seemed to buy it but this could have scuppered the deal.'

'Christ, you're a buttered-side down man, aren't you? A glass half-empty guy? For fuck's sake, I'll keep the money myself seeing you're against it in principle.' Then he laughed. 'Actually, *I will be* custodian of the money until we create a system of laundering. So you're going to have to trust me, mate.'

'I'm getting good at that. Oh, and by the way—what were you doing in the early hours of the morning?' The silence was audible.

'Same as you, mate.'

'So you were up early preparing for a board meeting?'

'Tucked up, sound asleep, bud. Pretty confident that such a masterful plan would get the go ahead.' That smug characteristic that Doug employed so well face to face also transmitted just as effectively over the phone. I could picture his expression despite his absence.

‘So you weren’t in Bearsden breaking into any mansions, then?’ Again, there was a split second gap before he replied.

‘Lost me there, mate.’

‘Charles Henderson—remember him? Likely to question or block the move? Delayed due to an early morning break-in at his home? Neatly missed the presentation and the vote? Amazingly fortuitous.’

‘Oh…right. There we are then, there is a God after all.’

‘I’ve just seen him entering the bank.’

‘He was probably the victim of a random thief. Happens all the time. A guy like that must be able to afford a small increase in insurance premiums. Water off a rich duck’s back if you ask me.’

Would Doug really have organised a break-in to ensure that the deal progressed? Surely he was beyond that? Then again, what sort of immoral exercise had we just encouraged a major bank to pursue?

I was complicit.

In some respects a break-in was small potatoes. Given the result in the boardroom, perhaps it didn’t matter, but there was a nagging concern in my mind about our ‘partnership’. If Doug had engineered this behind my back, and he was prepared to add another four hundred thousand to the bill for the bank, what else might he decide to do? It occurred to me that Charles Henderson could attempt to prevent progress. We’d only secured approval from the board ‘in principle’. Carole McLetchie, the Director of Compliance, had also voiced concern and the acting CEO might equally throw cold water on the plan, though Weir had suggested the opposite.

Mandy was next on my list. When I called, her number was engaged and I tried a couple of times before getting through. ‘Hi babe,’ I said offering the opening phrase she had often used on me. ‘I’ve got some good news.’

‘Your plan’s going ahead?’

‘Yip.’

‘Cool stuff. I was pretty confident that it would. No brainer from their perspective. So you’ll be spoiling me with riches?’

‘Well, it’s going to take a while. But—despite my advice—Doug threw in a demand for some up-front investment and that got board approval too. So there should be some rewards sooner rather than later.'

I agreed to postpone seeing Mandy until the weekend and hung up. The irony was that a large slice of the motivation for embarking on this devious ploy was to impress her—yet there was an inverse relationship between the time devoted to the project and that expended on Mandy. I returned to the Dosh Dome and bumped into David Moritano at the junction of the stairs and the elevator.

'Ally…hi. I was looking for you this morning. But I heard that you were at a board meeting.' He eyed me cautiously. He'd been circumspect with me since our earlier conversation about his potential career move.

'Yeah. The usual. There's always something moving. Just trying to duck and dive. You never know what's coming next.' More bullshit on my part.

'Right…well, I've made a decision on that job offer.'

'Okay.'

'I've decided that I'm going to stay here.' I nodded, not wishing to sound too despondent because I'd been hoping he'd take the move. That way I could massage my conscience with at least one member of the team.

'That's fine, David, it's your call. These decisions are always difficult to make. I'm sure it will all work out.' He raised his eyebrows, as if he expected me to say more: like how fantastic he was in his role, or how there would more rewards for him, but of course, to suggest anything of the sort would have been a downright lie as he was about to get the chop. He was going one floor up, but rather than join him on the stairs I nipped into the elevator. Normally I avoid elevators (a bad experience once as a child) but on this occasion it gave me a reason to take a different route from David—the second floor via the fourth.

I stepped out at the fourth only to see Charles Henderson in deep conversation in the corridor. He then glanced round, and given that I'd arrived under false pretences, I could hardly have enacted an immediate volte face for fear that he would interpret this as deliberate avoidance. He made distinct eye contact and beckoned me over as other board members began to depart.

'Hello, Ally. Missed your presentation earlier due to unforeseen circumstances.'

'Yes. Sorry to hear about that. Burglary, was it?'

'Yes actually it was. Gosh, bad news travels fast. I hadn't mentioned much detail to anyone here that we'd had anything other than a disturbance. But given you ask, there appears to be some things missing. My iPad's been stolen.' He shook his head as if dismayed by the state of today's society. Weir or one of the PAs must have spoken to Henderson's wife about the break-in. Then a sudden though also occurred: did Doug arrange for Henderson's iPad to be nicked?

I touched his shoulder, before stepping back, desperate to get away. 'Right…I hope that everything is resolved. The police are pretty good these days.' I made to leave.

He then stepped closer, speaking in low tones. 'Ally, I'm a little disappointed by your proposal. I've just been brought up to speed by a board colleague.'

He continued, bearing down on me. 'After our chat at the Caledonian, especially. You gave me no clue as to your intentions.' I felt my skin beginning to colour, the temperature suddenly feeling distinctly warmer. What could I say?

'Yes…I was meaning to talk to you about it, but it's been so hectic…and…Leslie asked for complete confidentiality until we had fully assessed the project…he was the main driver behind things…'

He looked me directly in the eye. 'That's not what's been reported here. From what I hear *you're* leading the charge. Your proposal's gone down well, it seems, with most of the board, but if I had been present I would have advised caution. The idea about asking customers for donations is an interesting if unproven innovation, but what I don't understand is why you need an outside agency—especially one based overseas— to distribute the funds? This is the sort of un-necessary risk that I've witnessed many businesses take. Throwing the baby out with the bathwater. '

'Yes. The reason—'

'It's not just about my granddaughter, you know. If the system is working, why would the bank pay an unknown quantity to run the show? These people might well be slick salesmen, but would they have the bank's interests at heart once a contract is signed? The kind of event you organised at the Caledonian probably wouldn't happen.' He stopped talking, awaiting a proper explanation. I decided to use an old variation of the principle of agreeing then countering sometimes used in negotiation: *Feel, Felt, Found.*

'I understand how you *feel.* The chairman *felt* the same…initially, though when I produced a full explanation of the rationale behind the new set-up he said that he *found* that he could see the advantages.' Henderson looked on sceptically, so I continued.

'You see, I feel that if we stand still, we will fall behind. Tom Knight actually said that he felt we weren't going far enough with the proposal.'

'Ah yes, Tom. He's always focused on short-term bottom line issues, even though he's Director of Strategy. I tend to look at things from a long-term strategic perspective.' He touched my shoulder again. 'You're an able executive, Ally, but even able executives can crash and burn.'

A dream-like quality engulfed the next period, with the sheer pace of events overshadowing other aspects of life. I couldn't tell you a news story from this period, or a football score. All my energy was focused on covering my ass. Actually, it's extremely awkward being a lying bastard to those whose help you need. Even the lies had a Machiavellian twist, as I had to legitimately deceive those about to lose their jobs, yet illegitimately deceive management about everything else: Lexicon Chartered, Doug, Mike Canavan, the Irish office, the Caribbean angle, and my own investment. I didn't feel guilty in my dealings with Leslie Weir—because he was a total prick—but the case was difficult with others where I was aiding the redesign of their lives for my own personal gain. That class in ethics I'd taken whilst a student now appeared to exist in an altogether different universe.

The one advantage I'd secured from Weir was a week out of the office. He never questioned my whereabouts when I was researching the last strands of the legend of Lexicon Chartered in order to meet with the compliance policy of the company and the government. Nor did he ask where so much of the information had been sourced. I presumed that he had either underestimated the work involved or he simply didn't care if I flogged myself to death in the process. Then again, he was due to benefit, presumably, though a bonus of some sort, so why would he question the source of this volume of work if it was in his personal interest? I offered the believable story that all this data and the related policy had been designed with the help of Lexicon—if this company was to be our new partner and secure a sizable down-payment from us, we were legitimately entitled to full-service. It turned out that the acting CEO had actually been happy with the full details of the proposal when Weir had met him and all he needed from me was a five-minute chat.

Unfortunately, the foundation team was also beginning to ask questions—I'd received emails and phone calls fishing for information as to what was happening. My absence had become an issue, raising obvious questions. My media contacts had also enquired about delays in response and non-appearance at one or two events where I would have usually pressed the flesh and pushed the company's key messages.

The Canavan angle still worried me too, as Mike Canavan would probably have to meet with Weir in Lexicon's "Irish Office" in Dublin to secure the deal. I was as yet unconvinced of Canavan's thespian skills, having now had two or three short conversations with the man where he clearly couldn't wait to get rid of me. Maybe he would turn it on once he was 'in character'? Doug had assured me any meeting in Dublin could be arranged in a way that there would be few questions asked.

Indeed, signatures were needed as part of the binding contract we were aiming to secure, and notwithstanding the subtlety with which Doug had manufactured this company (and the two other fakes that had now so easily been dismissed after the board meeting), there was still the requirement of compliance. Here we received good news. Weir reported that the legal team had given approval to Lexicon as a supplier. The Director of Compliance, Carole McLetchie, had also now given approval. The bank's responsibility included raising the donations from customers and Weir even volunteered to liaise with the relevant departments in order to speed up progress. The law on charities *themselves* had been tightened significantly in recent times because of scams where proceeds failed to reach worthwhile causes in sufficient quantities but the beauty here was that *we weren't running a charity.*

Then, at short notice Doug suddenly suggested that I get Weir on a plane to Dublin for our 'site visit'. Weir agreed straight away. He appeared to be buying into the whole caboodle, though I feared that Mike Canavan would blow the deal when we met. I'd agreed the script with Doug in advance. Just over an hour's flight from Edinburgh Airport was long enough in close proximity to Weir, aftershave and all, and the resultant journey to the Lexicon folly as I'd imagined it in my mind proved short and simple. The office was in a modern block about thirty minutes by cab from the airport, in the suburb of Dundrum. I'd enjoyed weekends in Dublin before, though on this occasion I wouldn't have time to enjoy the expensive if cordial banter usually on offer in the Irish capital.

The offices were within a fairly nondescript modern development that could have been anywhere in northern Europe. Canavan had briefed a few of his own staff to behave accordingly, and there was some Lexicon display material that all looked legitimate. Canavan answered all Weir's questions convincingly. In fact, he even turned on the charm. Weir, though not an individual normally influenced by such human warmth, real or fake, appeared content with the set up and the apparent personnel behind the project. I had feared that this would all go belly-up, but I felt a little more reassured that this lot could actually deflect inquiries if and when required. The fact that Canavan operated a genuine direct marketing firm based in the same premises added validity to the operational presence, despite the fact that Lexicon was in effect a shell company. We returned to Edinburgh and I endured a 'told you so' from Doug when I reported that the visit had gone so smoothly.

We were two weeks away from a formal announcement, and things were going well.

Then the merde hit the extractor.

Someone in IT—one of those who'd been sworn to secrecy about the restructuring—had been overheard talking about the project by one of the foundation's team at the company cafeteria. Weir, the board, the legal staff and I had all managed to hold our water, but not the tech folk. I had been on a phone call to Doug when, without warning, I suddenly had a posse outside my office, angrily staring in through the glass walls. I had instantly known that the story was out and there was no escape route except to break the outside window and leap from the building. The resultant dispute became heated.

I lied. And lied.

I felt very small. The worst aspect was that I'd been speeding towards a red light on this issue, knowing it was coming but hoping somehow that the light would turn green. These people were doing a decent job—they were part of the success of the foundation, and I owed them. Yet here I was, shafting them.

When were you going to tell us? What's to gain by outsourcing? Do we have jobs? Why weren't we consulted? Who's going to pay our mortgages? So, *your* job's safe, is it?

Weir was offsite at a meeting in London, Doug was conveniently immune to such moral enquiry, and there was no one to blame but me. As I asked them to move back down to the basement, David Moritano arrived, a belated addition to the lynch mob. He said nothing, but when I caught his eye, he simply shook his head as if I were the biggest wanker on the planet. The mood was mirrored by Kostas, who had witnessed much of the event from his desk outside, and who raised his eyebrows in sympathy with those whose futures were now in doubt.

Word travelled even faster out of the building. Weir gave me stick for the way the events had turned despite the fact that I had no control over what someone in IT had blurted. I was forced to give a number of 'no comments' to the media—something I hate doing as these tend to deflect journalists for only a short duration before more probing questions return under a new guise.

The next two weeks were hell. Only David Moritano and one other guy avoided the chop. David agreed to take a PR role on a short-term basis, but he still clearly blamed me for failing to advise him properly on his potential move to Glasgow. There's an old adage in business—people can cope with the expected negatives, it's the unexpected negatives that piss them off. I couldn't blame them, and I wrote personal letters to all of the team—hollow letters—though the guilt remained with me. Charles Henderson even emailed me to say he'd been disappointed. I said that I fully expected that the new set-up would benefit the same good causes that the previous foundation had, including support for kids' sport. I didn't receive a reply.

One person who was fairly supportive was Elise Stewart. She bought me a coffee in the cafeteria and intimated that in America this would constitute no more than a brief rumble. She'd been a victim of downsizing twice before and had bounced back. Said it was one of the best things that had happened to her as she thought inertia set in where folk had a 'safe' job. Clearly she wished to avoid making a cultural criticism, but she displayed an underlying sentiment that people here should learn to suck it up and get on with it. Kostas said that in Greece the entire staff would be out on the streets setting things on fire. Lighting me first.

We began to obtain donations, subtly directing new account holders not to electronically 'un-tick', whilst a small communications budget was created to request that all existing customers would become benefactors unless they specifically requested otherwise. Banks, eh? Bogging people down with deception.

Our planned alterations didn't even make a page lead in the business press. I had initially suspected that this would be a story—how a bank had skimmed its customers again—but no. Some other banks has been subject to severe criticism as they had disbanded charitable foundations in order to save money, but the key difference was that Scottish Chartered was continuing with the work, albeit with a new funding model. Clearly this didn't merit scandal status, which was a relief. Then one morning Weir and the company lawyer quietly signed the deal with Lexicon. Mike Canavan "signed" on behalf of Lexicon, and responded by registered snail mail. An electronic payment for four hundred thousand was transferred to an Antiguan account.

The only problem was that I felt like a lottery winner who had still to pick up the cheque, wondering if it would bounce.

Chapter 9

I began to enjoy being a successful cheat. Perhaps it was the thrill of having planned a seamless scheme, or the feeling of future riches, or the emotion of minor superiority over some of my more pompous work colleagues who were unwittingly aiding my success as they ploughed the banking furrow. Maybe it was the fact that I would be able to deliver a winning chunk of money to Mandy and prove my worth as a player. Who knows? All I did know is that my self esteem enjoyed a boost.

But feeling good also has its risks. There was often new legislation in banking because one scandal followed another—like devious children following dishonest parents. This had thwarted the life of the financial crook; made it more complex. Concealing money entails thinking what others don't and playing along with the rules so that nothing seems out of the ordinary.

Yet, the prospect of being caught seemed less real now that we were underway. It might seem odd, or very cocky, but the scam now seemed more secure. But becoming too greedy was not one of my plans as the reason everything was working was due to a slow, undetectable accumulation of money which people had willingly given away. The 'offices' in Ireland and in Antigua were processing money at a fair rate of knots.

This brought another problem, because so far I had witnessed not a penny of the income that had accrued to Lexicon, and I wanted to pin Doug down on the detail. I was monitoring the flow of money, and more than three million had now accrued through donations. And as Lexicon was due a 12 percent fee, a decent six figure sum had come into the coffers. It might have seemed crazy, but because of the hours I'd spent on delivering the plan within the bank, I had actually failed to nail Doug down on the specifics of how we would split the booty. I called him and let him know that I wanted to talk money.

We met in the White Hart pub in the Grassmarket. I'd always liked this place as it had a nice traditional feel. Mandy worked not far away, but I decided not to contact her. Doug and I ordered two pints and found a quiet corner, where I asked about sharing the rewards. Initially he was evasive, blaming Canavan for new fees.

I tried to stay cool. 'I thought he was only involved as he owed you a favour? Why should he be paid first?'

'Expenses.'

'How much?'

'Forty to fifty thou.'

'*Fifty thousand*?! This is way more than we agreed. He only had to buy a few signs and host a meeting. Answer a few calls. He hasn't invested anything in this, unlike me.' I shook my head.

'He needs to be incentivised just the same as *us*.' Doug sat back, arms folded. Here we go again, I thought.

'Sounds almost like a blackmail payment to me. What about *my* half of us?'

'What do you mean?'

'Why the cloak and dagger with the money now? You were quick enough to take my ten thousand without any receipts.'

'I put in plenty too. And what's the matter? Need some cash to keep your girlfriend happy?' He raised his eyebrows, entering new territory.

'She's got nothing to do with it. Money has.'

He leaned forward, a thumb under his chin. This was one of the poses he'd used when I first met him at that charity bash—as if mirroring a sort of academic stance and preparing to justify an obscure argument.

'Ally… you know as well as I do that there are strict laws on money laundering in this country. Remember, officially you can't earn anything from this venture, certainly as far as the Inland Revenue or the bank is concerned. So you need your share to be protected. I do too.'

'But I only have your word.'

'You'll need to be patient.'

I flinched. 'Patient? Canavan hasn't had to be patient.'

'Calm down. This is for your own good. We talked about this early on. What do you want? Your name all over the company documentation? Big posters up at the bank displaying your photo along with an Antiguan bank account number? The fraud squad at your door? We've gone to great lengths to keep your name out of it.'

'Doug, I *know* all this. I've taken you on trust all the way through this process. I should get a doctorate in fucking trust studies since I started associating with you. I want to know what the plans are for funnelling my share to me. I think that's only fucking reasonable.'

'If you want cash, I can't do anything right now. We dare not make electronic payments to either one of us in this country. But if you're going to set up an off-shore account it could blow the whole thing. There are reciprocity agreements between so many countries now in terms of governments sharing information, and there's no way we can risk discovery here because of tax evasion discovered through some dodgy foreign bank account.'

'So how come Lexicon is so secure?'

'Because Lexicon is registered in the Caribbean and technically has nothing to do with either you or me. I have, let's say, understanding lawyers. Lexicon is secure. And before you ask, we paid Canavan because he runs a legitimate business and presumably pays tax.' As he looked at me, I breathed in and out, trying to think clearly.

'Okay, Doug, I'll take some *cash* then. When are you off to Antigua, and by the way, how are you paying for that?'

'Oh for Christ sake, it won't be yet, and hell, I'll use my own money if it makes you happy.'

'Okay, okay.' I said. There was probably no point in pushing it too far at the moment. To an extent he was right. I might have been down a few thousand at this point, but I was in no way implicated in either tax avoidance or money laundering. A moment of silence occurred, and I looked out of the window of the pub, watching the passing drift of human traffic. Shoppers, commuters, people on the move with a purpose. I contemplated if any of them might be pursuing illegal ventures or arguing about how to distribute dirty cash sitting in the Caribbean. Then an orange coat caught my attention. I knew someone with that coat, and as the woman turned round in the street I made direct eye contact with none other than Mandy. I stood up and beckoned her in. She looked cold, and rubbed her hands as she made her way over to our corner.

'You really are a sad stalker,' I ventured.

'Hi. Yeah, I've nothing better to do with my time,' she said as I kissed her on the cheek.

'Out shopping after work?'

'Trying my best.' She glanced at Doug, and smiled hesitantly, before sitting down. She'd probably put two and two together and guessed his identity.

'Mandy, this is Doug Fox,' I confirmed.

Doug stood up, extending his hand. 'Ah, at last I get to meet the lovely Mandy. I see why you've been keeping her a secret.'

'Aye, right,' I replied. 'Corny lines like that went out of fashion twenty years ago.'

'Just being truthful, mate.'

'Yes. That's your middle name, truthful, right?'

Doug turned to Mandy. 'He's hard work at times, your boyfriend. You must have hours of fun together.'

She sat down beside us, looking him straight in the eye. 'Yes, it's riveting stuff, going out with Ally. Never a moment without, what do you call it here? Wit…and repartee? Actually, I should really thank you, Doug.'

Doug raised his eyebrows. 'Why's that?'

'All the hours you've had him working on this big mystery project have kept him out of my hair. You could actually charge for a service like that.'

Doug then grinned, so I spoke up. 'He's charged me plenty as it is. As a matter of fact I had been attempting to prise some cash *back* from Doug before you came in, but maybe we should leave that one until another day.'

Mandy viewed Doug cautiously before speaking. 'I would say he's got the look of a reasonably honest man, Ally. I'm sure your reward will come.' Doug stretched out his arms in apparent vindication.

'And I'm sure that you'll help me spend it,' I suggested.

'I've been called many things, Ally, but cheap isn't one of them,' she replied.

'Can't argue with that,' I whispered. 'There you go Doug. Now Mandy's on my case you can book that flight to Antigua to bring me back some laundered money.'

Doug's expression reminded me of a frustrated school teacher addressing a pupil who keeps asking the same question, but then he suddenly bit his lip, and cleared his throat. 'I take it that Mandy knows the full story here, and that I can speak candidly?'

Mandy and I exchanged glances and then she turned to Doug. 'If you're wondering if I'm trustworthy, the answer is, yes. If you want privacy I'm happy to leave, though perhaps I might even already be classed as an accomplice, of sorts.'

I butted in. 'So it's not in Mandy's interest to give away any trade secrets. Say what you're going to say, Doug.'

He leaned forward in a conspiratorial manner. 'You know, rather than stuffing banknotes into my boxers on the way back from St John's Airport sometime, I've just thought of an easier way that I could channel money to you…indirectly.'

'I'm listening.'

'We could use someone only loosely connected but with a different name and a different…business.' He then touched Mandy's arm, looking straight at me.

'*No way*.' I said, a little too loudly as a couple at another table stared in our direction. I lowered my voice. 'Why should Mandy take any risks? That's a crazy idea.'

'Hold on, Ally. Before you dismiss it out of hand, this could work. Mandy could be a *consultant* for Lexicon. Just like Canavan. You're in, what, PR, Mandy?'

'Yes.'

'Perfect. Legitimate business expense for Lexicon. Okay, you might have to pay tax once a payment reaches you, but it moves the money back home. All cleaned up.' I raised my hand in protest but Mandy took hold of it before interjecting.

'That *could* work, Ally. Providing it's all secure, which I assume it would be? I mean, before I came in, were you actually asking Doug to bring back a stash of dollars for you from the Caribbean?' Sarcasm seeped through her tone, irritating me, especially as this was in front of Doug.

'No, actually. I was going to request crumpled up *sterling*, Mandy. I know full well that I'd have to give personal details to exchange a large amount of US dollars here. I *have* worked in a bank for some years.'

'Well then you'll also be aware that you'd be unable to deposit a large amount in sterling either without having it flagged up.' She folded her arms, looking at me as if I was a complete idiot. Doug also folded his arms in postural echo. Unbelievable. They were ganging up against me.

'I had been intending to gradually make deposits and purchases of assets over a period of time. Spend less of my income. Do things, gradually.' They both still stared, clearly unconvinced.

Doug whispered again. 'Ally, you must know that with the money we expect to make out of this there is *no way* you could gradually hide it in normal bank accounts or stocks without drawing attention to yourself. There are lots of triggers used by the authorities these days. This is why I was asking you to hang fire. *To chill out about the money*. But seeing you want a result, *Mandy* is the perfect vehicle to legitimise the flow of cash. I don't know why I didn't think of this before—we could use Mandy's business to move money legitimately.'

'I'm really not sure that this would be a good idea.'

Mandy sat back, arms folded. She was now looking in the direction of the ceiling, lips pursed. She was taking this as a slight.

'What?' I asked. She slowly lowered those striking green eyes towards me.

'You don't trust me.'

'That's absolutely not true! This is not about trust. It's…it's the fact that I don't want you to take any…risks.'

She blew out some air, looking first at Doug and then at me. 'Ally, this has nothing to do with me, but I think that this is probably a safer way for you to make progress. Providing you and Doug can guarantee that this end is legal, and secure? It is secure, right?'

'Yes, or we wouldn't be suggesting it. All you'd need to do is produce invoices and receipts for work,' Doug said.

'Well, I could do it then. Providing that the other end is properly incorporated and I pay the tax, legitimately.'

I didn't like this idea. I *did* trust Mandy, but I was a little miffed that this conversation was happening in front of someone she'd never even met before. In Doug's case—well yes, I did have questions about his level of trustworthiness. He'd done a couple of things that I could question. I simply didn't want to involve more people, or generate unnecessary risks for my girlfriend. On the other hand, I wanted to stay with Mandy and this might strengthen our relationship. We'd not seen very much of each other recently, and she was genuinely offering to help. It might actually push her away if I steadfastly refused and looked like a right miserable bastard. Life is as much about perceptions as reality, after all. As a moment of silence passed I considered if I might relent.

'You wouldn't spend it all on clothes?' I attempted to deflect the situation through some crap humour.

'Absolutely,' she replied.

And then before really thinking, I replied: 'Well, I guess…that would be okay then.'

Mandy raised her chin, having won the argument. Doug scratched his forehead, trying hard not to smile. 'Well, it looks like we have some kind of a deal. I feared for the state those banknotes after seven hours wedged in Ally's pants on a plane from Antigua.'

She laughed. I didn't.

'Hey, don't complain buddy,' Doug said. 'You thought I was going to rip you off, didn't you? Well I won't. I'll get something set up via Canavan. Mandy can bill him for say, ten thou to start, followed by future payments of similar amounts?'

I nodded slowly. 'Okay.' Mandy raised her chin as if the natural order of life had been restored—the female of the species being treated with respect.

Doug took some basic details about Mandy's business, and said he would arrange paperwork to legitimise the first payment, which could be made in a couple of days. Mandy explained to Doug that her business was split into two companies, so she could undertake work on her own as well as with colleagues, and separate payments when necessary—ideal in the circumstances. We finished our drinks, and Mandy said she needed to get going. I suggested visiting her at her flat later that night but she said she needed an early night. Doug said he needed to shoot off too so I decided to head home.

It felt like a pyrrhic victory.

When Mandy and Doug finalised details the following day, the payment was transferred as planned. I felt a minor twang of guilt having not trusted Doug. He seemed like a loose cannon at times, but then he also found solutions to problems. Mandy showed me the transfer details and said it was best to treat it as her legitimate income and pay tax so as to reduce suspicion. This was rational, if a little frustrating. I had expected to pay no tax on this venture; dishonest, I know, but I'd figured that it would be the only way. I could hardly claim my ten thousand in expenses either, which was ironic. I wondered how much illegitimate money is laundered under the nose of the Inland Revenue, and how assiduous the authorities are in such cases, when they actually *get* their tax, versus those cases of straight tax evasion. I suspected that I knew the answer to this question, so Mandy's viewpoint prevailed. And then for the fourth night in a row I stayed on late at work in the evening, and as the last remaining colleagues disappeared I contemplated a simple question in my office: *what could go wrong?*

Then the phone buzzed. I let it go for three rings, before picking up.

Weir.

'Leslie?'

'What took you so long to answer?' It was typical—even if I went for a piss when Weir was looking for me, I suddenly morphed into Harrison Ford in *The Fugitive*.

I ignored his criticism. 'What can I do for you?'

'Need to speak to you urgently. But not on the phone. My office, now.'

I wandered up to his lair. The usually omnipresent Wendy had actually departed.

'Anyone else out there?' Weir observed me cautiously.

'No, looks like everyone's packed it in for today,' I answered.

'Right. I'm going to speak plainly.' He stared at me as if this were to be a novel experience for me. I said nothing.

'We've got a new CEO lined up.'

'Okay…so Peter Lawrence didn't get the job, then?'

'Didn't want it. Or so he says. But anyway, the new guy is a bit of a ball breaker. Martin Dodds.' Weir would be in good company, then.

'Oh,' I replied, non committal. I knew of Dodds. An Australian, he'd worked for RBS where he'd gained a reputation as a hard-nosed exec. 'Excuse me for saying this, Leslie, but you couldn't have told me this over the phone?'

'Stock market's not going to be informed until 7 am tomorrow morning.'

'I think I could have managed to hold my water until then.'

'Don't be bloody cheeky. But this isn't the main reason for speaking to you.'

'Okay. So what's up?'

'It's about your nice little Caribbean company.' Weir assessed my reaction, but I attempted to remain calm, as his choice of words appeared ambiguous.

'Not *my* nice little company, Leslie—but one that happens to have been hired on a fair, open manner.'

'Really? You could have fooled me.' He frowned, as did I. Where the hell was he going with this?

'I'm in the dark here,' I explained. 'What's the matter with Lexicon?' I felt a sudden chill. Things had been going so smoothly, hadn't they?

'Well…I think I might be able to circumvent Henderson, if for no other reason than the new set up is geared to work and should benefit the bank. I could make the case that there's no appetite for some kind of audit at this stage. The bank is going to save millions, and charities can still get something out of it.' Weir was going round in circles, so I asked the obvious.

'So what's the problem, Leslie?'

'You honestly think that I don't know?' He closed his eyes and slowly shook his head.

'Don't know what…exactly?'

'About your little fiddle?'

'Fiddle?' I swallowed, my face unavoidably colouring. *Fuck.*

'Look, perhaps you've got me down as some kind of *Peter Principle* typecast boss,' Weir continued, 'but you really are quite naive.'

'Look, Leslie, I haven't a clue what you're talking about.'

'Just shut the fuck up!' He said flatly, hitting his desk. '*I know all about this little venture*. Fake companies, shell companies. That quaint little mirage you set up in Dublin. Tried hard not to laugh my way around those premises.'

A bombshell had exploded.

'Leslie, I can expl—'

'Don't!' He hit the table again, leaning forward to grab my arm. 'You could do time for this. Once you've been *fired first*, of course. And disgraced. Or would *humiliated* be a better description? Pension rights removed. Colleagues shocked. Never work again in financial services.'

I was visibly shaking, as the consequences of Weir's revelation began to register. This was no simple imbroglio. It was a disaster. My mouth felt very dry, and my stomach began to experience churning gymnastics. I ran my fingers through my hair before I plucked up the courage to speak, if only croakily.

'How did you know?'

'Let's say that it's my job to be investigative. And let's just say that I'm aware of the nature of your deception. You haven't covered your tracks particularly well.' Weir stared, letting his explanation filter through my mind.

'You've known this for how long?'

'Long enough.'

'But…if you've been aware of everything…why have you waited until now to have a go at me?' He said nothing so I decided that attack might be the most apt form of defence. 'Surely you wouldn't have let the venture proceed in the first place? You could lose *your* job too for incompetence or accessory?'

He laughed sarcastically. 'This has had nothing to do with me. Yet.'

I stared at him, unsure of the ramifications.

'You're going to have me fired?'

'What do you think?' he said.

'I honestly don't know what to think,' I replied. 'I can pay anything I owe back…'

'Don't make me laugh.'

'So what is it you want?' I asked.

'*I want in*.'

Chapter 10

The last person I would have chosen to go into 'business' with would have been Leslie Weir. The very reason for the scheme was to make a financial return and *eliminate* people like Weir from my life. The emotional nightmare of being uncovered—however horrendous—appeared as a small blip compared to the reality that now faced me. I couldn't escape, as Weir told me he had evidence of my involvement at several different stages. What did he have? What did he know about me? I'd suggested that he would incriminate himself too, if he admitted he'd been aware of my plan, but he insisted he'd independent evidence that removed him from the equation, yet implicated me. I demanded proof. Unfortunately he then provided evidence—a short video clip of the meeting in his office where he'd appeared to challenge his own request about taking the foundation outside. I vaguely recalled him pointing a silver pen directly at me—a 'camera pen' it seemed now. He replayed a visual and oral reminder of the conversation, from his point of view.

'Ally. It's now the fourth of November, right?'

'And?'

'I have been thinking about, eh, restructuring.'

'Okay.'

'Well, this is all, eh, preliminary, but, there could be a way to save substantial costs and still generate effective public relations benefits for the company.'

'Oh, really? That sounds interesting…so can you outline this plan you've brought to me?'

'Yes. It might be possible to...re-organise the foundation, and fund it through a different vehicle, reducing the bank's exposure to PR costs...maybe go outside to undertake the work.'

'I see. How would this operate?'

And so as the tape continued: I had become incriminated.

Not Doug—*me.*

No wonder the accused squirm when shown recorded evidence of themselves by police. Was something like this admissible in court? As it stood it looked like Weir had incontrovertible proof of me suggesting that I was behind the plan. Thinking back, he'd pushed me into making changes due to boardroom pressure. But then, somehow he must have figured out what the plan had been and then manipulated me, first thing in the morning, into saying it was all my idea. I couldn't work out how he'd spotted the plan in the first place. Did he have me under further surveillance?

I attempted to reason with him that there were other players, and that his own career at Scottish Chartered would probably come to an end for incompetence if he incriminated me. But my arguments were weak and unprepared. He said smugly that he was strongly aligned to the *positive* elements of the venture—the new funding arrangements to save the bank millions, but that he had quietly put on record with the board that the recommendation for Lexicon had come *exclusively* from me.

My endorsement.

My crime.

Cunning bastard.

The cold air engulfed me when I left the building, yet it failed to calm the uncomfortable sweat that had remained with me during the meeting. There was an atavistic fear deep within me that I would be punished, disgraced. I desperately needed to talk to Mandy, but I knew she was attending a function, and that it would have to wait.

I tried Doug, and got through straight away.

'Hi. Can't speak. Need to meet. Major problem.' I signed off immediately having agreed to see him at his office, despite the hour. It had then occurred to me that my phone might be bugged. Doug's office might also be bugged.

Would Weir have such capability? Was I becoming paranoid? When I arrived at Doug's office on Forth Street the communal meeting area was free, so I suggested we sit there. I'd left my phone in the car just in case. Doug appeared a little ruffled, unsure about all the cloak and dagger behaviour.

'What's all this about?'

'Weir knows about the scam.' The words seemed very hollow, despite the truth behind them.

'You're kidding!' He jumped up, before looking at me sideways. 'If this is some kind of practical joke, you can fuck off.'

'It's no joke.'

I briefly outlined the discussion I'd just had with Weir; the accusations, the video evidence and the demands.

'This is a nightmare!' Doug marched around the room. 'How the hell did you let him film you suggesting changes and outsourcing the work? You'd think you were born yesterday.'

'Wait a minute! There's *no way* I could have known that he suspected anything at that stage. The guy was pushing *me* into making organisational changes, not vice versa. In fact, *you* were chipping away on one side when Weir was demanding things.'

'So a leak has occurred at your end and your first instinct is to blame *me*?' He shook his head, sitting down abruptly. 'Why would I do anything to jeopardise the very plan I dreamed up? Can you explain that, mate?'

'Yeah, fine, *mate*. But why would *I* do such a thing? It's *me* in the firing line here. *I'm* the one caught on film, for fuck's sake, not you. He's obviously looked into Lexicon, but he doesn't appear to know anything about you. I don't even know if my phone is bugged.'

Doug then stood up again, and wandered over to the window, facing away from me as he viewed the activity on the street below. 'So tell me again. What exactly does he want?'

'Half the proceeds.'

'What? Well, I'll tell you one thing for certain—if he gets anything it comes out of your share, mate.'

'Stop calling me *mate*. So I'm to be penalised?'

He turned to point directly at me. 'This problem has originated at your end. I don't even have contact with the guy, so how could it have been me? *You've* caused the problem, so you fix it. Negotiate with the prick and knock him down. That is, if you want anything for yourself.'

'This is ridiculous, Doug. Any payment to Weir has to be split between us. I have in no way compromised this operation.'

'You're the one on film, not me. If your phone's been bugged I suggest you have it checked out. But Weir's got nothing on me.'

'Yet.'

'What? You're going to shop me?'

'I'm not shopping anyone. But if he's somehow uncovered me, who's to say he can't trace you? He might have *your* phone bugged for all I know. And another thing. He knows about the office set-up. Canavan. So that could mean that the leak was at your end. Maybe he checked Canavan out and found that Lexicon really had no business history there. A few phone calls could have done the trick.'

'Impossible.'

'Why.'

'Because Weir accepted the back story without question,' Doug answered glibly.

'Really? If you're so sure of that how come he told me that he tried hard not to laugh as he made the trip round that office?'

'Which only goes to prove that he knew beforehand, so Canavan wasn't the leak—but *you* could have been.'

'I *know* I'm not. That's a fact. But here's another proposition for *you*. If he knew in advance, why didn't he blow the thing apart? Why not fire me right away? Looking back, Weir smoothed the way.' I looked at Doug, but his eyes moved away from mine. He clearly didn't want to hear this hypothesis, however rational. I pointed right at him. 'Weir aided and abetted every step of the way. Why did he approve Lexicon over the other fake bidders straight away? Why did he push me into an early presentation with the board? It even took place without the CEO, and that helped steer the project through. Then he rubber-stamped the Irish trip with a smirk on the other side of his face. The irony, Doug, is that in retrospect, it couldn't have been done *without* Weir. What have you got to say about that?' Doug simply stared at me, and there was a moment of hesitation before he spoke.

'This has *nothing to do with me* if you think that. It's a fucking mess, Ally. But you need accept that your take is going down. I'd love to meet him and give him a piece of my mind, but that isn't going to happen. You let me know exactly where we're going with all this tomorrow after you see him.'

And with that I went home, trying Mandy by phone but without success. It seemed that I had no one in whom I could confide. No one from whom I could obtain some insightful wisdom and recharge my own self belief. I felt very stupid. How could I have possibly believed that I would have remained undetected? I hadn't received a penny, and here I was up to my neck in it, being blackmailed.

The following morning I arrived at work having barely slept. Kostas said I looked like death warmed up, but I could hardly raise a smile.

I knew from negotiation training that trilateral negotiations are more complex, but can be used to one's advantage. I was piggy in the middle, and it was up to me to play off each side, if possible. And there is the often misunderstood concept of win-win, which originated in micro-economic modelling. Always, when you believe that there is no chance of reaching a mutually acceptable solution, consider that two or more parties *can* win, providing that it is demonstrated that their success is mutually dependent. If I could convince Weir that he had nothing without Doug and me, and explain the same concept to Doug, I should be able to find a win-win outcome. There was no way I would be truly content with any understanding with Weir, but right now I desperately needed such an arrangement.

Weir insisted on meeting off-site. We went to the Scotsman hotel and sat in the lounge bar. I had my mobile phone in my pocket, so I left it on record, and stuffed it behind a cushion on the chair beside me, pulling the chair closer so he would sit on the only other available chair at the table.

As if reading my mind, Weir asked me to remove my jacket. He checked my pockets and—as much as would not attract attention in a public place—padded me down. No phone on me, no magic pens.

'Satisfied?'

He simply grimaced as waiter appeared to take a drink order.

'Leslie, the way I see it, you are complicit. Even if there is no direct proof you must have known that we would be in this position right now. It was engineered. You *knew* that if I walked away right now it would not be in your interest.' I sat back, awaiting his response.

He held his fingers in a cathedral position under his chin. 'What if I agreed with all you've said? You're still stuck.'

'Not so,' I replied. 'For this to work to *your* maximum advantage, you *need* to incentivise me.'

'Losing your job, facing charges, humiliation—not sufficient incentive?'

'No.' I leant forward. 'Because if I lose, *you* lose too. *Prisoner's dilemma.* So let's get to your best offer. I don't believe that your opening gambit last night would be your last offer. Basically, my…*partners*… are willing to cut you something, but not half the proceeds.'

'What do you mean by proceeds?'

'You know the commission structure. I'm not going to lie. We can make all decent money out of this. You can have a quarter of the commission after expenses.'

'A third.'

'But that would leave me with less than….17 percent…'

'I'm being generous. You are really pushing it. The only reason I am even countenancing your little spiel right now is that…perhaps…you do need some kind of reward.' He pulled the cushion away from the spare chair to reveal my phone. I sighed.

Weir continued. 'Maybe if you got something, it might stop you trying little stunts like this? Who do you think you're dealing with here?'

'You filmed *me*.'

'No, you did this to yourself. So listen to what I have to say. You can have your miserable 17 percent. I'll take that third share. Your *partners*—as you call them—can have their fifty percent.'

Bastard. I had obviously over-estimated his position and offered him too much. He watched my reaction, smiling.

'Surprised? Well, I also want something else.' I shook my head. What exactly was he demanding now?

'I want the new foundation to direct funds toward a specific charity of my choice.'

I scratched my head, confused. 'Let me get this right, Leslie. Your aim's now to play Santa? Having screwed a third of the commission you've now emerged as a charitable benefactor?'

'Building up slowly, a percentage of the funds will be directly channelled into a charity called Kid World Funds.'

'Never even heard of it.'

'You wouldn't have heard of it.' And then the penny dropped.

'Ah…shit. This charity is new? In fact it has only recently been set up?'

'Maybe.' He retained the self satisfied smirk.

'And you are suggesting that we would award this charity how much?'

'Twenty, twenty-five percent.'

'What, *five or six million*?'

'About right. There will be some high profile cases of helping children in far off places, and some close to home, but…' His words tailed off, so I completed the sentence for him.

'But there will be huge tacit *administration* costs…meaning that whoever operates the charity makes a fortune.'

'Wishing you'd thought of it?'

'When did you set up the charity? The day you uncovered our plan?'

'That doesn't concern you,' he said dismissively.

'How are you going to convince the board to back an unknown charity?'

'You make an assumption. This would be coming from you.'

'Me?'

'Naturally. You came up with the restructuring plan so the recommendation for the next part will be a pushover as it comes from a *proactive* source. They will follow your advice because you're trustworthy. All you need to do is gradually channel more money into one particular direction.'

'I can't believe this! What about people like Charles Henderson?'

'I wouldn't worry about Henderson.'

'Why?'

'He's a bit player.'

'What about corporate governance issues? You know as well as I do that the law on charities is much tighter now. Registration is one issue, but so is accountability.'

'This charity is fully constituted. It fulfils all the necessary legal requirements. It's not the bank's job to regulate an external organisation to which it donates money—don't you see the beauty of that? And what's more, the finance from all this is coming from our customers, so the bank is saving millions. You will have to get media coverage for Kid World Funds and give…incentives to journalists.'

'What? I've got to offer bribes now? That's against the law.'

He smiled at the irony of my words. 'You've no choice. You know how it works anyway, back scratching, and making things worthwhile for those who help.'

'And I have to simply trust you on that—before I recommend to the board that our clients' money goes AWOL?'

'Yes, you will trust me on that.' There is was again, the word 'trust'.

'What about the real good causes?'

'Are you telling me that you've now had an attack of conscience? You're a fucking crook, and now you're worried that little Jimmy somewhere won't get money for his football strip? Give me a break.'

I slunk back in my seat. As this latest twist sunk in, I had to admit, he'd played me. Now he was manipulating me into a further swindle on his behalf. A substantially more lucrative swindle. This was worse than chess, this was my life. And every move I appeared to take had not only been anticipated by someone else, it had been orchestrated by someone else.

'I refuse.'

'You're snookered. I know it, you know it and you know I know it. You walk away and I inform the cops. What's that old adage? If getting screwed is inevitable, lie back and enjoy it. You're working for me now.'

Weir left and I made my way back to the office separately, considering my predicament. I decided to call Mandy first, rather than Doug. I'd been avoiding what would amount to a confession, but the time had come to seek another person's opinion. She answered on the first ring.

'For Christ's sake, Ally. I don't know how you could have been so naive!' I recalled starkly why I'd initially avoided seeking empathy from my girlfriend.

'Neither do I.' My response was meek.

'And when were you going to tell me about this mess? You assured me that this was secure. Remember? When we met your pal Doug in the Grassmarket I specifically asked if anyone else was involved. You said that there wasn't. I'm now laundering money on your behalf, in case you hadn't remembered. It was supposed to be safe.'

'I thought that you thought it was a good idea?'

'Yes, Ally. *To pay the tax*, not to give the game away. I'm part of a legitimate business, and paying tax is one way to stay on the straight and narrow.'

'But I thought that you seemed…miffed at me not trusting you?'

'That's unfair, and you know it. If I thought that your boss knew all about it there's no way I would have agreed!' She was correct, of course, but what could I say?

'I know, I know, Mandy. I'm in the thick of it. And I have no idea how this happened, how Weir found out. I thought we'd covered our tracks.'

'But obviously not well enough.' There was a cold silence.

'Mandy. I promise I will sort this out. You will be absolutely in the clear.'

'You'd better.' I stared at my phone. She had hung up.

Chapter 11

I had arranged to meet Doug later in a public park—the Meadows—as I was still concerned about surveillance. An odd thought had occurred to me: *I had no tangible evidence about Doug's involvement in this scam*. All the risk appeared to be centred on me. Hell, Doug didn't appear in as much as a photograph I possessed. Thus, I arrived early and parked my car some distance from the meeting point, specifically to use my phone to get a decent shot of him before he was aware of my presence. Call it paranoid, but I sat in the bushes until I got a clear line of vision, and then took three or four shots of my accomplice. I would copy these later. Proof of something? No. A record of complicity? No. Proof of Doug's existence? *Yes*.

I then parked beside his Mercedes and we leaned against the respective car boots. There were towering beech trees above, gently dancing in the breeze. When I explained to him what Weir had outlined, he said virtually nothing. I'd expected anger, but Doug was seemingly oblivious to the moral issue of diverting charitable proceeds to the unworthy. Was I really surprised? So I then told him that I shouldn't be penalised with my cut but he refused to budge. Inwardly, I considered that I could tell Weir who Doug was, but something stopped me making this threat. Then I mentioned to him my concerns about Charles Henderson.

'Henderson's got more to worry about than a trivial charity issue. He should stay out of this.'

'What do you mean by that?' I asked.

'Henderson should have been paying his taxes.'

'I'm not sure I follow you, Doug. Has there been something in the media? This guy's clean. Is he being charged with something?'

'Not yet, mate.' Doug looked away.

'Look, what's the score here? What do you know?'

'I know that Mr Squeaky Clean has more than one offshore account, including one where there is a looming dispute with the Inland Revenue.'

'What?'

'Oh, this isn't public yet.' There was another silence as I considered how he could know this. Then I remembered the iPad.

'The iPad. This information was on there, wasn't it? You got some petty criminal to do it, didn't you?'

'Oh…I wouldn't say it was petty. Insurance never is, Ally.'

'So you lied to me! I specifically asked you if you had anything to do with Henderson's break in, and you denied it, point blank.' Doug looked at me as if I was a total criminal novice.

'So what? It was in your own interest. You were the big shot making the presentation to the board, and you didn't need to be distracted by Henderson. I did you a favour and we hold a trump card, so stop fucking complaining.'

'So Doug, we've now got breaking and entering, and what is it to be—blackmail?'

'Happens every day in business. Thought you'd know that from the world of PR. Big corporations are guilty. Politicians are guilty. The cops are guilty. We won't get caught, as it's not in Henderson's interest for that to happen.'

'You threatened him?'

'He's simply had a warning not to make waves at the bank, full stop. Vote neutrally, avoid complaining, and fuck off, basically. Suitably vague, but strangely effective for someone of his age with a lot to lose. He won't have a clue where this is coming from.'

I let this filter in. Shit, this was taking another nasty turn. But then again, it could make my life easier. I had a task of deception to complete, and it would be much simpler if there were no investigator on my back.

'Should I tell Weir?'

'Tell him if you like. You've still a chance to make a packet, and what's done is done. Maybe your percentage can be reviewed once we're up and running.'

Back at my flat in Stockbridge, the first thing I did was check Weir's 'Kid World Funds' online. A very inspirational website blossomed before me: details of what looked like a successful hands-on charity. It was registered abroad—but of course still functionally able to receive donations from domestic corporations. The site contained 360 degree film footage of apparent projects, testimonials from happy children who'd received money, parental endorsements from smiling faces in a number of countries and various—believable—claims as to what had been achieved over the past two years. *Two years.* Had Weir been running this on the side from before I met Doug? This seemed improbable, but then he was such a twisted bastard it wouldn't have surprised me that he was involved in some fiddle to con kids out of money, and had suddenly found a way of exploiting something extra via the bank. On the other hand, given that this was a sham, maybe he had simply invented the back story just as Doug had done with Lexicon and its fake counter bidders. I had a quick look at the home page, noting that the website had been designed by a company called Indisweb; not that knowing who undertook the web design was going to make any difference as to whether the charity looked bona fide. However, I did contemplate whether this firm would know anything about the nature of the con that they were helping to market.

I opened a beer before collapsing on the sofa. To date, the foundation really had made a difference to people's lives, and if Weir managed to siphon off what he aimed to do there really would be a morally reprehensible element to the scam. This left me cold, but both Doug and Weir had no such guilt, which left me exposed. As my thought process drifted, the moral philosophy class I'd taken years before at university permeated my consciousness. I recalled the lecturer, a chubby professor called Hobbs, who wore glasses with lenses that greatly magnified his eyes, giving the impression of him peering at you in an odd, disconcerting manner. One of his mannerisms was to swiftly spin round from the whiteboard, and challenge students about one moral dilemma or another, a favourite being: *when is too far*?

Had I gone too far?

Mandy and I had lunch in a little Italian place in Hanover Street the following day. We sat at a corner table, a little distance from the nearest customers. She clearly didn't want to be there, and made very little eye contact with me during the meal. Busy restaurants are supposed to offer the social lubrication that allows us to be personal in public, the chatter of others providing an eclipse for our own confessions or insights. However, the iced cola was distinctly warmer than my girlfriend who raised a disapproving eyebrow at each passing comment I made. Initially, I tried to make small talk, explaining that there was still a good chance of making money out of the scam. This received a pained response, as if I had just farted at the table. Mandy was pushing food around her plate, never a good sign. Then I offered the details of Kid World Funds.

'What? How could you let *this* occur?' An angry whisper.

'It was hardly my choice, Mandy.'

'You, of all people? A supposed PR specialist? This simply increases the chances of being caught.' As I suspected, Mandy was more concerned with evasion than scruples. However, her basic premise was accurate—it had gone too far, yet I was forced to argue the opposite of what I believed, playing devil's advocate.

She continued. 'How did Weir find out?'

I protested. 'I have no idea. He won't divulge anything.'

'That's so reassuring.' I tried to ignore the sarcasm, but she continued. 'You know Ally, when I agreed to do this laundering thing; you lied to me saying there was no one else involved.'

'Yes, but that's what I thought at the time.'

'At the time? That's great, isn't it? You know, I actually went along with Doug's suggestion because I felt it would bolster your position. I said it needed to be secure, but now it turns out your boss even knows.'

'I can assure you that he's the only other person,' I said, defensively.

'You can *assure* me? Really?' She sat back looking towards the ceiling. I touched her arm with hand, but she pulled away.

'It's not ideal, I know. I can hardly go to the police, can I?'

'Even you are not that stupid.'

Then suddenly I thought of a brilliant defence. 'Mandy, I can understand how you feel. But you have to admit, having Weir on board offers some kind of insurance.'

'Insurance? What do you mean by that?' Her elevated voice had now attracted attention.

'Please stay calm. What I mean is that I don't have to spend my time looking over my shoulder at my boss, because he's in on it. It might actually help me—*and you.*'

'Me? I don't think that you give a damn about me.' She drew her eyes off me.

'Mandy, this isn't about you.'

'No, it's about *you*. It's always about you, Ally.'

The couple at the nearest table glanced briefly at me again, noting the domestic that was on show. I lowered my voice. 'If you give me a minute, I'll explain.'

'Explain? That's all that you do. Explain your career—or lack of it. Explain money or your lack of it. Explain your stupid little ploys that fail. All I've heard you talk about for the past few months is *you* and *your* fiddle. And now, the minute I've offered to help you, you've compromised me. Do you know how hard it is to build up a business, and then have yourself exposed by someone else? My own boyfriend?'

'We can reroute the money another way.'

'There are now records connecting me so it's going to look ridiculous if I say that there will be no consultancy job. I'm stuck in this too.' I considered what she had said before responding.

'But Mandy, don't you see? This means that there's something to motivate *you too*.' Instantly, I realised that this comment was a mistake, as she picked up her handbag from the floor, stood up, and leant close to my ear.

'Ally,' she whispered, 'why don't you just piss off?' I watched her stride from the premises, unable to prevent her departure, yet too embarrassed to run after her.

Afterwards I decided to let her cool off for a while. Those green eyes sometimes contained a fire that could not easily be extinguished. I felt aggrieved that I was supposed to take all the blame for twisted events and I had also failed to remind her in the restaurant that she'd encouraged me into the venture. When Doug had suggested that she help launder the money, she'd been insulted at my initial rejection. But no doubt if I had explained there and then that Mandy herself had aided and abetted, she would have lost the plot in a public place, which could have been a more acute humiliation.

If I was honest with myself, maybe there was an imbalance in our relationship: that she was too good for me. That I would always have to chase and cajole to please, that I could easily lose her to a predator. I fancied her rotten, and I genuinely didn't want to lose her.

The first time we'd met I'd been hooked inside ten seconds. It had been at a PR event organised by the bank at the Prestonfield in Edinburgh, where we'd given an open invitation to public relations specialists to mingle with our staff—a kind of interactive fishing expedition. The second I'd locked eyes with her she'd given me an intense come-on—a kind of "I know you want me, and I'm letting you know that you might just be able to have me". Everyone's had it at some time or another, but mostly we don't act on it as we're so surprised, otherwise involved, or simply too un-nerved by such sexually charged behaviour. Yet I'd been so turned on that I pursued her the next day, just as she'd probably expected.

Much as I'd wished to charge after her at the restaurant, I also had to remain focused. My life had become exponentially more complex. That previous corporate boredom—the flat lining I had experienced—would now have been a welcome walk in the park.

By email the next day appeared a communication from Kid World Funds. No mention of Weir, but a nice message from their head of communications "replying" to my letter of enquiry about the possibility of the foundation donating money to the charity. I hadn't sent any such letter, but no doubt Weir had, complete with my "signature". He was such an impatient prick that he hadn't even had the courtesy to ask. He simply expected me to jump. What was I to do? Ask awkward questions to cover my back, and risk being shopped by Weir, or take the morally defunct approach and facilitate the whole exercise?

I elected for the latter option, replying to Kid World Funds asking for details of their bogus claims to fame, some of which I'd already witnessed on their website. I was fully aware that the minute we began gifting money to Kid World Funds we would have to reduce the support given to others. As I sat with my hands in my head, attempting to work out how to reply to them, there was a light knock on my door. Elise Stewart smiled at me through the glass.

'You look like you've just lost a winning lottery ticket,' she said in her dulcet Carolina tones.

'Yes, Elise… and that little win would have been enough to buy the pills for the overdose.'

'That good?'

'Not really, on reflection I'd probably have to cheer up to commit suicide.'

'You Scots really are a happy bunch. If it's not the constant complaints about the weather, it's moaning about money or English football commentators.'

'I wouldn't get complacent if I were you. That Stewart DNA will soon evolve from absorbing to adapting, and before you know it you'll hate everything. What can I do for you?'

She smiled warmly again. 'A little favour, if possible.'

'Shoot.'

'Never say that to an American.'

'Firearms are illegal here.'

'Apparently,' she added, alluding to the gun crime that occasionally existed in parts of Scotland. 'It was some advice I was looking for. You're originally from near Oban, right?'

'Don't start making sheep-shagging jokes.'

'What's shagging?'

'Forget I said that word.'

'Okay… my Stewart ancestors were from Appin—you'll know it?'

'Of course. Lovely wee place, just north of Oban.'

'That's right. Actually, I came here partly to undertake genealogical research in my spare time. My grandmother partly raised me and she was born in Appin before her family emigrated.'

'You really are connected. And ancestral research probably beats working here. You can change your job, but you can't change your antecedents.'

'Very profound, Ally. Well, I'd been hoping to achieve more of this roots thing, but then in the short time I've been here it's been non-stop work, and I'm just not getting round to it.'

'How can I help?'

'Well, I went online for local help in arranging some research in the Appin area, but I seem to have come up short. I was wondering if you happen to have any contacts up there that might have local records of this sort of thing. There's a genealogical centre in Inverness, but I wanted to be more hands on—cemeteries, access to places my ancestors lived, and ruins. Something real.'

'So if I can find you some 95-year-old crofter to show you about, you'd wear a ghost buster outfit and soon produce a new client for the cemeteries?'

Elise grinned, revealing her perfect teeth. 'Oh, I'm not that dangerous.'

'But you're serious, Elise. I'm impressed. My folks still live not far from there, and they'll know some older people there, so I can try them. And there are a couple of guys from that area who I know from Oban High School—those not convicted yet—that I bumped into at the Oban Hogmanay extravaganza last year. Hold on a minute,' I took out my phone. 'I'm sure I took a couple of photos of these guys at New Year—totally and completely sober.'

I flipped through the photo files in my phone, before locating the said characters. 'What do you think?' I asked. Elise took the phone and laughed out loud at two inebriated guys, bare-chested in the snow, each holding bottles of assorted booze. 'They look just dandy, Ally. Must be close relatives of mine.'

'There's more—just flip through. Forewarned is forearmed.' Elise rolled over some further photos, shaking her head, before pressing a button in error. 'Ooops, that's wrong. I seem to have opened another folder.' She looked at a picture, frowning. 'Hey…I recognise *that guy.* He won't be from Appin.' Surprised, I took the phone back to see to whom she referred.

Doug.

A sudden rush of fear engulfed me. 'You know…*this* guy?' How could she know Doug?

'Well I don't know him. I said I *recognise* him. Odd picture, though. Is that taken through bushes or something?'

'Eh, yes…but that's another story. Nothing sinister. So where do you, um, recognise him from?' I tried to sound unconcerned, but my voice suddenly felt a little raspy, the moisture having inexplicably evaporated from my system.

She looked again at the picture. 'Yes, he's definitely the guy that spilt the coffee. I always remember faces. So who is he?'

'Oh… I think he's a guy that used to supply us with some contract work. A consultant. Nobody important.' I hated to lie to her, but I had no choice.

'So why do you have a picture of him on your mobile phone? He's not your gay lover, is he?' I laughed and she responded in kind.

'No, you're safe enough on that front, Elise. Or unsafe, depending on your viewpoint…no, the picture was sent to me. By, eh mistake. Another consultant sent it. Not important. Forgotten it was even there. So, tell me the coffee story. Was this outside in a cafe somewhere in town?'

'No, right here in the Dosh Dome, as you guys call it. If the guy's a consultant, that would explain his appearance. I think Kostas was there too, and a couple of others.'

'Kostas?'

'Yeah. The coffee trolley had come round a corner and in a split second an entire jug of coffee splattered over this guy's suit.'

'Hilarious,' I ventured.

'I shouldn't have laughed, but he got angry as he cursed the coffee lady. The guy must have a short fuse. What's his name?'

'Oh, Donald, David, or Douglas something,' I said, attempting to appear nonchalant. 'So was this recently, was it?'

'A few months ago—not long after I started here, actually.' This could have been the day I met Doug outside, when I'd asked why he'd been there. 'I figured that you would have known him better.'

'Why's that? Because of the photo?'

'No, because when he got covered in coffee, he'd just come straight out of a meeting in Leslie Weir's office.'

Chapter 12

When Elise disappeared from my office, a cold sweat enveloped me. Weir and Doug in cahoots? Viewing things through the other end of the binoculars, some signs had been there. But were they in it together from the start? In fact, now that I thought about it, the day that Weir had been gunning for me about pressures from the board to reorganise the foundation was the same day I'd met Doug in the car park. I'd been so consumed with anger at Weir about him questioning the set up that I'd failed to recognise the obvious fact that Doug's solution was uncannily fitting and seamlessly timed. Did this constitute proof of complicity?

I'd actually been pounding my brains to discover how Weir had known of the plan in the first place. How he had known to film me in his office, how he had played along with rejecting the fake bids, yet tacitly concentrated on forcing me to convince the board about the merits of change. Had all of this been an act? One designed to implicate me as the designer of the sham that was Lexicon Chartered?

And what of those 'pressures' from the board? Weir had deflected my questions about which board members had pushed for change. Probably none of them. And the concept of customers paying what Scottish Chartered's shareholders had paid up to now was brilliant. But most of the board had probably been pretty content with the in-house structure and how the PR was generated. If they hadn't, they'd have spoken out before now.

The set of events reminded me that all illusions rely on a decoy. A *deflection.* A plan to tap customers had blinded the board to the underlying illusion—the *means* by which the proceeds would now be distributed.

If Weir and Doug had set me up, Weir probably knew Canavan too and might have been instrumental in setting up the Antiguan angle. Henderson had now been silenced, and the old CEO—who would probably have knocked back the whole move—was looking like history. Weir had precisely timed the Lexicon intervention when there had been no one steering the ship—even the acting CEO had been off site the day of the board meeting.

The only thing I didn't possess was any direct proof of their joint complicity. They would simply deny it even with Elise's coffee story. Not that possession of proof of a relationship was much good to me as my own role had been intertwined with Doug and Weir. I paced back and forth in my office, oblivious to any observation from beyond the glass.

Then, the name Indisweb suddenly came to mind—the company that had designed the Kid World Funds website. I checked online and found a perfectly normal web design firm touting for business. I don't know why I made the connection, but there was something familiar about the layout of the site, something that had stirred when I'd first seen it but had registered on a subconscious level: offset photography, and moving pop-ups at the bottom of the page. Then I remembered where I'd seen the same configuration of tricks: Lexicon Chartered's site. I'd had nothing to do with the promotion of the bidders for the foundation's work as Doug had insisted that I didn't get too close which now made me even more suspicious. I searched for the Lexicon Chartered site, but was given the 'site under redesign' message that Doug had insisted was placed there.

I placed a call to Indisweb in Manchester and politely said that they'd been recommended by a couple of clients. The voice asked what parties had recommended them. When I responded by suggesting the name Kid World Funds, she affirmed that Indisweb had designed the site. I then suggested that Lexicon Chartered had also recommended them, and she hesitated, before asking me to hold. A supervisor came to the phone, and asked how I knew of Lexicon. So there was a link? There was one chance in a thousand that Doug and Weir had used the same web designer in a city in England three hundred miles away. I said we'd done business with them, but the man asked if I had a contact number, as Lexicon owed Indisweb money as their site lay in abeyance. So the bastards hadn't even paid the bill yet.

I don't know what felt worse; my own sheer ineptitude in not spotting the connection, or simply that I had been played by two absolute wankers. Perhaps it was a combination of the two, but did it really matter? Why is it that the most obvious things elude us at the most crucial of times?

The only glint of hope was that they did not know that *I* now knew. I might be able to strengthen my hand if I could garner evidence of their relationship. Obviously, I did not wish to involve Elise or Kostas, who were genuinely innocent bystanders, even if they were main witnesses to the two meeting at Weir's office. I might also threaten to undermine the whole process—say by leaving—but Weir had threatened prosecution as he held evidence against me rather than vice versa. I considered the benefits of doing nothing—playing along and banking my share. Each day I would dig a deeper hole. If I had to sift through a mountain of logistics about payments, processing of charitable donations, and assessing the conundrum of how to legally 'incentivise' journalists to cover Kid World Funds stories, I would presumably have to remain personally motivated despite having been conned myself.

When I finished work that day, my jumbled thoughts returned to Mandy. There had been no conciliatory call or text. Initially, I'd felt that she would come round; we'd had conflicts before, and time usually healed things. The more pensive I became, however, I thought, stuff it, I would make the first move. I would opt for the traditional apology and pick up a grand bouquet of flowers to surprise her at home. It might not be greeted with acclaim, but it might just soften her up. I also badly needed someone to talk to, however I was received, and Mandy was the only person in whom I could confide.

When I arrived there, Mandy's flat mate, Laura, answered the door, but her expression remained passive despite the fact I was holding an impressive bouquet. She didn't move to let me in, however, which surprised me.

'Aren't you going to invite me in?' I asked, casually.

'Not much point, is there?' Her expression conveyed minor hostility.

'Laura, look, I'm sorry if I've come at a bad time, but what's the problem?'

'Mandy's left.'

'*What*?' My own confusion suddenly gathered pace.

I asked if this was some kind of joke. I said that I wasn't really in the mood for daft games, and Laura made to close the door. When I apologised, she reluctantly let me in. I sat in the large leather sofa that I had occupied on more than one romantic occasion with Mandy. Then Laura brought me the note bearing Mandy's distinct handwriting.

L

I'm out of here.

M.

When it dawned on Laura that I'd also been blindsided by this revelation, she offered me a coffee.

'Look Ally. I'm sorry for being abrupt with you. This probably isn't your fault. It's just...you can understand why I'm pissed off.'

While she made the coffee I tried Mandy's number but got a 'number unobtainable' message from the network. Shit. I then checked my own emails and text messages to see if she'd been in contact with me independently in case I'd missed something. Nothing. My initial hope was that this was a wind-up, though I knew from experience that such was not Mandy's style. Secondly, I'd considered that there had been some kind of misunderstanding, and Mandy would appear at the door any second. When Laura appeared back with two mugs, she explained that she'd contacted Mandy's office and they'd confirmed that Mandy had taken leave. The staff would not add anything further on the basis of confidentiality. She'd chucked her job too? This was bizarre. A horrible knot began to develop in my stomach. If she'd left the flat and her job without any discussion, had she left me too?

When Laura returned with the coffee, she said that there had been no warning, and that there was the question of rent. Both Laura and Mandy earned good money, but this was an expensive pad, and they'd agreed to share the costs for three years or until either of their circumstances changed. It appeared that circumstances had changed, though not the way any of us expected. All of Mandy's possessions were gone. I asked Laura about any forwarding address—but she said that Mandy had left nothing. Presumably Mandy would have to redirect her mail to another address, but where? I didn't even have a family number as she'd be quite guarded about her past in the Czech Republic, often changing the subject when I asked.

Laura promised to contact me if she made any progress or suddenly obtained an explanation from Mandy. As I made my way from Murrayfield towards my own flat in Stockbridge every traffic light seemed to turn red in front of me. I turned on the radio to hear a song by the *Australian Doors.* Doors? Exits, more likely. Obviously I'd spent too much time on the scam, and not enough on Mandy. But was it even about me? Could some other disaster have occurred in Mandy's life without my knowledge? Perhaps something happened at home in the Czech Republic, requiring a return visit. What I did know is that there was no text, and when I listened for an elusive electronic beep on my home answer machine, again, nothing.

The following morning I made an excuse to leave the office and drove over to Mandy's office. Liz Fleming, a colleague of Mandy's, was noncommittal when I asked for help. Embarrassed as I was, she politely ventured that data protection laws prevented her from giving me any forwarding address. I lost my cool a little, which didn't help. She said she didn't want any kind of incident, so I left.

Sure, I'd been in relationships before that had ended, but usually there was at least an opportunity to have your say. Mandy could be feisty, but she normally possessed an underlying sense of rationality. I then made a call to the police, and the desk officer at Fettes Avenue Police Station took my details, and those of Mandy. The officer said that such domestic issues happened every day. It did not sound like a missing person case as there was a note, and an agreement with an employer. People had the right to privacy, so I could not harass Mandy's colleagues about her whereabouts. Again, I got a little flustered, only to be told to cool it unless I wanted to be charged with wasting police time.

The problem was that I was aware of comparatively little about Mandy's background. Most of my previous girlfriends couldn't shut up about their siblings, mothers and fathers and school experiences, but Mandy had been more of a closed book.

Being raised in Prague had brought obvious cultural differences, but she had also been reluctant to share details with me when I enquired; alluding only to having lost her mother at an early age and having been encouraged in sport and academic pursuits by a driven father who was now dead. She had no siblings, no obvious roots that she had volunteered to me as she'd moved schools during her formative years on a number of occasions. And since she'd arrived in the country, her sole close friend in Edinburgh outside of the work circuit, was Laura. I considered calling one or two of her work colleagues other than Liz Fleming, but the sheer embarrassment of it all stalled further consideration.

Then I was hit by another problem as I arrived back at the bank.

On the *Herald* website, I dipped into the business section only to see an article about Kid World Funds, and how they had secured a major charitable investment from Scottish Chartered Bank. The donation was 'imminent'. My name was mentioned, though there was no quote from me. Weir. I hadn't even had a call from the *Herald*, let alone an interview. Weir had jumped the gun.

This was running out of control.

I knew he was in the building so I ran upstairs.

Wendy was having a chat to a 'hair director' about an appointment. She frowned at me before shaking her head. I held my hands out wide in enquiry as to Weir's whereabouts. She shook her head, as if I had no right to ask, but then dismissively pointed upwards. Boardroom? In with the new CEO? I had nothing to lose so I entered the stairwell to advance to another floor. Upstairs I spotted Weir leaving Martin Dodds' office. The slimy bastard was probably forcing the guy into some agreement before the paint was even dry in his new office. Weir's speciality: bumping people into commitments before they had time to consider what they were doing. As I hovered at the end of the corridor, Weir turned towards me, projecting a false smile in my direction. Martin Dodds was standing at his doorway.

'Ah, there's Ally Forbes, Martin. Ally, I don't think that you've met Martin, our new Chief Executive?' I stepped forward and shook hands with the Australian, and we made pleasant noises. Then Weir interjected. 'I was just telling Martin all about your work in recommending Kid World Funds as a major recipient of our charitable funds. Pity that you couldn't have made the meeting early this morning, but don't worry, I've filled Martin in on all *your* plans, and how all these children will benefit from the support of our valued client base.'

'Mmm. I was just reading the article in the *Herald* website about the project. Hadn't realised that it would be in the media *so soon*, Leslie.' I stared at Weir.

'Ally…you must be losing your touch.' He slapped me on the shoulder, patronisingly. 'Didn't you just say to me yesterday that the media coverage would be excellent with this and the bank could expect a burst of positive commentary from today? Your phone will be ringing off the hook! You'd better come downstairs with me.'

Martin Dodds raised a hand, offering a deep Adelaide drawl. 'Keep up the good work, Ally.'

'Oh, he's good at spending other people's money, Martin, but I keep him in check.' Weir pushed my back from behind, and only spoke when we entered the elevator.

'What the hell are you doing up here?' Weir spat the words.

'What the fuck are you doing making media announcements without consulting me, you cheeky bastard?' The time for being polite to Weir for fear of being sacked had clearly come to a conclusion.

'So you think you're running the show here, do you? You never were, and you never will be. If I want to make any announcements about charitable donations, I will.'

'Aye, to your very own benevolent fund.' The lift reached the ground floor, but Weir closed the door again when it opened.

'Keep your voice down! Your own greed got you into this. You were stalling on the Kid World Funds move, and you know it. And remember, you're being paid too.'

'That's a joke.' Weir looked me straight in the eye, almost puzzled, though I wasn't buying it, so I continued. 'And as far as Kid World Funds is concerned, I was simply trying to make the whole thing believable. It's quite a departure from previous charitable work. I've had three or four organisations on the bell asking if this will endanger what we donate to them. What do I say?'

'Tell them what the hell you like. And get on with thinking of every angle to make Kid World Funds make the media. You'll be receiving photographic material shortly that will be excellent for generating stories, now the donation has been cleared. Get your act together, Forbes.'

We parted outside the elevator. A few suits passed and I put on my professional smile, while I really wanted to pounce on Weir's lanky frame from the back and smash his head in. Not since I had been in school had I been so worked up, violent thoughts entering my mind. I had to steer some kind of course though troubled waters. Mandy's departure had left me feeling low—nauseated—by a sequence of events which had perfectly highlighted the fact that my own naivety had brought me to this point. Weir had reminded me that I was due to receive money, and I was bloody sure that I would at least obtain what I was due out of a bad situation. Money.

I called Doug.

'We've already sorted the money thing.' was Doug's stark response. 'You know how the payments are being routed.'

'But that's just it. I haven't seen any money!' I half shouted down the phone, exasperated.

'The money's been getting paid in. At least fifty grand has now gone into your girlfriend's account.'

'Fifty thousand has gone in? Are you sure?'

'Do you honestly think I wouldn't know if I'd sent fifty grand to someone? Give me a break!'

'Right.' So Mandy now had *fifty thousand* of my money.

'You should speak to your girlfriend, mate. Surely she hasn't spent the lot already?' He laughed, which irritated me further.

'This is not about Mandy.' I decided to tell a lie. 'Though she feels…totally exposed now due the turn of events and I can't say I blame her. I—we—demand that the payment be made another way.'

'You're impossible to please! I went out of my way to set up the payments through your squeeze, and the next thing that's no good. I've even upped your cut because of your moans. What do you think I'm doing with my time?'

'You're making plenty out of this and you know it.'

'So are you. Shit, she was in favour if I remember correctly. You sort it out.'

'Yes, but with this bombshell about this Kid World Funds thing, I feel much more exposed.'

'But your share is coming from Lexicon Chartered. Kid World Funds is nothing to do with us.'

'Oh really? Nothing to do with me, maybe. But what about you?'

'What do you mean by that?'

'You got me into all this.' Something just stopped me making the full accusation.

'You were going nowhere, totally pissed off with your job. You told me yourself, you were looking for some action. Don't blame me if you saw the money and jumped.'

Enough was enough.

'Doug, I know for a fact that you were in Scottish Chartered's offices meeting Weir before I even agreed to your plan. Spilling coffee over the place. Remember? So what have you got to say about that?'

Silence.

'Alright, I was checking him out.'

'You really expect me to believe that? You have repeatedly told me that you did not want to meet Weir. No fucking wonder. You already knew him!'

'That's the exact reason that I couldn't see him again. He'd have recognised me.'

My own indignation left me shaking as I gripped the phone. 'Doug, this is futile. You're really pissing me off.'

'You're barking up the wrong tree here.'

'Well what about Indisweb?'

'What about them?'

'I know that they designed the Lexicon Chartered site.'

'So?'

'Do you think I am an idiot? I know that they *also* designed the Kid World Funds site. I spoke to the staff in their Manchester office myself.'

'That must just be a coincidence. Big company.'

'It's a fact. And it makes perfect sense. You've set me up. I know about you and Weir, and I'm not taking any more shit. And I'm going to let Weir know that very fact too.'

I bumped him off my phone, trying to breathe in deeply. My anger carried me upstairs towards Weir's office.

'Where is he?' I demanded of Wendy.

'Where is whom? I don't like the tone of your voice, young man.'

'And I don't like the shade of your lipstick. But maybe you can use these same podgy purple lips to give me a fucking answer.'

'How *dare* you speak to me like that! I'm going to make a complaint to *Mr Weir* about your attitude. And your language. And if you're referring to Mr Weir, he's just left for an external meeting.'

I rushed downstairs hoping to catch Weir. As I arrived outside, I spied him wandering towards his Jaguar in the car park. He was alone, so I rushed over towards him.

'What do you want now?'

'I just want to tell you what a prick you are. I know all about you and Doug Fox, by the way, so you can cut the shit, the demands and the blackmail.'

'You really are a clown, Forbes. I don't really care whatever ludicrous accusations you are making. Just do your little bit like the underling cretin you clearly are,' he said, turning towards the Jag.

I lunged at him, grabbing his lapel and forcing him back against his car. He slipped slightly on the wet surface before attempting to thrust back at me. I side stepped him, moving towards the rear door, my anger building.

'I'd like to smash your fucking head in!'

'You haven't got the guts, Forbes,' he said, adjusting his tie.

'You just watch me. I'll wait my time.' As I spat the words, I realised that I was shouting. I turned towards the car park to check if we were alone, only to see Wendy making her way over with a small package.

'What on Earth's happening? Are you all right, Mr Weir?' She sneered at me. 'And I saw what *you* just did to Mr Weir. That's *disgraceful* behaviour for someone working at this bank. You should be fired.'

I turned away from them both, seething.

Chapter 13

That night, I was consumed with a synthesis of rage and confusion about what to do. To take my mind off things I called my mother about Elise's request for any information about the Stewarts of Appin. When I signed off, I checked my work emails. The standout email was in relation to Kid World Funds. It had just been confirmed that the fake charity had received payments totalling more than *six million*. This seemed unbelievable. The speed with which this had happened astounded me. Just like that. A further quick scan down my in-box resulted in an enquiry from Kostas. Where had I disappeared to? Did I fancy a pint?

MacVarish's Bar is the kind of place that you can drown your tears, allowing a small degree of privacy in the back room.

I needed a drink. Once we had ordered two pints of Deuchars IPA we moved into the back room and he asked after Mandy. As someone married with two children, Kostas liked to know that others were going to follow the same familial path. On this occasion, I came clean.

'She's disappeared?'

'Yes. Gone, without a trace.'

'Shit.'

'That's how I've felt since I read the note.' I explained how my life had changed on the strength of a small piece of paper, while Kostas listened intently. He waited until I had finished.

'I see where you're coming from,' he said flatly, resting a thumb and finger under his chin. 'With no note you'd be really worried—facing a missing person's investigation, in fact. But it looks as if she's simply taken off. Where?'

'Does it matter now? *I* didn't even get the courtesy of a note. Laura got the note.' I sat back staring into my pint.

'But surely Mandy would stand to lose, business-wise, too?'

'She could have set something else up for all I know.'

'This is crap. Nice looking girl, too.'

'Thanks, Kostas.' He held his hands up in an apology, realising that such observations wouldn't help. A couple of old guys wandered in and sat not far from us.

'So what are you going to do?'

'I think I've already given up. The last time I saw her we had words anyway.'

'Right...but I'm surprised you're not going to give chase. You're normally a more determined character.'

'There's nothing to chase, apparently. I have no forwarding address, she's changed her phone number, and I suspect I'd be wasting my time and money getting a private detective to look into it. I guess that all I can do is hope that the 'acceptance' stage of the psychological process arrives as soon as possible.'

'Well, I'm sorry, Ally. But in the circumstances what you probably need is a rebound candidate. At least to cheer you up?' He cleared his throat. 'Now, stay with me here. There's a really huge girl called Molly in the Accounts Department. She's single, if you can believe that. She's a catch, assuming...you didn't drop her. Good child-bearing thighs, a head for numbers, and she'd never ask if her bum looked big in anything because you couldn't find an item of clothing large enough to cover her fully anyway.'

I gave an empty smile in response.

'Oh come on. There are plenty more man-eating sharks in the sea. Give yourself a break! Hey, your work's going all right. You've survived your re-organisation and emerged smelling of unfertilised roses. You must be in line for a juicy big bonus with all that money you've saved the bank. You're the gold-plated boy at work! Look on the bright side.'

He viewed my impassive face.

'This girl's really gotten to you, hasn't she?'

'Kostas…there are…other things. My problems don't begin and end with Mandy, unfortunately. I could probably live with her disappearance if that was all I had to worry about.'

'And I was merely looking forward to a bit of banter after work. I didn't realise that you'd sold your sense of humour on eBay.' He stood up. 'Want to talk about it?'

He went down to the bar to order two more beers, as if aware that I needed a couple of minutes to make a decision about confiding in him about something else—something even more serious than Mandy's exit. I trusted Kostas completely, but would it be fair to off-load my guilt onto a friend? Would he too become complicit in the scam? I was sure I'd read that the term 'accessory after the fact' wasn't used in Scotland, but was called something else. Art and Part, or something like that. Would I regret bringing in another party, one employed by the bank? And would he, even as a trusted friend, inadvertently give the game away?

Kostas returned with the drinks. Even though Deuchars is a relatively low alcohol pint, I could clearly feel the effects of the first beer before taking a sip from the second. Kostas then suddenly raised his new pint glass.

'To Leslie Weir.'

I folded my arms, exhaling air.

'Come on, the guy has some redeeming qualities. If my Athenian intuition serves me well, *he's* actually the reason you agreed to go out for a pint with me. Correct?' He looked me in the eye, raising one dark eyebrow.

I nodded.

'And?'

'There is something that I haven't told anyone about.'

'You're having a gay affair with Leslie Weir?' He punched the table and employed a self satisfied grin.

'Seriously, Kostas. I need your absolute assurance that this goes no further. Not to Elena, or anyone else. If you have any doubt about keeping a secret then we'll call it quits right now and talk about the Olympics or some other shit.'

'You really are being serious?'

'Yes.'

'The Olympics are *not* shit…but I can keep a secret, especially if it helps you. You're a good friend. Okay?'

And so I told him the story.

My first confession.

Sitting at the back of MacVarish's, on a wet Tuesday night in Edinburgh, amidst the casual chat of other punters moaning about football, or their wives, I confessed that I was a greedy crook. He remained silent for most of the tale, shaking his head from time to time, asking me to confirm or deny only the occasional detail.

'What a fuck up. I thought you were an honest guy.'

'I knew you wouldn't approve.'

'I don't really. Though it is a brilliant scam, if you take out the part involving Weir. He's such a dick. But what on earth possessed you to get involved in something like this?'

'It seems crazy in hindsight, but I was being pushed by Weir—threatened about my job—and the pincer movement was being operated by Doug Fox. Even Mandy was telling me to get the finger out and do something with my life.'

'And now she's out of the picture?'

'Yes. And her disappearance now feels even worse when you think about the money. I didn't want to consider that aspect too much, but I don't think I'll be seeing that fifty grand now.'

'I think that you've been stuffed,' said Kostas dryly. 'Jesus, there's millions being siphoned.'

'But as yet, I haven't actually *stolen* anything. Sure, I've lied to my employer about fake companies bidding for work. I've lied—by omission—about my connections with an agent to whom the bank is now paying commission. However I have not actually *received,* personally, any illicit money.'

'Should I know this Doug guy?' he asked, and I realised that I still had the photo of Doug on my phone and Elise's story. I showed him the image.

'Looks familiar, right enough,' he said, scanning the photo.

'Yes, you've met him, I believe. Briefly. I forgot to mention that Elise recognised Doug right away when I showed her the picture.'

'Elise Stewart? She's involved too?'

'*Of course not.* Keep your voice down, please. No, I showed her the picture by accident and she explained that she recognised Doug from a visit he had to Weir's office. He spilled coffee in some incident. Remember?'

'Yeah, vaguely.'

'Well, Doug claims he was only checking Weir out, but I know that the two websites—one set up by Weir, and one set up by Doug—are designed by the same company in Manchester. It's more than a coincidence.'

He scratched his chin. 'You know, Ally, I really wish you'd confided in me earlier on. I would honestly have stopped you. I realise that hindsight's a great thing, but as a friend, you've excluded me from a situation where I could have helped you.'

'I'm sorry,' I said downing the pint.' 'I think that we both need another pint. When I returned from the bar, Kostas was looking at his phone.

'I've just been online to see.'

'What?'

'What the likely custodial sentences would be for you.' Kostas mimed a person being handcuffed, as I struggled for a sensible response. 'Will I begin with famous historical cases? Alan Sanford, Conrad Black or Bernie Madoff? Which one do you think most closely reflects your case?'

'Kostas, please. This is a *crisis*, and you're taking the piss out of me!'

He placed a hand on my shoulder. 'Ally, this is *not* a crisis. Third world poverty is a crisis. Civil war is a crisis. AEK Athens winning the Greek league is a crisis. Come on, let's go through this…minor mess.'

'Okay…I'm listening.'

He cleared his throat, as an inebriated man passed our table on the way to the toilet, almost knocking over our drinks. We waited until he had staggered past.

'Firstly, you have not stolen anything, as you just said. Your crimes are against your employer rather than against the state. Your track record in the sector is excellent, so you could easily find another job, at least at the moment. I'm no employment lawyer, but I suspect that if you consulted one, they would advise you to resign and hope that the bank would sort this matter out itself to save corporate embarrassment. I know of a well known Scottish business that had to let its director of digital security go with a payout — despite proven internal embezzlement—in order to avoid being laughed off the park by its competitors.'

'Who was that?'

'I'm not telling you.'

'Why?'

'Because I can keep a secret. Remember?'

'Okay, good point.'

'Look, Scottish Chartered takes great pride in its image. You *know* that. It's your very raison d'être at the bank. So it would be *likely* that the bank would want this to disappear if at all possible, assuming that they ever found out. So far the directors probably know nothing. In fact they are pretty much delighted as the plan appears to be saving a fortune. Remember what I said just a few minutes ago? They must see you as gold-plated. There would always be a risk of a problem later on, but this thing could go away, if you're prepared to concede two important points.'

'Which are?'

'Money and pride.'

'I'm pleased that they're not important things, Kostas.'

'Stop being facetious and think about this logically. Objectively. You have your health, and your freedom. And your reputation is still intact. These are the important things. Forget the money. Tell Weir to stuff it, and chuck the job. There's no way he can actually incriminate you without incriminating himself anyway. Sure, he wins. And so does this guy Doug. You've been set up, and you've been used as your position at the bank helped facilitate the whole scam. They needed you as you had a squeaky-clean record and are respected for your work to date. If they're in cahoots, fine. But I think that you have to cut your losses and get out while you can.'

'What about Weir's recording of me? That the whole thing was apparently my idea?'

'Looks like a bluff to me. How the hell is Weir going to explain to anyone why he was secretly filming you about a business idea, then fully supporting you about it in front of board members? It's ridiculous! His credibility would be on the line immediately. If he'd had any legitimate concerns, he would have had to take them upstairs before you even got started. Don't you see? He'd lose his job if he even dared to say he'd filmed a direct report without your knowledge. As long as you aren't trying to double cross Weir in some way, the film's a red herring, a piece of flimsy insurance that's no longer valid. Weir will know that, but he's been trying to create an illusion that this is somehow crucial to your position. If you walk, the film's meaningless because if he used it he would simply incriminate himself.'

I rubbed my eyes. 'I think I've been too close to this to see the obvious. So I forget Mandy too?'

'You're not eighteen. Sorry to be hard here, but let her keep anything she's been given. That way it's not connected to you should the shit hit ever actually hit the fan later.'

He was right, of course. But pride had always been a problem for me, since I'd been a child. Kostas could see a bigger picture, one where losing a couple of battles allowed the peace to be more enduring, but I just felt so angry.

'You look lost, Ally. Decorating the room with your thoughts? Am I talking sense?' Kostas peered at me, every bit the Greek philosopher.

'Yes, but…'

'You just need to manage your exit. You said that Kid World Funds was Weir's idea, but he somehow managed to implicate you in the selection process?'

'Exactly. He's a bastard.'

'Well, if you decide to resign, you need to make it clear with senior people that you aren't happy with the new direction—the inclusion of overseas charities. Put it on record that you think this will not generate good PR. Make it a business reason. There is no financial connection between you and this organisation, right?'

'Right…'

'Good. Then you should be in the clear.'

'Thank you, Kostas.' I offered him a drunken hand. 'But see Weir? I still want to get the bastard back.'

Chapter 14

When I woke the next morning I felt like shit as the raw emotions of guilt and fear hit me like angry vindictive twins. My head throbbed. It was as if sandpaper had been rubbed against the inside of my skull. I just wanted to block the world out and my recollections of the conversation with Kostas and the rest of the evening were all extremely hazy.

Shit, once this was all over I should give up the booze, but right now I needed to be present at work.

I arrived at the Dosh Dome later than normal, my attempts to treat the headache having failed. I was operating on autopilot. At the end of the corridor along from Weir's office, two of the directors—Carole McLetchie and Niall Kidd—were in close discussion. I ventured into Weir's office, as I might normally do. The area was free from the usual waft of cologne. In plain sight sat Wendy, and a sight she certainly was. Her cheeks were severely reddened, moist with tears, mascara smudged as she dabbed a hanky to her face. One of the other secretaries, Linda, was sitting beside her, and angled her head towards me, also clearly upset.

'Eh…have I come at a bad time?'

Wendy began to cry, facing downwards. I motioned with my hands to Linda—*what's going on?* She quietly stood up and took me outside the door of the office.

'Ally…you won't have heard if you've just arrived.' She swallowed slowly. 'Leslie…has died.'

I blinked. '*My God*...what...what happened?' The sentence kind of trailed off as I watched her.

Linda tearfully shook her head. 'Some kind of freak accident, it seems.'

'This is unbelievable. A *freak* accident?'

'Well, we spoke with his wife, who was understandably in shock. It's not entirely clear, but it seems that he was run over by a hit and run driver. He was found at the side of the road not far from his home in Morningside.'

'That's...awful. When did it happen?'

'Well, Lucy didn't give many details but we think that it must have occurred when it was dark, very late last night. I think she'd wondered where he'd gotten to, and then there was a commotion...when someone found... his, eh, body by the road side.' Linda's eyes began to fill up.

I left Linda to comfort the beleaguered Wendy, and shortly spotted Kostas sitting outside my office. He saw me immediately and made his way in, pulling a long face.

'Hear the news?' I asked.

'Amazing, Ally. It's spread like wildfire in here. There's going to be an announcement at ten, apparently. The new CEO is drafting something with the directors right now.'

'I saw some of them congregating upstairs.' I shook my head. 'I was cursing the man stupid last night.'

'Still considering resigning?'

'I don't know...I can't think straight. Things have been so pressured lately. Now I'm not sure.'

'Tough call, I guess. Especially right now. I know the bloke's body is scarcely cold, but I wonder what will happen to his fake charity now. How much did you say it had received from the bank?'

'Over six million.'

'Wow. And the charity doesn't really exist.' Kostas scratched his chin, before looking at me directly.

'Are you thinking what I'm thinking?'

'Don't go there, Kostas.'

'So I'm right. You *are* thinking the same thing, aren't you?'

'Coincidence.'

'Coincidence?' Kostas lowered his voice and checked if anyone was outside of the office window. 'Look Ally, given the way your little venture has spiralled out of control, would another twist really surprise you? Last night in the pub it was like listening to the plot of some zany movie. But just consider the facts here. Weir receives over six million illicitly, and then he's flattened by a hit and run driver? That doesn't sound like a coincidence. It doesn't even seem like fate. It looks like murder.'

'Murder! Come on now, Kostas. That's a huge leap.'

'Is it?'

I massaged by temples with my fingers. We both stared outside to the street below, cars meandering by. Kostas thought Doug Fox actually killed Leslie Weir.

Kostas touched my arm. 'Correct me if I'm wrong, but didn't you say that Doug Fox guy already threatened Charles Henderson, and arranged a break in at his house?'

'That's...different. It's just too farfetched.'

'Where's the money gone, then?'

'It must be sitting in some account. I think this one is offshore too. I could ask the finance people for details, though that's going to lead to possible suspicion.'

'I'm not attempting to alarm you, but you know a lot here. Too much, maybe. I think that you're going to have to watch your back.' I was about to reply when there was a knock on the door and we both turned round to see the CEO enter the room with Carole McLetchie, the Director of Compliance. Kostas nodded to them and politely left the office.

'Terrible business, Ally.' Martin Dodds spoke with his pronounced Adelaide accent.

'Shocking.' I couldn't think of more appropriate words.

'I've spoken to Lucy this morning. She's totally distressed, of course. Can't prepare for things like this.'

'I couldn't agree more.'

'Yes, it makes us think about what we're really about. But we do have to consider the business, in the interim. The market is sensitive to things like this. They always want stability. Certainty.' He was showing his true form as a banker here. Weir's body was barely cold, and we were to concentrate on the bank. He placed a hand on my shoulder. 'You're the obvious candidate to help bridge the gap. I'm asking if you'd cover some of Leslie's role, at least in the meantime. Carole's taking some things on, but you're knowledgeable about much of what Leslie was involved in, so perhaps the pair of you can liaise?'

I cleared my throat. 'Of course, eh, Martin. Anything I can do to help in the circumstances.' Carole gave me a strange look as I considered the absurdity of events.

'Seriously,' he then continued, 'you're the safe pair of hands we need round here. That's what Leslie would have wanted.'

It was the last thing that Leslie Weir would have wanted.

'Yes, Martin. I suppose that's what Leslie would have wanted.'

Then Carole spoke, curt as usual. 'There are some *issues* I need to discuss with you before this afternoon, Ally. I'll need to see you later on. Are you here this afternoon?'

The pair left my office, with Carole McLetchie promising to get back to me, no doubt to stack a load of work on my lap. And what exactly did she mean by *issues*? The Director of Compliance, of all people.

If I resigned at this instant, Kid World Funds would surely be exposed as the sham it was, and the evidence pointed, at least indirectly, to me. Weir had ensured that I had appeared involved in the selection of this 'good cause'—he'd even faked that letter. And any investigation could grow wings to delve into the murky reality of Lexicon Chartered, so I would need to sort that out.

Carole McLetchie had a reputation of being dedicated and assiduous at work, one of those compliance individuals who actually took her profession seriously. She seemed a disciple of rules and regulations, particularly if she felt that any breach of such would damage or influence the bank's standing. She was someone I'd avoided since I'd embarked on this scam. The thought of her prying into the whole quagmire made me worry because I had heard stories of where she'd worked right through the night to tackle some niggly problem; a dog with a financial bone. No close family and married to the bank, or perhaps, the law.

The other concern was contacting Doug or Canavan. Perhaps they would see the value of cutting their losses. However, Doug had used Indisweb, the same web design company as Weir had. How could they not have been involved? Doug had told me so many lies over the piece that he enjoyed no trust from me whatsoever. If he was complicit with Weir, then it was possible that he could be seen as a beneficiary of Weir's death, even if he had denied all knowledge of Kid World Funds. If Doug was connected, he could stand to make six million, not counting the residual fees that Lexicon Chartered had received to date. That was a substantial incentive for the police to look at if things blew up.

I called Doug from the office car park, paranoid at being overheard at the bank. The automated message, however, left my mouth dry; *this number is no longer in use*. What the hell did *that* mean? A cold shiver swept over me.

I had to be sure, so I made my excuses at the bank—I said that was going out to order flowers for Weir's wife Lucy—and drove into town towards the office Doug rented in Forth Street. There was no answer on Doug's personal intercom, so I waited until someone entered the building and then made my way upstairs. His office was locked up when I tried the door, so I knocked on one of the doors adjacent to the communal area that the small businesses shared.

A blonde woman in her fifties appeared, and I asked her if she'd seen Doug.

'The guy with the curly hair? And the designer glasses?'

'That's him. Have you seen him recently?'

'You mean before he left?' I felt myself placing my tongue between my upper front teeth and my upper lip. So the bastard had done a runner.

'Right, yes. When did he leave?' I asked, perhaps pointlessly.

'Yesterday. He had a couple of boxes and a tablet. Said he'd found a better vocation.' She shrugged, as if we could all have done with a career change. I rubbed my forehead.

Shit.

'Can you tell me who owns these premises? Is there a caretaker I could speak to—or an office I could call?'

'Are you the police? Is this guy in some kind of trouble?' No, dear, but I am.

'No, not at all,' I lied. 'I simply owe him money for a job, and I want to make sure he gets it.' It was an old line but in case Doug had slipped her some kind of bribe I figured I would lie anyway. Deceit was becoming habitual for me. And easy.

She popped back into her office, and returned with a business card for *Upwards Property*. I thanked her and made my way downstairs, dialling the number. I asked if they could give me a forwarding address for Doug Fox. After explaining that such was confidential, I employed the same lie about repayment of a debt. The man reluctantly said he'd access the details. The Business Q centre? In Forth Street? I replied in the affirmative.

'No such client as Doug Fox.'

'But one client vacated just yesterday. Perhaps he used a...business name instead?'

'Hold on a minute.' There was a gap, while I heard a keyboard being tapped. 'Yes, someone did leave, but they'd paid up for the next two months.'

'What was the name, if you don't mind? It's in his interest.' This was bullshit, because why would I owe money to someone whose name I didn't know? But it was worth a try.

'I'm really not supposed to divulge names, as I said...but seeing it's about repaying a debt...'

'Yes?'

'Hang on. Here it is. The name he gave me was Forbes. Ally Forbes.'

As Billy Connolly would have said, *fucking brilliant!* I was certainly having the piss taken out of me. The only other remaining player was Canavan, with the exception of the two people in Antigua. However, as Doug had dealt with them, they might have evaporated too, if they ever actually existed. I dialled Canavan's number in Dublin, which rang out. I then checked the Republic of Ireland directory on my phone, looking for a general number for the business centre I'd visited with Weir and Doug. Surely someone with a business the size of Canavan's couldn't hide?

A young man sporting an Eastern European accent of some kind replied. I gave the name of Canavan's company. He'd never heard of it. I pressed the point in case he'd misunderstood my question. They've got quite a large number of employees, I argued. A direct marketing company? There were no direct marketing firms located here, he said.

As the cold wind blasted at the front door, the sheer numbness inside me competed with the weather, and won easily. No Canavan either? But then, on my short trip to Dublin I had been so concerned about the deception of Weir that I had completely failed to notice that there genuinely was a separate illusion being perpetrated in the background. Was the entire venture a facade, designed primarily to fool me? And only me?

As I walked back to my car, I had yet another unpleasant thought. I had counted three missing participants; but there was also Mandy. There had only been five people who knew directly about the scam, and I was the sole dancer left spinning about like a fuckwit.

Chapter 15

On the short journey back to the office I had a sudden attack of conscience so I stopped at a flower shop to order flowers for Lucy Weir. What must she be thinking? From her perspective it would seem bad form if one of her late husband's closest colleagues didn't make contact, and I sensed that she might possibly know nothing of Weir's dealings. Lucy had always been pleasant, and I reflected on the mismatch that their partnership represented. It's an odd thing when someone you can't abide dies—sympathy for the bereaved still remains. The Weirs didn't have children: we used to joke in the office about imagining having to call Leslie Weir 'Dad'. That was academic now. And I suddenly realised that Lucy Weir would now have to make one of those lifestyle adjustments for which people can never be prepared, so I wrote some words to that effect on the card and arranged delivery.

On return to the office, I once again absorbed the horrible problem of Kid World Funds. How the hell was I going to explain the missing money? The last lot of blurb I had received from the fake charity contained all sorts of visuals of projects that the charity had apparently 'assisted'. Altruism personified. Weir had instructed me to make a number of splashes with this stuff. The problem I had, however, is that I would falsely be aiding a scam on its last legs, deceased in fact. There was only so much I could achieve without more material from the fake outfit, so I would run out of time and opportunity to cover the tracks. And this would simply help Doug disappear.

Carole McLetchie would surely be on my case to pick up what was in effect *Weir's* work with Kid World Funds, yet I had only one contact detail for the outfit, which I suspected would also provide a dead end. I would probably have more chance of making contact with my great, great grandmother through the Scottish Paranormal Society. There was also the distinct possibility that any investigation into Kid World Funds would throw up an inspection of Lexicon Chartered. The stark reality was that I actually had to distance myself from the whole mechanism. But how? I was the remaining human, apparently, representing that very mechanism.

What I needed to do was buy some time. That meant obtaining the key to Weir's world, identifying where the money had gone and perhaps uncovering the ultimate connection to Doug Fox, however dangerous that might be. Perhaps I could even argue that the foundation should be brought back inside, though I might well be fired for such a volte-face.

And just as I considered how I could avoid Carole McLetchie, the very demon appeared, as if by magic. 'Ally, *there* you are.' That curt smile again. 'I need ten minutes of your time. It really is quite urgent.'

'Yes…we must get together. I've a heck of a lot right now, what with—'

'I'm sure that you do. But I need to ask you some questions *right now.* Let's go to my office.' She looked over her half moon glasses, superior and uncompromising.

I followed her to the elevator, like a child awaiting chastisement. She said very little, perhaps waiting for the privacy her office afforded before blasting the cannons. Her office was slightly more austere than most of the others; no artistic decoration on the walls, and a solitary silver picture frame sporting a photograph of a glaring black Doberman. I was certain that it would rank higher in her judgement that most human beings.

'Coffee?' Why not? She ordered two cups and her PA arrived instantly—who'd keep Carole waiting?

'This is a touch delicate. What I am about to say is confidential, needless to say. Are we absolutely clear about that?'

'Of course.' I swallowed some coffee and the lump in my throat.

'Good.' In a few seconds of silence she followed my eyes as if assessing whether I was already aware of whatever it was that she was about to tell me.

I retained eye contact until she raised a finger in my direction.

'Is there anything you have to tell me, Ally?'

I quickly digested her question. Fishing trip, or opportunity for a full confession prior to interrogation? Maybe she'd set her dog on me.

'I'm, eh, a little confused. You were going to tell me something?' Pass the hot potato back.

'You know, Ally, people misunderstand my role here. I'm not the police. Far from it. My role's more akin that of, say, your lawyer.'

'Right...'

'Assuming, that is, that you're a full team player at the bank, if you get my drift?'

'Team player, of course. You've got a difficult job here...I understand. How can I help you?' I was talking rubbish as I held her gaze.

'Are you bullshitting me?' She took off her glasses.

'Bullshitting about what?' I was fairly sure that she was testing me, unsure of her ground, but with a purpose of some kind.

'You see, that's what I mean. Answering a question with a question. What you just did?'

'Did I?' She didn't smile.

'That's not going to wash with the police, Ally.'

'Police?' I kind of gurgled, before clearing my throat.

'Yes, the police. They have been in contact about Leslie's death. Very quickly I might add, given that he only died last night. I presume that it's just in case there is a connection between what happened last night, and the bank.'

'But it was an accident. A hit and run. That would mean that his death was totally...' I hesitated, 'tragic, but unconnected to the bank.'

'I very much hope so. However, they appear to want to explore all possibilities. They have requested that I compile a list of employees with the greatest involvement with Leslie, based on what he was working on recently. Connections. They would like to interview these people as a first trawl.'

'So I'm on your list?'

'You're *top* of my list.'

'Oh.'

'So, I repeat, is there anything I should know before you speak to the police? Anything odd about Leslie's work, that you think could potentially lead to something like this happening?'

I cleared my throat yet again, coughing, buying time in order to compute a decent reply. 'Cold coming on. Time of year. No, to tell you the truth Carole, you couldn't have met a more *upstanding individual* than Leslie. He may have been the victim of a tragic accident, but I'd be amazed if this accident was connected to his work here at the bank. The man was a straight as they come,' I said, without a flicker of an eye. She stared straight back.

'Excellent. That's *exactly what I was hoping to hear you say*, so sincerely. Because I have to guard the interests of…this corporation, you understand. Now, the police will be here tomorrow morning at 8:30 a.m. I've got you pencilled in for half an hour from 8:45 a.m. Right after Wendy, Leslie's secretary.'

'I'm due at an event in town tomorrow morning.'

'Cancel it. Don't mention the police, either. Completely confidential, remember.'

'Okay.'

'And there is something else I want to make absolutely clear. If an unexpected negative were to emerge as a consequence of a police investigation, it could be damaging to the bank's interests.' I nodded, and then she stood up, indicating that the meeting was at an end.

'Anyway Ally, anything that damages the bank's reputation would almost certainly damage the reputation of an individual member of staff like you even more.'

Back downstairs I chewed the fat about Weir's demise briefly with a couple of colleagues, before beckoning Kostas into my office.

'Cops are coming in tomorrow.'

'Cops? Weir? That's quick.'

'Yes, yes, and yes.'

'Who told you this—Carole McLetchie?'

'Right again.'

'Boy, the cops are off their mark. Must be suspicious about something.'

I scratched my head. 'Appears so. And Commandant McLetchie just grilled me, told me that I'm top of the list for interview.'

'She's suspicious of *you*?'

'Woman's a nightmare. She's suspicious even when there's nothing to be suspicious of, so she's having a field day now. But, apparently, I have nothing to be concerned about *providing* that the bank's interests remain intact.'

'She's a company *man*, through and through.'

'Yip.'

'So what are you going to do?'

'I believe that's the third time you've asked me that in the last 24 hours. I *definitely* can't resign now.'

'No, you can't. But I could hardly know that the police would be onto you when I advised you last night, could I?' Kostas looked a little peeved.

'Fair enough. All I can do is say how *wonderful* Weir was, and how *highly* I thought of him. A pile of shit, but it seemed to work upstairs with Carole McLetchie.'

'But will it fob off professional detectives?'

A poor night's sleep left me drained. Perhaps a certain kind of fatigue had manifested itself now—from what direction would the next missile emanate? At 8:44 a.m. I sat at the assembly point awaiting my meeting on the fourth floor. Precisely one minute later, Wendy's bulbous frame appeared and waddled towards me. I looked away as she passed though I could hear muffled tears. Surely she hadn't been crying for the past 24 hours?

The two plain clothes cops sat side by side in our 'Mackintosh' room—a conference room usually deployed by the directors for small group meetings with corporate guests. The room boasted two original pieces of CRM furniture, and normally exhibited an aura of peace and class. The CID personnel appeared slightly incongruous in the surroundings. Although seated, both were clearly elongated characters, one balding with a thin moustache, and the other with cropped sandy-coloured hair and a ruddy complexion. What is it about police? You could place them in g-strings selling flowers on a street corner, yet they would still look like the police, smell like the police, and sound like the police.

'Mr Forbes,' said sandy, ruddy. The deadpan expression surveyed my face and a finger motioned to his partner. 'Detective Sergeant Barker, and I am Detective Inspector Wilson.'

No handshakes were proffered. Bad cop, worse cop?

'Alasdair Forbes,' said Barker.

'Alasdair Forbes,' repeated Wilson.

'Yes,' I replied, slightly hesitantly.

'Bit odd isn't it?'

'Odd? No, not really. My grandfather was called Alasd—'

'No, *no*,' Wilson interjected.

'No,' Barker repeated.

'What?'

'What? Well, that *is* strange. So you don't think a hit-and-run accident perpetrated against a senior member of staff at one of Scotland's largest financial institutions is odd?'

'I didn't say that.'

'Well why did you question it?'

'I'm not questioning it at all.'

'See? That's what I mean.' He turned to DS Barker, who shook his head almost imperceptibly. 'He's not questioning it either. A hit-and-run, unquestioned.'

'Look,' I said flatly. 'Of course I think it's odd. Leslie Weir was my boss. There's obviously been a tragic accident.'

The two shared a knowing glance, as if telepathically communicating some kind of secondary text which I had no prospect of deciphering. Wilson shuffled some papers on the desk, before staring directly at me.

'Well, we don't think so, Mr Forbes. It *is odd* that you *assume* so, however. Very odd.'

I began to sweat, and a minor but noticeable itch emerged on my nose. I was determined not to touch it: body language for deception. My head thumped. Bring back Carole McLetchie. Wilson stood and walked to the window prior to suddenly swivelling round and pointing.

'Why did you have a heated argument with Leslie Weir in the bank car park the afternoon before he died? ' He looked at his notebook. 'Tuesday, 4:35 p.m.?'

I swallowed. 'That's not true.' I looked up, mentally accessing the necessary facts. It was true. 'No, that's definitely not correct. We did speak briefly about a work matter, but we distinctly didn't argue.'

'What did you…discuss?'

'I can't recall, exactly.'

'The phrase "can't recall" is the most common line used by villains.'

'I can't *remember*, then.'

Wilson snorted. 'Just two days ago?'

'Just bank stuff. Nothing important. But we didn't have an argument. I would have remembered that.'

'Well, someone else did *remember* it.'

Shit, Wendy.

'He or she witnessed you grabbing Mr Weir by the jacket outside in the car park. What have you got to say about that?'

'What? Well, whoever that was must be mistaken. We were having a bit of a laugh, actually. A joke.' I spoke as assuredly as possible.

'Security cameras will be the judge of that, Mr Forbes.'

'Security cameras?'

'Security cameras,' Wilson repeated, as if such would provide irrefutable evidence that I had murdered Weir in cold blood.

'That would demonstrate motive, Mr Forbes.'

'Motive? For what, exactly?'

'You tell us.'

'I'm not sure that I follow you.'

'Where were you at 12 midnight—Tuesday night?'

'I was…asleep in my flat.'

'On your own?'

'Yes.'

'He was on his own,' said Wilson. The two shared another look, a clear measure of disdain and suspicion focused directly on me.

'No wife. We know that,' Barker said, looking at his notes. 'No girlfriend to back up your story?'

'No.'

'Doesn't have a girlfriend,' Wilson said. 'Boyfriend, perhaps?'

'Look, this is ridiculous!'

'We have to cover all the angles, Mr Forbes. We don't discriminate. We don't care if you're homosexual.'

'I am not homosexual.'

'So you're more bothered about that than the fact we think you've a motive for murder? That's incredible.'

'Murder? I do *not* have a motive for murder! This is absurd. And I hate to use a cliché, but I can't see why you're wasting your time harassing me instead of catching real criminals.' Wilson smiled, as if he'd heard this line a thousand times before.

'So what were you arguing with Leslie Weir about? I very much doubt if you've forgotten what you talked about. An intelligent guy like you? Come on, you're clearly concealing something from us. So if you're innocent, spill the beans.'

'There *wasn't* an argument,' I said deliberately, mentally calculating if security camera footage would really catch me grabbing hold of Weir to back Wendy up. 'I remember discussing one of our upcoming events. We were having a laugh about it.'

'Ah…you were having a *laugh*,' Wilson said.

'Really funny place to work, it seems,' Barker replied, scratching his head. 'So, you grabbed his jacket in a playful, fun manner? A bit of horseplay? Whilst having a laugh about an event?' He raised his eyebrows.

'Yes…that's actually about right.'

'So why did you lose your temper and swear at Miss Turnbull?'

'That's not right.'

Barker continued. 'Ah, so you were just having a laugh with her too, before having a right hoot with Mr Weir?'

'Look. Obviously you know things that I don't. But this meeting is going nowhere.'

'If that's the way you want to play it, fine. A man has died—your boss—and you're not willing to cooperate. You'll be hearing from us, once we review those security tapes. Oh, and by the way,' he stood up, looking out of the window. 'Is that your Audi down there?' I stood also, and peered outside. There were two uniformed officers and another man taking photographs of my car in the car park.

'Yes, that's my car. Have your people been inside it? You'd need permission—a warrant in fact—to do that.'

Barker smiled again. 'We're aware of the law, Mr Forbes. We *are* the police, remember. No, we have not entered your vehicle. Yet. But we have taken some pictures, which is perfectly legal.'

'Any reason why would you need to photograph my car?'

'I believe that there's a bit of a dent in the front wing of your Audi. Looks recent.'

'Right…hang on.' I considered the dent. 'I hit a rubbish bin about a week ago.'

'Rubbish bin? And I don't suppose that you would have any witnesses to corroborate this story?' I shook my head.

Wilson stared at me. 'No surprise there. And I bet you were on your own when it happened,' he said, motioning for me to leave. 'We'll be in touch.'

Chapter 16

The phone call from Lucy Weir came just after I'd just crashed out in my flat. Her voice carried a low, earthy and sad quality, the trauma of the week's events having taken its toll.

'I just wanted to thank you for sending the flowers. It was very thoughtful.' She let her words hang.

'Not, not at all'. Suddenly I felt very sorry for her. Very guilty. 'It was the least I could do. Dreadful business. It must have been such a shock.'

'Nothing prepares you for a time like this,' she said. 'Excuse me.' There was a brief silence before I heard her blowing her nose in the background. Another few seconds elapsed before she spoke again.

'Sorry about that. It's just, well you know...'

'Of course.'

'It hits me every time I speak to someone...about Leslie...for the first time. It's a little surreal, I suppose.'

'I understand. You certainly deserve to take it easy in these...awful circumstances.' I spoke slowly, struggling to know what else to say: I'm sorry for you even though your husband was a greedy, manipulative bastard?

'It would be lovely to take it easy, Ally, but I've had to deal with the police, which on top of everything else...'

I swallowed. 'I suppose that they've got to be thorough in cases such as, eh, this one.'

'They seem to think that someone might have hit Leslie... deliberately.'

'Right…I'm sure that they don't really *believe* that. I mean, it's almost certainly been an accident. A *horrible* accident. It must be truly dreadful to be in your position. It's even probable that someone knocked Leslie down without even being aware of it. Maybe a truck or a bus? I'm sorry…' The scenario seemed cruel however it was described, but what else could I suggest?

'I think it was an accident too. You might be right. But perhaps,' she said, sniffing audibly, 'it was some guy with no morals slinking off, not even returning to the scene. How could someone do such a thing?'

'I don't know. I'm sorry.'

'But then, the alternative is worse. The police say it could have potentially have been *murder*. Isn't that ridiculous?'

'Did they say that to you? That's ridiculous.' I'd used the same adjective to the police.

'But why would they think that? I mean, Leslie didn't have any enemies.'

'Of course not,' I lied. 'I'm certain that they're just being thorough, Lucy. It must be terrible for you having to answer questions.'

'It is. But they're going to make full inquiries at the bank too. You haven't met them yet, per chance?'

'Eh, yes. I met them briefly today, actually.' My throat felt a little dry, more guilt for not mentioning this fact.

'And what did they say to you?'

I cleared my throat. 'Oh, they were wondering if there was anything at the bank that might…potentially…on the *off chance*…be linked. But honestly, Lucy, I think that this is a formality. Procedural. There is probably a strict process for them to follow. I'm sure that they do this all the time, however horrible it is.'

'I suppose.'

'It's as much a shock to me as everyone else here. Leslie was such….' I paused briefly to choose a truthful phrase, 'an experienced professional. Everyone knew him. I hope that the police confirm it was just a horrible accident.'

'Well, I hope that they catch the culprit, Ally. But, I have to ask you, honestly, do you think this is connected to anything Leslie was working on at the bank? I thought you might know as you were such a close colleague.'

'Oh, not really, Lucy. I honestly don't think so.'

'But there was all the recent restructuring, and all the new, what might you call it…changes in strategic direction, for good causes. You know?' Maybe she wasn't as naive as I'd hoped. What did she know? The line went silent for a couple of seconds.

'There are always things going on, Lucy. Nothing much was different about this week,' I said before she explained that the funeral would be held off for a few days to allow time for forensic analysts to interpret the post mortem results.

When she ended the call, I sat down, trying to clear my head. Practicality had to come first. I needed to bypass Lexicon Chartered imminently, to delay payments to them and at least temporarily stall the flow of cash outside the business because Weir's death and Doug's disappearance had changed everything.

A bottle of Pinotage looked at me invitingly from the oak mantle piece.

I grudgingly peered back and then surrendered, filling one of those over-sized glasses that encourage people to treat red wine like Ribena. Or maybe that was my excuse. Sifting through the snail mail, I found an envelope containing a small pack of information from my mother—details of some local history and an outline of some contacts in Appin for Elise Stewart's genealogical project. I made a mental note to bring it into work for her. Then the phone rang again. Another female.

'Hi Ally, it's Laura.' Mandy's flat mate sounded a little distant. 'Have you heard from Mandy?'

'No, I haven't heard from Mandy. I'd have been in touch.'

'I was simply checking in case. You see, I'm moving out of the flat. Did a deal with the owner of the flat to mitigate against penalties, but the time is right for me to buy, so I've had a bid accepted for a nice pad off Lothian Road.'

'You've been off the mark. I hope it all goes well.'

'I'm a professional person and I should really own my own property, so here I go.'

'Fair enough.'

'There was one other thing. I found a data stick in the flat as I've been clearing things out. It was in Mandy's room, wedged under the carpet in the corner. We re-carpeted when we came in so it doesn't predate our tenancy.'

My mind leapt. 'Do you know what's on it?'

'This may seem a little dishonest, but I looked out of curiosity. Mandy did leave us both high and dry, after all. However, it's full of encrypted files. Not really my thing, though I wondered if it might be of interest to you?'

'Sure, I could have a look at it. I could pop round and pick it up if you like?'

'That's fine.'

'I've had a couple of glasses, but hell, I don't care. My boss died this week…in an accident…so any diversion would help.' Another diversion was probably the last activity I needed, but maybe this offered a means of contacting Mandy. Why would she have a data stick containing encrypted files? Work stuff? She definitely owed me an explanation, and fifty grand said it was worth a look.

Kostas had been in the midst of one of those IT strategy sessions in which large businesses seem to specialise. He noticed me peering in the window of the training room—one of these featureless venues that forces minimal distraction while corporate brainwashing is administered. I pointed at my watch, miming the drinking of coffee. He held up ten fingers indicating a break was due soon. We met in the cafeteria.

'Thank you for rescuing me from those idiots.'

'Come off it Kostas, you love those sessions as much as the other tech-heads.'

'Really? If someone else says that the "dynamic has changed" one more time I swear I'll throw them out of the window.'

'Good point.'

'So, how's the world of corporate deceit?'

'Would you mind keeping your voice down?'

'Sorry. I take it that you saw the police? There are rumours.'

'They say I have a *motive*, because that cow Wendy witnessed me having a go at Weir earlier on the day in the car park. Probably never got off her fat arse and looked out of the window in her life until that moment. They're trying to dig up the security camera footage to confirm her view of events. You couldn't make it up.'

'They're probably just fishing, Ally…big cheese at a bank is flattened on the road. No one stops. It's probably a drunk driver who's taken off. But *possibly* someone who has a financial motive…'

'Thanks for that. Even Lucy Weir was on the blower last night asking if her husband had any enemies. I didn't know what to say.'

Kostas took a gulp of coffee and sat back. 'That there's a long list? He must have annoyed hundreds of people during his time. You're in good company.'

'In good company, but hoping that there's no usable film footage from the car park. It's one of those rare times when I would support mindless vandalism. Hopefully someone spray painted the bloody camera last week and it's useless.'

'And how's your investigation into Doug Fox, and your fake foundation? You must have had time and opportunity to pursue this line of inquiry in between consoling the bereaved and assisting our noble constabulary.'

I produced the data stick and placed it on the table.

'Obsolete,' Kostas stated flatly.

I shook my head. 'I wasn't enquiring about its efficiency as a means of data storage. It's encrypted.'

'Where did you get it?'

'It was Mandy's.'

'Oh. I'd almost forgotten about her. She's been in touch?' He appeared surprised.

'No, but her flat mate Laura found it in the flat. I can see what types of files are there, but can't access them. I need to decipher what's on here.'

'That's your priority?'

'One of about ten priorities, Kostas.'

'What type of files?'

'Something I hadn't heard of—ellon.'

'Ellon? Mmm. Are you sure you want this uncovered? I mean, you're not going to have to kill me if I decipher your data?'

'I'm not really in the mood for humour.'

'Fair enough. I'll have a look at home tonight. Best to keep this off any work-related computers, just in case.'

In a whirlwind morning I cleared up some of the backlog, delegating where possible and sifting through what I could fix. I knew that it was a matter of time before insiders would ask about Kid World Funds and where the money had gone. There was also Lexicon Chartered to consider, which might now cease to exist. I decided to pull in some favours. A large slice of contrition was needed on my part, so I needed to make two contacts. First up was the PR department, where I phoned David Moritano.

'Ally, how are you?' His voice modulated minimal enthusiasm.

'Shocked about Leslie's death, as we all are.'

'Yes, I guess you can never tell what's coming in life.' I was unsure if this was a reference to the restructuring, as we hadn't communicated as much by phone or in person since the shake up.

'Good point, David. It's left us numb, but also on a more prosaic note, in a practical dilemma.'

'Let me guess, you want my help?'

'David, I'm not going to be evasive. Yes, I do.'

'You know, it crossed my mind that if things went awry, you'd be in touch,' he said quietly.

'No one could have predicted Leslie's death, but that aside, there are other issues.'

'So the off-shore dream hasn't produced the promised results?'

'It's not been a disaster in any way....but...it was *Leslie's* desire to push through the maximum change. That's why I urged that the best people—such as you, obviously—were retained with...new opportunities.' I cringed as I delivered this nonsense, though I spoke with as positive a tone as feasible.

'Look Ally, I do have a job here, though it's not as bright as the one I used to possess, or that one I *could* have taken. But forget that: what can I do for you?'

'Thank you. David, I think that the bank should reconsider running the foundation internally.'

'You must be kidding.'

'No. Please hear me out. Not where we raise money, but rather how we disperse it. I am partly to blame for the changes, I accept, though Leslie was also putting a lot of pressure on me too.' There was silence on the other end of the line.

'Are you with me?'

'Are you offering me my old role back?'

'Possibly.'

'Right.' Non committal.

'I'm sorry about the way things worked out. It wasn't fair, and it was rushed through. But right now, I'm going upstairs to seek a provisional review. This is confidential, so I'd ask you not to discuss it at work please, but before I do it I wanted to know if I could count on you to help me if we brought the thing back in house at some stage. What do you think?'

'It worked perfectly well before, Ally. I'm just surprised about your about-turn.'

'So you're not against the idea, in principle?'

'No, I suppose not. I thought the externalisation was a crazy idea in the first instance, if you don't mind me saying. So admitting an error and being prepared to regroup is probably a good thing.' I smiled to myself; he was of course correct.

It felt good to have made minor reparation for previous failures. I called his new line manager and asked for a bit of slack for him—that he was helping me with some confidential stuff, but that there would be benefits for the Marketing and PR departments in due course. Providing that there was something in it for them they were fine about it. Then there was a call to the Finance, asking them to copy David into emails about funds received, as he'd be taking some responsibility in this area. I had already asked Finance to cease charitable payments to Lexicon Chartered even though the agent still received its fee. This led me to my next awkward point of contact: Carole McLetchie.

I went upstairs.

'I can give you five minutes,' she said curtly. 'I've a conference call from Malaysia at 1:30 p.m.' She checked her watch as if this statement in itself had taken up more valuable time.

'Just a note about Lexicon Chartered.'

'Yes?'

'Well, this may seem a little surprising, but I think that we could do better.'

'You mean use another organisation?'

'Return to in-house management.'

'This is a volte face.'

'It may appear so, Carole. But...Leslie was actually keener to outsource than I had been.'

'Really? That's not the impression you gave when you presented to the board.' She peered over those glasses, every bit the dour headmistress.

'Well, you see, when I approached Leslie about the idea of our customers funding the venture—saving the bank millions per annum—*Leslie* pushed the idea further, and sent me to investigate options. So I assessed some agencies that might fit the bill, following his instruction.' I slowly delivered this lie, praying that she wouldn't recall the order of events before Weir was actually involved in the scam, or wouldn't have the inclination to go digging.

'Ally, you're treading on thin ice.' My heart momentarily fluttered. Had I misjudged my ability to bullshit someone of her nature?

'Leslie has just died,' she continued. 'And we haven't even had the funeral yet. However, you're casting doubt on the legitimacy of decisions you say Leslie supported—rather than you?' This was a separate point, so I took a breath.

'Not at all. I wouldn't ever disrespect the deceased. Leslie was having similar thoughts himself, I think.' She couldn't disprove such hearsay so I continued, somewhat hesitantly. 'It's just that in practice, I feel that the distance, and potential loss of control...in the medium term, should be revisited. The old structure actually worked.' I made direct eye contact with her, though she remained impassive.

'As you will remember, I argued a very similar point when you made your presentation. It's in the minutes. Don't you remember? Given that you presented your case like a slick salesman, I assumed that you had the resilience to make your plan work?'

'I do, Carole, though the essential element of the restructuring was the cost saving by engaging customers—and look at the results—it's made a difference to the balance sheet already.'

'You're still in sales mode, Ally. What is it you want?' She checked her watch again, and I glanced at that sinister photo of her dog on the desk. It looked likely to leap from the frame and attack on sight.

'I'd like to consider the old structure. I have provisionally asked one of the staff to look for best value for us.'

She stared at me. 'You can undertake a *provisional* report. Now, on more pressing matters, what did the *police* ask you when they visited yesterday?'

'Oh…nothing much,' I uttered, before a hearing a faint knock on the door. Carole's PA appeared and smiled politely, noting that the conference call was now waiting.

'Right, Ally. I'll catch up with you about this.'

I escaped her clutches having secured a small break. However, I'd been forced to play down the line of questioning about the police interview for the second time within twenty four hours and as I made my way back downstairs, a cold layer of perspiration seemed to envelope me. The security camera thing bothered me, because if the police had evidence of an argument this may well be the deciding factor in pursuing a more thorough investigation. Then there was the dent in the car wing—was this simply another procedural grey area that would demonstrate nothing conclusive either way? I was ignorant of forensics or indeed regular police tactics.

So I had to make the call.

'I've a couple of questions for you actually, Mr Forbes,' DI Wilson said before I could speak.

'I'll try my best. Is this call, eh, being recorded?'

'Why? Would that be important?' I could feel the sheer suspicion in his voice.

'No. It's just that after the interview you had with me I felt that there were some, let's say, misunderstandings, and when you're not face to face with someone, sometimes that can happen more often.'

'Would you prefer to come into the station tomorrow?' Given that I had no idea how he was going to reply—or what he might ask me in return—it probably didn't matter.

'No, no, that won't be necessary. So...have you found who hit Leslie yet?'

'Our investigations are ongoing,' Wilson said dryly.

'Okay. And you were concerned about a misunderstanding of an event in the car park at the bank?'

'Have you something to tell us?'

'I am just concerned that a colleague had misinterpreted a conversation that is completely unrelated to subsequent events.'

'I'm not sure that I can comment on that.'

'Well,' I kept on digging. 'I'm sure that you can't have found video evidence of anything in the car park because nothing of any note actually occurred.'

More silence.

'Am I not correct, officer? Surely I have a right to know?'

'Not really. The surveillance material in the car park may be useful in our investigation.'

'In what way?'

'We can conclude, for example, exactly when Mr Weir left the premises.'

'And that's it?'

'And that's what, Mr Forbes?'

'Am I on the tapes?!' I blurted it out, anxiety launching into my voice.

'Not...conclusively.' I could hear the frustration on the other side of the line too. 'Though there may be cameras at adjacent properties that we can still requisition.'

'Well, you won't see anything there either, because nothing happened.'

'We'll see. We're not finished with you.'

Chapter 17

When Kostas called me at home after work I'd temporarily forgotten about the data stick. He said he'd found something and that he'd come over to my flat immediately. However, his characteristically affable demeanour was missing when he placed his jacket on the sofa, opened up his laptop and looked me squarely in the eye.

'What?' I asked, suddenly unsure of what he might tell me.

'This is really none of my business, Ally.' He held the data stick, as if it were poisonous.

'What's on it, Kostas?' I folded my arms.

'Well, it was cleverly encoded. There's an old encryption trick, where you can encrypt different sets of files, using an *almost* identical set of codes, to confuse a prospective decoder into believing that they have found all that there is to find.'

'But you weren't fooled?'

'No. There are two levels of files here, an obviously encrypted set, and another set of hidden files. The first level is trivial stuff. Lists of prospects for Mandy's business, an assessment of the potential of each one—a bit of strategy plus some numbers. Of no more than minor interest. Business planning stuff.'

'What about the rest?'

'I'm not sure that you're going to like this.' He showed me the laptop screen. 'Ally, it's possible that I misunderstood your story about the order of events when you set up your scam, but I don't think so. You've been completely straight with me, right?'

'Of course I have.'

'That's what I thought.'

'Kostas, what is it?'

'Look, these hidden files indicate a different business plan. Sensitivity analysis, projections, inputs....and much more detail. But it's not about Mandy's business.'

'So what's it about?'

'The scam in which you have been involved.' I tried to remember what I might have given Mandy. I hadn't recognised the data stick, but I had shared some information with her, and perhaps she'd duplicated it for some reason.

'Yes, Doug and I did quite a bit of work on this stuff. We had to make the case to the board. Maybe Mandy got a copy of this stuff after we involved her in the payment thing.'

'I don't think so.'

'Why not? Let me see.'

Kostas accessed one file. I viewed a spreadsheet, scrolling down to see if it was familiar material. However, the categorisation and projections differed from what Doug and I had worked on. In fact, this read like a contrary take on the same project. There was a lot of detail, and sets of assumptions that Doug had not discussed with me. I glanced at Kostas, who sat with a furrowed brow.

'I see what you mean,' I said. 'I've never seen this stuff before.'

'Yes, and Ally, this file was created some time ago.'

'When?' He pointed to the creation date.

'But that's...before I started dating Mandy.' This felt like a punch to the stomach, even if I'd already feared it coming. Kostas watched me carefully, an expression of sympathy on his face.

'Yes. And I'm afraid there's more.' He opened up another file, which was an ordinary presentation file entitled 'Profile'.

Then I saw a picture of myself.

The photo had been taken at a work event, though I hadn't seen it before.

As I read the blurb, I realised that it all focused on me. Someone had done a very thorough job. There was a CV of sorts, but also much more: more than you can find on social media. Likes, dislikes, interspersed with factual stuff such as where I banked and my finances, who my friends were, which pubs I drank in, the people who were my key business contacts. There were appraisal scores for all sorts, and then a SWOT analysis. Under 'weaknesses' there was a sub-section headed 'character flaws'. Some of it was very negative. I continued to view a set of 'strategic options'. Kostas remained silent as I scrolled further down to read more. There were actually recommendations as to how I could be targeted, groomed and systematically exploited. How my 'ego' could be used against me, especially where a good looking girl was concerned. There was even a suggestion that I could be hooked-in most believably, and easily, at a work event.

This was exactly what had happened when I first met Mandy. I sat back in the sofa, hands behind my head.

'I'm sorry, Ally.'

'For fuck's sake.'

I then held my head in my hands, shutting my eyes tightly. I could feel the blood pumping in the temples; a force out of my control. This just wasn't fair, adding humiliation to insult. Kostas remained silent as I considered whether I should bother retaining consciousness. Then I opened my eyes.

'Obviously, I knew about Weir, and I'd figured that I'd been set up by *Doug*.'

'But not…' He let the sentence rest.

'No. I knew that she probably took off with the fifty grand. But a total set up?'

'Understandable. She's a good looking girl.'

'That's not helping.'

'I am genuinely sorry. Look, if it's any consolation, I think most guys could fall for the same thing.'

'That's not any consolation. I mean, was she actually screwing Doug?' I whispered the words, though the resonance in my own head could have been deafening.

'You don't know that, Ally. Maybe it was just a business thing.'

'The guy's such a supercilious prick. I mean, obviously I've been turned over, but what the fuck could she have seen in *him*?' I iterated the cliché automatically.

'I don't know, Ally.'

'You know, Kostas, it explains a couple of things. She kept egging me on to do something, even though she hadn't apparently known Doug. And then she actually turned up when I met him at the White Hart in the Grassmarket. Stupid bastard as I am, I thought it was simply a coincidence, given that she worked close by. But then, if I remember correctly, *he* suggested the place, and before we were finished, she was arranged as the recipient of *my* share. Another bloody pincer movement. And then she takes off the moment that Weir was officially involved. But then, she gave me shit for the Weir thing, and that seemed genuine. What an actress. Anything else on the data stick?'

'No names, except for you, and the others who were on that potential hit list.'

'Doug was using a fake name anyway, at least for his office rental, so he'd hardly go to that trouble only to display personal evidence on a data stick, even if they did leave it lying under a carpet by mistake. Mandy left in a hurry. Yet, Doug kept me going *until the bigger money came in*.'

Kostas nodded as I digested this fact. 'Have you spoken to the cops again?' he asked.

'I called the guy Wilson today. I think that he's still intent on nailing me.'

'You're on the CCTV footage?'

'Not in the car park, but he now looks fixated with checking other possible cameras just to see if by magic that joyous meeting with Weir has been captured for posterity. Next they'll be investigating if it's been filmed by fucking satellite. So they can set it to music and make me dance to it.'

'What are you going to do?' He pointed the data stick at me.

'Track that bastard Doug down.'

'I don't think that would be easy.'

'Mandy might be easier to locate. I know that I could probably have tried harder to find her, but to be truthful I think I just wanted to forget all about her. It's the sheer embarrassment. But Doug's different.'

'Why?'

'I want to get *even*.'

Weir's funeral was held on a quintessential funeral-type day—uncomfortably chilly, a cruel north easterly stabbing at the mourners as they made their way into the church. I had no idea if Leslie Weir had been religious, or whether this was simply the default position as played out by countless bereaved relatives without a preconceived script. Certainly, he had embodied a distinctly uncharitable demeanour in life; but then such hypocrisy was hardly uncommon because everyone's a hero in death.

The church—a large red sandstone edifice off Queensferry Road in Barnton—was about three quarters full. The ceremony embodied a generic Church of Scotland service, where I switched off. I'd heard it all before anyway. *In God's house there are many rooms.* Years before there had been many *mansions*, so there might have been a drive toward austerity at the church, or perhaps a touch of political correctness. I wondered what they honestly thought of him, but then that was a moot point. I couldn't stand the man yet I felt guilt. Maybe everyone feels guilty at funerals. One thing for sure though, there was one vacant room at the Dosh Dome as a consequence of Weir's demise. One vacant room and a nightmare for one Ally Forbes to address.

As the congregation exited the church I observed the crowd. My eyes moved from Lucy Weir, who appeared sedated, through several people whom I didn't know, then towards two plain-clothes policemen—Wilson and Barker. They were already staring at me when I noticed their presence. I nodded slowly though neither reciprocated.

Wilson then approached me as I left the church. 'Mr Forbes?'

'Yes.'

'Anything to tell us?' What did they hope to attain, a chance confession? The case solved before the coffin was lowered into the ground?

'No, actually I'm at a funeral, in case you hadn't noticed.'

'There's no need to be offensive, Mr Forbes.'

'I'm trying to stick to the facts.' I looked him in the eye.

'So you insist that you didn't have an argument with him on the day he died?'

'Yes.'

'Yes you did? Or yes you insist you did not?'

'This is getting us nowhere. He was my boss, and if you don't mind I'd like to pay my respects.'

'Respect. Yes, that's an interesting term. So, can you shed light on any aspect of his work that might have been connected?'

'No I can't, actually.' I lied again, as this was the other problematic avenue of investigation. I was fairly sure that Carole McLetchie would not have divulged confidential bank details unless really pushed by the police. Legally pushed.

'Just remember, we are only a call away, if you think that you can assist in our inquiries. And remember, *you're* not out of the woods yet.'

He joined Barker in an unmarked car. I felt slightly relieved. No surveillance evidence, then, just trying to bump me into giving the game away at a weak moment.

After the committal I headed back to the office, not wishing to participate in the wake at a local hotel. The first thing I did was dig up the PR material that Weir had sent to me for Kid World Funds. What I'd figured was that should Carole McLetchie ask, I was simply doing my job coordinating the publicity material in which we had invested. There were numerous shots of smiling children in far flung locations. Testimonials and stories about how the charity had been 'helped'. God knows where Weir had procured the stuff, but ironically, it all appeared realistic. I daresay that an immoral individual could create such material—and the related blurb about projects—at a fraction of the cost of the real investment. Indeed, there was an attached plan suggesting when and where these 'stories' should appear over the coming months, with ideas as to where I should incorporate the bank's name into the story. Notably, all this was to appear *after* the bank's investment, despite the appearance of this material before we had spent a penny. If I had gone upstairs with this now, it would have triggered an internal investigation that would have implicated me rather than Weir.

Weir had created the impression that I had recommended Kid World Funds, not him. And although Weir was now dead, there was nothing to stop me briefly following the plan to buy some time. The stories were all from overseas locations, under different legal jurisdictions—difficult to trace, or disprove. The Kid World Funds website was still operational, and consistent with the sort of material I had in front of me. There were strict rules for processing charitable donations in the EU—compliance and governance issues being under more scrutiny than in the past—but there was less chance of observation of activities in distant lands. Ironically, all businesses banks themselves were the most expert corporations in operating covertly in distant locations far from the gaze of homeland supervision.

Therefore despite the fact that there might well be *internal* repercussions I took the morally challenging position of working through the evening to write about how brilliantly Scottish Chartered had supported Kid World Funds. I took care to employ careful language and I ensured that any queries about the apparent activities should come directly to me. However, I then emailed David Moritano suggesting while Kid World Funds was all well and good, we could use some evidence to steer the strategy back towards home-based projects. I asked him to put something together to aid a report I was writing for Carole McLetchie.

I contacted Lexicon Chartered's 'Antigua desk'—what a farce—and received a cursory reply saying they'd get back in touch. So, Doug actually still had a body present even if the operation was purely a sham. The man had some gall but then he had me in a tight spot. This, of course, was eating away at me. With each payment to Lexicon Chartered, I was still complicit in subsidising the con that had been perpetrated, each penny enhancing the lives of Doug, Canavan, and almost certainly, Mandy. What if Carole McLetchie, or one of the other big wigs asked to visit one of the projects? How could I possibly set that up? If that happened, curtains. Equally, there could be an internal audit at some point, and just possibly, an independent audit. I could only hope that the production and dissemination of a solid media release on Kid World Funds would buy some time.

By the time I had completed the relevant spin, the office was virtually empty and I suddenly noticed Elise Stewart appear outside my office, dressed in a cream overcoat.

'Boy, are you one sad guy with no life,' she said, displaying that winning smile. It was difficult not to respond in kind.

'I was just thinking the exact same of everyone else who works late here. Doesn't apply to me, of course.'

'Aye, right,' she said in a mock Scottish accent.

'So you're picking up the lingo?'

'Only the really stupid phrases that no one would understand if I used them back home. Busy, eh? I guess with Leslie Weir's death.'

'Shocking. I haven't really spoken with you since it happened. But we'll have to get on with it...we've got an agent in the Caribbean and I need to kick ass.'

'There's no word as fast as 'slow' out there. My ex-husband used to do a lot of work in the Caribbean.' She pronounced the word in the American style, with the emphasis on the 'r'.

'Ex-husband? I hadn't realised that you were a divorcee.'

'Just got lucky, I guess. He spent so much time in the Caribbean, that it almost felt as if I'd never been married. Another banker, I'm afraid. No kids, me free to travel, and him still married to the bank, or someone else.'

'It's nice to hear of a happy ending.'

'I prefer to call it a new beginning. Back to the future, so to speak.'

'Good point. Talking of which, I have an apology to make to you.' I reached to my desk drawer, taking out the pack my mother had sent on the Stewarts of Appin. 'I'm sorry, but with Leslie's death this has been sitting in my desk drawer for over a week. I'd completely forgotten about it. My mother put some stuff together for your genealogical research. She even sent a bunch of postcards she bought in Munro's shop in Benderloch, which is down the road from Appin. Her hand writing's bloody terrible so that's a second apology I owe you.'

'Not at all, this is so kind,' she said, leafing through the blurb. 'I must repay your mom in some way.'

'No need.'

'Well let me at least buy you a drink on the way home?' Now, that was an offer. I attempted to remove the grin that had suddenly manifested itself on my face.

'I'd heard that American women were forward...but I never refuse a drink.' She smiled back, and I agreed to meet her in the lobby in ten minutes. Stuff it, the final detail on the Kid World Funds spin could wait one more day.

I had a *date*.

Elise insisted on drinking a glass of beer to mirror my order. We were perched on bar stools in the XYZ club, a glitzy bar on Chambers Street which sported a jazz pianist and impressive gantry. I'd been in once with Mandy.

'This could be any city in the Western World,' she noted, surveying the decor.

'You're probably right.'

'Nice, though.' Her eyes wandered around the bar, taking in the scene. An audible buzz permeated the place despite the time of the week. Then I asked the obvious question.

'So Elise, have you met a Mr Right since you came over here?'

She hesitated slightly, before running her fingers through her hair. 'A couple of dates—guys recommended by colleagues—but neither were my type to be honest.'

'That's never a good idea, is it? I mean, being subject to someone else's judgement in respect of your love life. Puts you off the people who wrongly recommend others, you know—thinking you'd actually be compatible with some clown that they feel sorry for.'

Elise ran her tongue along her lips, and I raised my glass. 'You see, Elise, I can tell that you agree by your reaction, but you're too polite to say it yourself, right?'

'I try to insult only those who are robust enough to withstand the pressure.'

I laughed. 'Was you ex-husband not robust enough?' This was a little cheeky, but I couldn't resist.

'Actually he was, so I gunned for him all the time. But then he went and cheated on me.'

'Oh, I'm sorry to hear that.' I didn't know what to say. The guy must have been mad.

'So what about you? You have a girlfriend, don't you? Kostas mentioned someone.' Thanks, Kostas.

'I did. But that's history now too. I don't think that we were compatible either.' I considered Mandy for an instant but then caught a subtle response from Elise—an expression of one woman considering the judgement of another woman by a male.

'So here we are,' I said. 'Two sad singles, drinking after work. What would those Stewart ancestors have made of it?'

'Oh, they'd probably have been fine. But my ex wouldn't have had time. You've no idea how often he'd come home with bottles of rum he'd received as gifts in the Caribbean, and they'd never get opened.'

'Where did you guys meet?'

'Through work. We'd both worked for Bank of America in New York, though we first met in the Caribbean. At a banking conference at one of the big hotels in Antigua, actually.'

'Antigua? Really?' I considered the irony here, having sent an email to the sham Lexicon Chartered less than an hour previously. 'Interesting place for bankers.'

'Yes, my ex—Alan—spent a lot of time there setting up deals, and one affair, unfortunately. If there's a mover or a shaker in Antigua, he knows them.' This was interesting.

'The outside agency that we've been using for the foundation is actually registered in Antigua. Minimal presence on the island itself, but located there for tax reasons.' I used a white lie.

'Yes, I know that you weren't too popular in bringing in outside help, but then as I said to you before, if nothing changes we never move on. Everyone thinks that strategy is easy. You're simply trying your best.'

'It's odd you say that. I was thinking—and this is confidential if you don't mind—of re-establishing the foundation in-house again.'

'Really, so quickly?'

'Hush, hush, though at the moment.' I touched my nose.

'Again, I think that's fair enough if you think the gamble didn't pay off. The Caribbean can be a frustrating place to operate with the pedestrian pace and lack of accountability, not to mention the bribery. Alan used to spend half his time on the dodgy side of the banking business. But in your case, if you think you've made a mistake, I think that it's good that you took the risk in the first place. That would get you points over in the States, though I am aware that the culture is a little more risk averse here. You appear to have saved the bank a substantial sum through your donations idea, anyway, so I think you're still the golden boy.'

'Golden boy?'

'The staff say you're *in* with Carole McLetchie,' Elise grinned again.

Chapter 18

Within 48 hours I had generated enough media coverage for Kid World Funds to keep Carole McLetchie at bay. I'd only briefly seen Elise again, but hoped that another opportunity would arise. David Moritano had also come back to me with a comprehensive report and the irony was that I agreed with every single argument he made an in-house team for the foundation. I needed to dissolve the connection with Lexicon Chartered, yet something was bugging me. I knew instinctively that there was some kind of solution, though my conscious mind couldn't place it. I closed my eyes and let my thoughts drift but was soon interrupted by a loud knock.

Kostas stood outside my car window, squinting in. I opened the window of the Audi.

'Are you all right in there? Sleeping on the job is it now? The rest of us are knocking our pan in for the loyal customers and shareholders and here we have the elite staff slinking off and dozing in their cars.'

'Actually, Kostas I was… mentally programming.'

'What? Looks pretty mental to me. Wanna coffee?'

We went round the corner to that little Italian cafe Doug and I had gone to several months before and ordered two coffees. Blues music echoed sadly in the background. Kostas had the appearance of a psychiatrist meeting a patient who was making little progress.

'So what's this programming nonsense? One minute you're telling me that you want to get even, then you're sleeping in your Audi.'

'I was wondering how to get the money back.'

'And?'

'As long as Lexicon Chartered is actively receiving payments, there may be an electronic money trail. A means of locating Doug, and possibly Mandy.'

'Including the Kid World Funds money?'

'It's a possibility.'

'Long shot, Ally. Money moves instantly today,' he said flatly.

'Yes, but here's why I have a small opportunity. I think that Doug is a cocky bastard, and I know that the payments to Lexicon Chartered are still going through. He knows that I can't grass myself up, so he may figure, why not continue to milk this situation? He must be pissing himself laughing at me, yet that might be his biggest weakness—leaving clues in place because he thinks I'm a coward with no room for manoeuvre. They've already made mistakes—look at that data stick.'

Kostas sighed. 'I have a strange feeling that you're about to ask me for help.'

'I'm so glad you offered.'

'I've got kids, Ally. I can't afford to lose my job.'

'I understand. But the thing is, Kostas, I'm attempting to make amends.

'I don't know.'

'It's for the general good.'

'Your motivation is mainly to get even. You said so yourself.'

'That hasn't altered. Look, I'll tell you what I'm thinking. It can't do any damage for you to hear me out.'

'Okay.'Kostas checked his watch, and made a brief call to his team saying that he'd be delayed in getting back into the office. 'Right Ally, more coffee, and let's hear your plan.' He spoke briefly with the waitress, before I began.

'You've done some hacking in your time, right?'

'Oh, here we go again. I was a post grad student and it was a long time ago. One drunk conversation with you two or three Christmases ago and I'm tarnished forever. Where's this going?'

'There are two things I want to know. Firstly, where does the Lexicon Chartered money end up being routed after it arrives in Antigua, and secondly, where are the Kid World Funds?'

'Simple questions, Ally. Complex answers.'

'Yes, but you managed to move money before, albeit for a joke. I know that the Greek finance minister must have had pretty good security. No one spotted what was happening before the banking crisis.'

'Thanks for the reminder. That was years ago, and we returned the money. And online security these days is much tighter.'

'So you won't help me?'

'I didn't say that. It's just that in today's world, these things now come with greater penalties.'

'But we'd not be looking for money that anyone thinks is currently missing—so who's going to prosecute? And you could hide your identity like you did before.'

'Bloody hell, Ally. The way this is sounding you'd think I'd been a bigger crook than you.' I looked at him, and for the second time in ten minutes we began laughing again.

'It's not funny,' he said.

'Yes it is.'

'Hmmm. In any case, with the Greek minister that time, we had some inside help. One of the guys worked in the department. How are you going to get help in the Caribbean?'

'I might be able to get some help, if I can trace Doug's real identity first.'

'How are you going to trace his real name?'

I explained how this might be achieved. Lexicon Chartered and the other fake bidders for the foundation work all had directors' names listed. The stupid company names that Doug had concocted: Jerusalem Saviour and Gold Star. I was pretty sure that it would be difficult to set up a company—even a shell company—without real identities for the directors. I outlined my idea of visiting the Companies House website, and checking if there were any cracks. If real people were the directors of these companies, maybe Doug had crossed one of them or maybe they could give me a lead.

'And who's going to help you then if you discover Doug's real name?'

'You, hopefully. And maybe...Elise Stewart's ex-husband?'

'*What?*'

'I'll explain once I get a step closer.'

Carole McLetchie's email threw me. She'd actually praised me for the coverage we'd just received in the press for Kid World Funds, ending with the line: *excellent publicity for the bank*. Damn. The pressure simply wasn't going to abate. I accessed the Companies House website, to check the directors' names for Gold Star and Jerusalem Saviour. Both were classified as having 'ceased trading', which was a laugh, given that neither had ever traded in the first place. Several different names appeared, none of which I recognised. I searched online for the first name—Paul Lennon. There was the usual array of Facebook references for Paul Lennons, one was a man who'd written a children's storybook, but no one famous or business related.

The next name—Derek Torrance—I found as a football coach in Renfrewshire, but he did not appear in terms of any charity scam leads. Duncan Blethan proved more useful. Although there was more than one such character, several references to the same individual appeared. Duncan Blethan had been in PR, and had run his own consultancy in London before being charged with fraud. Media articles cited the case as having been unusual. Essentially, this guy had been caught defrauding the tax authorities in England, and had appeared in court, but the case had been dismissed after a single day due to a technicality. Blethan's lawyer had argued that the Crown had been timed out for having failed to process some elements of the charges in sufficient time and with sufficient notice. Could this be the same Duncan Blethan that Doug knew?

I continued my search, using alternative key words in conjunction with the name. Apparently, he had started a new firm called Blethan Associates and had interests in other companies, some in PR. So, I called the number given for the business and asked to speak with Duncan Blethan.

I also chose to tell another lie.

'Mr Blethan, I'm William Hillcoat from Companies House. We're running through some changes to company registrations at present and I'm checking if you were a director of a firm called Jerusalem Saviour?' A momentary gap ensued before Blethan replied.

'This is a little unorthodox.' He spoke with a polished, private school accent.

'Not at all, Mr Blethan. We run random registration checks on firms that have traded for only short periods of time. Nothing of concern, simply a routine enquiry.' There was another, notable silence.

'What did you say your name was?'

'William Hillcoat.'

'Hang on just a minute.'

'Of course,' I replied. I then waited another moment.

'Well that's odd, *William.* Because I'm...just accessing your website at present, and there is no one of that name listed under staff.'

'I've only recently begun working here, Mr Blethan. Now if you could just confirm the answer to my question?' No answer was forthcoming as the line went dead. A PR guy hanging up the phone? I'd withheld my number, so I doubted if he'd be able to trace me, and of course he hadn't admitted anything. However, the strange thing was that he hadn't *denied* anything either. Surely someone with no connection to a company—someone who'd never heard of it—would *instinctively* tell the questioner that very fact? A denial based on the truth—I was good at that myself. Only those with something to conceal evaded a straight answer. I called back but the number ran onto voicemail.

The next name on the list was Jennifer Sloan. A basic search again generated a selection of individuals, some on business or social networking sites. This appeared to be a more common name, as there were several different characters. I wanted to avoid emailing people, as this would leave a more obvious trail, so I began with those for whom there were business phone numbers. Again, I posed as an executive government researcher, asking routine questions. The first three Jennifer Sloans were either not connected or were very fluent liars. One became quite worried, so I assured her that I probably had the wrong individual. I was placed on hold for the fourth Jennifer Sloan, an executive in an insurance firm in Bristol.

'Hmm,' she replied. 'Gold Star Charity Liaison?'

'Yes, that's right.'

'You're not really from Companies House, are you?'

On this occasion I broke ranks. 'No actually, I'm not. But you were a director of the same company, correct?'

'If I'm going to discuss this, you should at least have the courtesy to identify yourself.' Bingo.

'Let's just say, that I am a victim of a scam.'

'Well, that makes two of us,' she said. This, I had not expected.

'Okay…I'd rather not say who I am, and I promise that I am not going to identify you to anyone else. You have my word.'

'You're not a journalist? Because if you are it would not play well for me where I work.'

'I can assure you that I am not a journalist,' I said.

'But you won't say who you are?'

'I'd rather not give my name because I occupy a similar position to you, which I think you might respect. And I promise I won't use your name.'

'Okay, this is unconventional, but I'm prepared to speak for a couple of minutes.'

'Thank you. Do you know someone called Doug Fox?'

'No. Who is he?'

'The man who set up Gold Star.'

'Okay…then I might know him, as I think that the person who conned me was using an alias. Can you describe him?'

I cleared my throat. 'Mid thirties, Scottish, five feet ten, brown curly hair, designer glasses, cocky, sarcastic.' I was surprised how easily I could sum Doug up.

'Yeah, that's him. Though he managed to drop the sarcasm when he was doing the sell.'

'That sounds about right. So how did you meet him?'

'He approached me at a dinner, and began a big spiel about supporting charity. How it can work wonders for company PR. It progressed from there.'

'So he asked you to become a director of Gold Star?'

'Yes.'

'You must have come to know him...well...if you agreed to that.' A brief silence ensued.

'He was very...persuasive. It's a bit embarrassing, actually.' I could hear the bitterness creeping along the ether. Doug must have seduced her.

'Okay, I'm sorry. So he actually got money out of you personally?'

'Yes, I was brought up as a Quaker. I believe in charitable giving, though I realise now that this was not an actual charity. And to make matters worse I got the company I work for to match what I donated—it is company policy if you make the case properly. I put in five thousand and the company gave another five to help set it up. It was going to be the real deal. There would be real beneficiaries.'

For a brief moment, I digested this fact. Doug had evidently coined it in during various stages in this project. He'd probably invested nothing himself, funding each element with a new scam via unwitting victims. Jennifer Sloan really had been done if she'd attempted an altruistic gesture with no hubris or greed on her part and I felt genuinely sorry for her as I honestly had known nothing of this when Doug had set up these fake entities.

'Jennifer, let me guess. After an initial splash, our man then disappeared without trace, and subsequently Gold Star was wound up?'

'Yes, that sums it up. And I've been lucky to keep my job.' I instantaneously considered how lucky I had also been to date on that front, if Jennifer Sloan had been carpeted for just five grand?

'Have you heard of Kid World Funds?'

'No, I don't think so. Is that another fake charity?'

'I'm not sure. It could be okay,' I lied. 'So what alias did he use with you?'

'John Reynolds. It makes me sick every time I think of the name.'

'I see. Look, I realise that this is a long shot, but do you have any idea of this character's real identity?'

There was another pause on the line. 'One of the documents we signed had another name on it, and it wasn't one of the other directors' names. The name was...let me think...the first initial was D. But not Doug Fox as you noted. Maybe still Doug...let me see...Mundell? I wondered afterwards who that was as he whisked the sheet of paper away from me when I saw it.' She spelled it and I wrote the name down.

'Jennifer, you've been a great help. I'm hoping to get even with this guy if at all possible.'

'Good luck. He deserves everything he gets.'

Chapter 19

My search for Doug Mundell then began. If this was his real identity, to what extent might he have been able to rewrite his own history? Which pieces of his life would be awkward for him to evade?

Social media secured no leads of any value. He'd clearly avoided detection this way by staying clear, at least with his real name. I managed to find no corporate references but then I considered universities. These were official bodies and they kept details for years. Indeed, graduation lists were regularly published in the media without any permission sought from the graduates themselves. I estimated that Doug was probably about a year or two younger than me, which would narrow the timescale required in any search. I also made an assumption that he was indeed a computing graduate and that he had studied at a Scottish university. After my fifth year at high school, I'd had a change of heart in terms of my future career and had initially considered studying computing when leaving school so I attempted to recall the universities that had offered degrees in this area at that time. I remembered four such institutions in Scotland, so I searched for the relevant alumni societies.

I was attempting to make progress with all this when Elise popped her head round the door. I smiled in response before offering her a seat.

'Your mom says "hi",' she stated in a matter of fact manner, surveying my face to compute my reaction.

'Ah...so you contacted the old dear, did you?'

'Less of the old—she's only 65 as you well know—and yes, she's certainly a dear.'

'She's always pleasant to start with, but then devours people later when they let their guard down. So, did she give you any help, or just interrogate someone from the *new world* when she had the opportunity?'

'No, actually she was charming, and said I could visit any time I liked. Doesn't see as much of you as she'd like, however.' My face reddened a little, a home truth having been delivered by someone who'd never even met my folks.

'I go up as much as I can…so anyway, have you unearthed any new contacts in Appin?'

'I can tell you all about it at lunch, if you like. On me?'

This was my 'in', so I accepted and we went out to lunch. What I figured was this: if Elise's ex knew the bank in Antigua with which Lexicon Chartered dealt, and that account was still active, he might be able to help.

But how could I bring this up?

I didn't think she'd shop me, but I feared that she might be disgusted with me, evaluating me as a loser who should be fired. We talked about her genealogical project for a while before a short silence in the conversation arose.

'A penny for your thoughts?' she said, whilst assessing the prawn salad she'd ordered.

'I…was thinking about your ex-husband, actually.' The truth never hurt, did it?

'I see. You're probably wondering if I was telling the truth. That perhaps he was a lovely guy, and I'm actually some crazy bitch that destroys men once she gets her claws in?' I laughed as she held her finger up like claws.

'Yip. Crazy bitch has a ring to it.'

'So what were you really thinking? About Alan?'

'Oh…how could he have let someone like you go?' While I'd previously considered this, it hadn't been my current priority.

'You must have heard that line in a few movies.'

'So what's a nice girl like you doing in a place like this?' I replied.

'Having lunch with the office enigma.'

'Enigma?'

'Come on. You've a lot going for you, but you don't give a lot away. Currently single...good looking guy...decent sense of humour...good career. Okay—old wheels for some reason—but hey, that can be fixed.' She tapped her fingers on the table, meeting my eyes. I liked the part about 'good looking'.

'The car's not old. It's ancient. But apart from that, you're being kind.'

'I'm being truthful. But I feel as if there's something else about you that I can't fathom. As if you're concealing some big secret.'

I hesitated a moment before responding. Guilt is a strange thing. 'If I were concealing some big secret, would you still give me points for the other things?'

'So there *is* something.'

'Oh, loads of things...it's difficult to know where to start.' Then I attempted to re-establish the original direction of the conversation. 'So is your ex-husband, eh, Alan still active in Antigua?'

'Alan? Yes, as far as I know. Why do you ask?'

'I—we—have been having some problems with our agent over in Antigua. I'd been thinking of investigating, but it's difficult at a distance.'

'What kind of problems? Financial?'

'Yes. Isn't it always the case? Seeing you'd mentioned that Alan was connected over there, I'd wondered if you'd mind asking him for a favour.' This was really pushing it, I knew.

'Okay. What's the bank called?' Just like that. I'd been expecting a rebuff, but there you go.

'Caribbean International Consolidated.' She jotted the name down.

'What do you want to know? I mean, I presume that you need to investigate something on the QT, or you'd be doing this through Carole McLetchie?'

'Eh, yes. This would be strictly between *us* at the moment. Ultimately I will need to provide recommendations for her, but first I want to be better informed. After Weir's mur...' I realised that I'd almost said *murder*, 'eh, death, I realised that there were some gaps in my knowledge about how this was all run.' I embellished the truth again.

'I don't mind contacting him. He cheated on me, so he owes me. After I found out about his affair I visited a shrink who said the best exit strategy was not to hold a grudge, and to move on. I accepted this logic and when I explained it to Alan, he was amazed. Most American wives would take a cheating husband to the cleaners financially, but I chose not to and I think that he genuinely appreciated that.'

'Wow,' I said. 'If I ever dated you, it would be fantastic. I could do whatever I liked and you'd forgive me every time!'

'Don't push your luck, buddy.' She leant over and poked me on the chest. A sparkle then entered her eyes. 'But you don't date someone until they actually ask you out.'

'Good point,' I replied. She held my gaze for a second, but then my phone buzzed. It was an inconsequential call from a journalist but it broke the spell. Elise checked her watch and we paid the bill before setting off back to the bank. She promised to contact her ex-husband to enquire if he'd do a little snooping on my behalf. I was going to have to decide how much to tell Elise Stewart, yet subconsciously I felt I was irrevocably heading for another full confession.

On return to the office I found that one university had responded immediately, but negatively. Another had provided a generic response but noted that they would get back to me, and was I interested in donating money to them? A third—the University of Edinburgh—said that they did not give out names of graduates directly, but that they could provide me with a complimentary access code for their alumni association as their mission statement aimed to encourage collaboration and networking, and those registered on the site had given permission to be contacted. None of this helped me directly, but I used the access code to search for Doug Mundell. As expected, there was no entry. Out of curiosity, however, I briefly searched for other IT graduate profiles from the same era, but there were no matches. Some of those profiled were overt networkers—the type of people who regularly go on social fishing expeditions, just to see what happens. Some had all sorts of elongated points of reference. One, interestingly, had placed class pictures of his era on the site. This prompted a further search under class pictures, pointing toward several rogues' galleries. I scoured those from around a decade previously.

Nothing.

Perhaps 'Doug' was neither Doug Mundell, nor a computing graduate. I decided to attempt to replicate the Edinburgh search with the other university that hadn't yet replied to me—the University of Strathclyde. Here too, I found an alumni association that encouraged networking and collaboration. I followed a similar route, phoning to ask if I could look up old friends. I used a name I'd garnered from an earlier Facebook search and posed as this graduate in order to gain a temporary access. Again, no reference to Doug Mundell. I then used another search to view class pictures, and found that a number of graduates had placed such images on the net. Some were labelled with names, others exhibited facetious captions. None of the faces staring back at me looked like Doug.

But then one label jumped off the screen.

Doug *Mundel.* Spelled with one 'l'. I'd assumed that Jennifer Sloan had given me a correct spelling.

I witnessed a young man in his early twenties sporting glasses, a light brown beard and long curly hair. I peered at the face. Despite the time lag and the facial camouflage, I smiled to myself—because Doug Fox was indeed Doug Mundel. Some comments were noted underneath, with three or four related posts. I scanned these, noting a Doug Mundel mention: *I can't believe this plonker shares the same birthday as me.* I checked the profile of the guy commenting, and noted his birth date.

Now I knew Doug's real identity, where did it actually get me? Sure, I could try to research his work history, but somehow I knew that there would be a break at some point where he would disappear. Did he have family, and so what if he did—what was I intending to do, kidnap them and make death threats? As there had been no social networking record for Doug *Mundell,* I briefly checked with the new spelling—and found nothing. This was no surprise. I considered if it would be easy to find if he owned a property in his own name. Would there be a central record of such ownership? A home address? Surely he would have had a bank account somewhere in his own name. Even crooks don't keep all their pecuniary loot in safes or biscuit tins—these days everyone has some electronic wealth, but the question was, where was Doug's?

The following day Kostas came into my office for a chat. He'd seen me the day before coming back into the office with Elise, and he cracked a joke about transatlantic romances, which I rebuffed, though perhaps not too convincingly. Then I explained what I'd found. In hushed tones he listened to my detective work, and then I mentioned that favour I'd asked Elise and my desire to track the money down.H

'I can't believe this,' he said. 'First you hint that my hacking skills would be needed, and now you're about to spill the beans to two other people.'

'Sure, but I might not need to tell the whole story, and I trust Elise. Don't you?'

'Yes, but she might let something slip. Who knows? She's quite the femme fatale, by the way.'

'Don't start.'

'Office rumours have begun already.'

'Fuck off. Now, are you willing to help me or not?' I lowered my voice further, even though the office door was firmly shut. 'If I can get more detail about that account you might be able to investigate any trail.'

'Ah, me. I can see what you're doing here. Breaking me down bit by bit. No wonder you've had a career in spin.'

'So that's a yes, then?'

Kostas smiled sardonically and left the office, shaking his head. Interestingly, he'd provided predictable objections about my plan, but this time he hadn't dismissed it out of hand either. After three hours burying myself in the backlog, Carole McLetchie then appeared at my office.

'Ally,' she said sternly, as she shut the door firmly behind her. 'I've just had one of those policemen on the phone again. The inquiry into Leslie's death is still live. They're asking questions again about Leslie's day to day activities before the accident. They're almost implying that it *wasn't* an accident, which is shocking. We need to be open with the authorities, but not *unnecessarily* so. Did you say anything about bank business to them the last time?'

'Eh, no. Nothing out of the ordinary. I explained that we were going about…our usual business.' She moved to the window and gazed out, as many visitors to my office seemed to do. She was facing outwards when she continued.

'They want to know about this Kid World Funds charity. You put quite a splash in the media about it. Now, naturally I explained that Scottish Chartered was very proud of its charity work. So, I need to know from the horse's mouth, did you say anything to the police about these donations?'

My heart leapt, a sudden burst of pressure flooding my temples. She then spun round to glare at me, akin to a prosecution lawyer in court.

'Well?' The woman was abrupt. I took a deep breath before taking the offensive.

'Carole, in all honesty and sincerity, as far as I am aware there was *absolutely nothing* amiss with that charity. Leslie selected it himself, and I'm amazed that the police should question the integrity of the deceased without good reason. You saw yourself the kind of coverage which can be gained with that kind of benevolent activity. It's our bread and butter. Yes, going forward we should find new home-based causes for donations. But I'm damned if we should have to defend our charitable actions to a couple of nosey plods with conspiracy theories. Even Lucy Weir is certain that Leslie was the victim of a tragic accident, and the last thing we want—as you said yourself—is for the reputation of this solid institution to be tarnished by *erroneous speculation*.'

'Good,' she said flatly. 'That's exactly the kind of robust answer I was looking for. I said to DI Wilson that you'd call him back as soon as possible. Stick to that script. However, I *would* like to see a review of all donations to charities.'

I wiped my brow when she left, perspiration having suddenly appeared during my mini interrogation. Kostas caught my eye from outside of the office and made a gesture with his finger at his throat as Carole walked past him. I waved him off and immediately rang the number for DI Wilson, on the basis that the quicker I moved the less suspicious he might become. He answered with that monotonic police voice.

'Mr Forbes? What can you tell me about Kid World Funds?'

'Kid World Funds...it's a charity that assists underprivileged children in various parts of the world. Leslie was keen to pick something bold for the foundation to support, something more international. He believed that this sort of thing met with the strategic goals that we had set.'

'Mmm. Don't you think that it's odd that Scottish Chartered granted such large amounts to one organisation, such a short time before Mr Weir's death?'

'Not really...these types of decisions happen all the time. Did someone at the bank provide you with figures? There have been lots of occasions where we have given multiple sums to one beneficiary. I can give you other evidence if you want.'

'So you've given more than six million in less than a month to other organisations in the past?' There was awkward silence as I attempted to conjure the most appropriate response. In PR, the golden rule is to say that you'll call back once you've thought about what to say but in the circumstances this would create more problems.

'We've certainly given multiple donations,' I said slowly, but surely. 'And sometimes large sums. This one was really Leslie's choice, though I can't see that there was anything wrong with the choice of charity.' I hated saying this, as it was clearly a crock of shit, but I felt I had to protect myself. 'I mean, we were able to generate quite a lot of publicity out of this charitable work.'

'So I noticed. All over the media. So that's the purpose? You solicit donations from customers from whom you already derive your profits, and then use their money to generate more profits?' Sarcasm seeped through his voice. 'Sounds like another banking scam to me. Amazed that it's legal.'

'DI Wilson, I understand that many people are cynical about banks and indeed charity work. But someone has to give—so why not a large bank? We do this sort of thing all the time, and many, many thousands of people have benefited from our work. Contributions from customers are all voluntary.

Not a penny is raised without permission. Just look at the kids in this city alone that have achieved sporting excellence directly due to the sponsorship from Scottish Chartered.'

'That's my point. This Kid World Funds thing is a departure, and it coincides with a suspicious death.'

'I realise that it must come with the territory to be suspicious, but you have nothing to worry about. Now, if I can help further, you know where to find me.'

I ended the call, silently praying that they would not begin an investigation into Kid World Funds. Wilson was a nosy cop, and the irritating thing is that he was right—totally right. Then, as I stood at the window observing the Edinburgh skyline in the rain and contemplating my life, another knock diverted my attention to the door. Elise.

She took a seat, and spun around in the chair. 'Do you try to make visitors to this office dizzy, Mr Forbes?' She seemed to have a genuine gift for minor innuendo—insufficient to be intrusive, but sufficient to make a male such as me take notice.

'Nope, only you. However, I advise against having dinner whilst dizzy.'

'Oh, I had a very late lunch so I might just barf in your office.' She giggled. 'I can't believe that I just said that...sorry.'

'No offence taken.' I was eager to hear if she'd spoken to her ex-husband, though I didn't wish to appear too desperate. 'So how's it going?'

'All the better for seeing you. And I also have some good news. I spoke with Alan last night. Caught him at his work, five hours behind us, so easy enough.'

'I appreciate that this must be awkward for you.'

'Awkward for him, perhaps. But he's willing to help.'

'That's fantastic. Did you mention the Antiguan bank?'

'Yes. And he knows it. Though he said that he was surprised that Scottish Chartered would have any real dealings with a bank such as Caribbean International Consolidated.'

'Why's that?'

'You don't know?'

'I've have really only been involved with the charity part. The bank's simply the conduit through which we remunerate the agent we use. What's the problem?'

'But it's the bank you want to know about?'

'Yes…I want to check some…things out.'

'Perhaps you should. Alan said that this bank might come under investigation. This is not unusual in the Caribbean—jurisdictional issues arise from time to time. But the US authorities might order an investigation because of accusations of money laundering in similar banks. If those here take a similar view to those in the US, then Scottish Chartered would be unable to send funds via this bank.'

I digested what Elise had said for moment. 'What type of money laundering accusations are we talking about?'

'Everything and anything. Organisations fronting illegal activities have probably used that bank. Grand Cayman has greater difficulties, of course, as the level of capital travelling though the Caymans is much greater, but perhaps that's why Antigua has been off the radar. Probably they don't ask the probing questions but either way they attract those with something to hide.'

'I really owe you one. So how about dinner?'

'Tonight?'

'If you're free.'

'Maybe.'

'Playing hard to get?' I scratched my chin.

'It's not that. I'm just a little concerned.'

'Why?'

'I mentioned to Alan that you'd wanted a favour. He became a little suspicious when I mentioned the bank's name, but said he'd try to assist if possible. So…you'll need to tell me what it is that you want him to do.'

'Yes…I can do…later…'

She viewed me subtly. 'This *is* dodgy, isn't it? Okay, I agree to have dinner with you—on one condition.'

'What's that?'

'That you tell me the whole story.'

Chapter 20

Given the nature of the conversation that I was about to have with Elise, privacy was the order of the evening. The suggestion of a take-away meal and a couple of glasses of wine at my flat was received with a raised eyebrow. She quipped that I sure knew how to treat a girl, so I used an old line of mine—*you should see what the 'market prices' are like these days for take-away giant panda in platinum sauce.* I'd never had a great response from Chinese people with this line but Elise grinned.

She commented on the 'Zen' nature of my pad. She asked questions about the faces staring at us from the photo collages on my toilet wall, a potted history of my life abridged into random images. We kind of slumped into the soft chairs in the lounge, but then the food arrived more promptly than anticipated as it was mid week. We sat at the creaky old beech table in the kitchen and tucked into Chinese minus the endangered species and the rare metal sauce. I opened a pre-warmed bottle of Torreon de Parades Merlot from the foothills of the Andes.

Then I told her almost everything.

When I reached the part about the police, she simply gawped. 'I'm stunned. And this Doug guy? Is he the person you showed me the photograph of in your office?'

I swallowed. 'Yes.'

'So you lied to me then. About his identity.' Her jaw tightened.

'I'm sorry. I simply couldn't say anything about this guy at the bank. I didn't want to involve anyone else. Please understand. I was shocked that you'd seen him and I was greedy and stupid, but ultimately I was set up. Now I want to make amends.'

'I'm dumbfounded by all this. You're a whole lot more dangerous than I initially thought, Ally. I figured—here's a guy who gets by making jokes about donuts in the canteen. But now I find you're a serious crook planning revenge. And before I say anything else—this is *genuine*—not a wind-up?'

'If only it were.'

'Just resign. Distance yourself from the whole thing.'

'Seems obvious, but it would just catch up with me now. And with Leslie Weir's death and everything, how could I sleep at night not knowing what each next day might bring?'

'I suppose when you put it like that...and the only other person who knows is Kostas?'

'He's the only other person I could trust enough. I've been deceived by three other people I *thought* I knew, so you can understand my reluctance to have faith in anyone, least of all myself.'

'Well, I guess I should thank you for your confession—and inclusion in your *circle of trust.* Millions missing?'

'This is where you come in.'

'Oh shit.'

'Oh shit. Frankly, I'm amazed that you haven't walked straight out of that door.'

'Yet.' She stared at me, suddenly showing signs of worry, as if the ridiculousness of my scenario had taken a minute or two to digest.

'Elise, what I need from you is some more detailed information—through your ex, Alan. Correct me if I'm wrong, but he's in the position to extract favours in Antigua? You've explained that he's a bit of a player out in the Caribbean. I'm not looking for a favour that would cost money, but one that might give me my life back. What I need to find is where the money from Lexicon Chartered's bank account has gone. Private, transactional information. I know that their account number is still active as we still pay a monthly fee to them, though this is probably about to finish. If it's a dodgy bank, and there's an imminent investigation, there might only be a brief opportunity.'

'This is way beyond risky—maybe I *should* walk straight out of the door. And even supposing Alan agrees, and can pull some strings—how would this help you? How would knowing the destination of funds exiting from the bank help you?'

Kostas would kill me, but then, in for a penny.

'If I can identify the ultimate destination of the funds that have gone to Kid World Funds, I have a friend who may be able to, eh…repatriate…the funds back to Scottish Chartered. You know, preferably through our agent, returning the money before it is actually defined as having gone missing.'

'A computer hacker?'

'Yes.'

'Kostas?'

I said nothing.

She shook her head. 'Ally…'

'It's not as bad as it seems. I shouldn't tell you this, but he's actually done this before, as a student prank in Athens, years ago. This is my only hope.'

'The pair of you could do real time for this stunt.'

'But we'd be stealing from thieves. They can't report it to any authorities because this is all tarnished money. And Scottish Chartered has saved millions so far with the new fund raising programme from customers, so there's a chance this might work, if everything's returned to normal with the bank still a few million up courtesy of the customers providing the charitable donations.'

'You're making the assumption that these funds can be tracked down. That they haven't been liquidated,' she said.

'You may be right, but I have to try. I admit that I was totally taken in by Doug, but I still think that he won't be sitting on this sum in one hundred dollar notes. My hunch tells me that he's been building up an electronic nest egg somewhere.'

'Okay, then. I'll ask Alan what he can do. Obviously, I will swear him to secrecy. He does owe me a favour.'

'That would be fantastic, Elise.' I held her hand. 'And that means a massive favour would be owed to you.'

'Right…it might be difficult to pay me back if you're sitting in, what's the place called? 'Bar' something?'

'Barlinnie?' I grimaced. 'That's in Glasgow. Or Saughton, the prison here in Edinburgh.'

Elise left, significantly more pensive than she when had arrived. In ordinary circumstances it would have been the ideal occasion to make a move and for her to stay over. Yet I could hardly blame her if the subtle interest she'd shown in me had been blown away. Once she'd slept on it, she might well change her mind about any involvement and simply wash her hands of me. After all, she owed me nothing.

My final awkward task of the day involved a call to Kostas at home. He quietly moved the call to another room away from his family, not having fully shared news of my deceit with his wife, for which I was grateful. Kostas, perhaps tired and weary after a day's work, agreed in principle to help though I could hear resignation at the other end of the phone. When the call ended, I felt a twang of guilt—realising that my old spin tricks had ensued again. I'd played each of them off against each other, placing in danger the two people at the bank whom I held in most regard.

The next morning an email from Lucy Weir caught my attention sandwiched between two communiqués from Carole McLetchie. I opened Lucy Weir's message first, and it contained a pleasant, if generic 'thank you' for having attended the funeral. A personalised addendum, however, asked if I'd heard anything further from the police. Naturally, she wanted to put her husband's death to bed. I once again remained guiltily noncommittal about discussions with Wilson and wished her all the best for a clear resolution—the very opposite of what I wanted.

Carole McLetchie on the other hand had now issued a deadline to produce a report for the changes I'd suggested. *One week.* The woman had probably become like her pet dog: ready to attack. I laid it on thick about strategy and tactics—bullshit—but worded it in a way that made the plea for more time appear like a necessity. I received a reply by return. Amazingly, the one week deadline had been stretched to two weeks!

Then Elise appeared at the door. She spoke quietly after having closed the door firmly. 'I've just had a call from Alan. He'll do it.'

'Wow. That's fantastic He must be some guy.'

'Don't be too effusive in your praise. He's not that great.'

'Sorry, Elise…it's just that I'm really grateful. I won't ask how he's going about it.'

'That's okay. I mean, you're hardly going to report him, are you? Just like everyone else, he's owed favours too. I think that he can help this bank avoid a future investigation. He's got contacts at the Federal Reserve too. Although Antigua is a separate jurisdiction, the US financial net can sometimes be cast wide, as you'll know. Help from an external ally can be a powerful incentive from a small bank with something to hide. I've clarified what you want, and he says he can hopefully get back by late tomorrow.'

The heightened sense of expectation gripped me for the entire afternoon. I had no idea whether the emancipation of data on financial flows from Lexicon Chartered would ultimately produce a lead to Doug, but it was worth a try. When I arrived back at my flat after work, it was already dark. I grabbed a beer, and collapsed into the sofa, kicking off my shoes. Then my phone rang.

'Ally, Charles Henderson. Sorry to bother you at home.' This was unusual. What did he want?

'Charles, what can I do for you?'

'I think that we should meet. I'm in the city tonight, and I'd like to talk to you.' Shit, not another problem.

'Charles, no offence, but I'm a bit washed out. The volume of work at the bank has been horrendous. I'm not trying to be rude, but couldn't it wait until tomorrow?'

'This can't really wait. I need to speak to you…off the record. It's in your interest.'

He suggested that we meet in the members' lounge in the Lenders' Club—a stuffy, old boys' club in the New Town dating back two centuries and originally set up by the Edinburgh banking forefathers. When I arrived, I noticed that the decor hadn't changed in the past decade since my last visit, but then it possibly hadn't changed since the Great War either.

'I've been a member here since leaving university,' Charles said, touching those unkempt sideburns. Why didn't his wife instruct him to tidy them up? He ordered a glass of brandy. I followed suit. 'Actually, Ally, I took out a loan to pay the joining fee. Over the years the networking opportunities paid that investment back many times.'

I smiled politely, though my impatience must have been more obvious than I realised.

'Okay, you're wondering why I've dragged you out for some clandestine meeting.'

'Yes.'

'There's a big problem.'

'What problem?' I attempted to appear nonchalant.

'A problem looming at the bank. I'm pretty certain that you *know* what that problem is, but I want to hear it first-hand.'

'Charles, I'm really tired. Can you explain what you're talking about?'

'Kid World Funds,' he stated. I hesitated for an instance, just sufficient for his gaze to interpret my thoughts; that I did indeed know that there was a problem. A multi-million problem.

'Go on,' I said, flatly.

'*I know—and you know—that this organisation doesn't exist.*' I just stared back at him. 'Sure, Ally, there's a shell, and an administration system for electronically routing donations. But in essence, there's nothing else, just a veneer. There's no genuine references to this organisation dating beyond two years. There is no charitable benevolence. There are no real projects, no children given new hope, nor did schools or sports teams develop in distant lands, and no clean water projects. Just a clever piece of online spin. Bollocks, basically.' He sat back, awaiting a response.

'Do you have proof of all this?'

'Ally, be serious. *Do you have proof of these projects? There's* the question.' I remained silent, guilty. 'There's no point in you denying knowledge of the problem. I have investigated this charity. It's taken a little time, but trust me, I have left no iffy stone uncovered. I may be the only single person at the bank who has done so, however.'

'I'm not sure what to say, Charles. Kid World Funds was not my doing. I can prove that. But that would mean delving into the death of Leslie Weir…which I don't think is a sensible avenue to pursue. Leslie Weir directed me, *very specifically*, to sponsor this charity. That is a fact. He'd even set the donations in place before I'd agreed.'

'I…believe you, Ally. But Leslie Weir is no longer alive and the responsibility for a substantial series of donations lies with you.'

'I realise this, Charles. The last person who wants to see more funds going to Kid World Funds is me. Yes, I placed the stories in the media, but what option did I have? I had no proof that these projects were not real.' I lied. A white lie, but a necessary one in a quick fire conversation. 'And Charles, Leslie Weir provided me with all this material from the organisation before he died. Carole then expected a splash. As recently as last week I spoke with Carole about changing direction.'

'I know.'

'She contacted you directly?'

'No. She's a difficult woman as I'm sure you know, so I subtly asked about the project yesterday and she mentioned that you were unhappy about it. That you said Leslie had pushed for it behind the scenes. This is the only reason that I am having this conversation with you right now—the fact that you wish to distance yourself from Kid World Funds gives you some credibility.' I considered what he was saying: my discussion with Carole McLetchie had provided a modicum of insurance.

'Okay, Charles, why the clandestine meeting?'

'Because no one would benefit from making this public, or even divulging such information internally at the bank, as it would ultimately come out in the media. Think of how our image would be tarnished? Rivals would have a field day denigrating an institution that has made a big play about helping genuine worthy causes. The positive aspect of the new foundation—raising money from our customers—would be blown apart. Which customers would donate their hard earned cash to a bank that gave millions to some shoddy shell of an overseas charity—*apparently* without checking? Or maybe deliberately? People routinely repeat the mantra that charity begins at home. If this fiasco became public, donations would dry up. Real projects like the one my granddaughter benefitted from would definitely miss out. And business at the bank would be grossly affected. Customers would question our credibility and I can tell you from experience that image and trust are everything in banking. The share price would take a hit, and any hard working innocent employee with shares or options would lose out. What would be the point of that? And let me state the obvious: your career would be over, Ally. Despite this Kid World Funds thing, I believe that you are a decent individual and I'd like to give you a second chance.' He took a large sip of brandy as I tried to digest the implications.

'Why?'

'Because my reputation stands to be tarnished also. I don't wish to ask you too many questions, and I ask the same courtesy in return.'

'Right…I'm shooting in the dark here. You're going to have to fill me in.' I had a hunch where he was going, but I patiently waited for him to continue.

'Okay…okay. I will tell you. I had, let's say, the possibility of a problem with tax. I have always considered myself to be a reputable individual, but a couple of years ago I was caught out in a variation of a Ponzi scheme. This left a black hole in my finances. This is very embarrassing, so these details must remain confidential. No fool like an old fool, I know. I have expenses like everyone else, and a duty to my family, my grandchildren. I could have been ruined. So I was forced to use some funds earmarked for a future tax bill to save my bacon. In order to buy time to correct the situation, I decided to avoid the tax, for a period.'

'So you didn't declare earnings? That's illegal.'

'Yes, thank you for pointing that out. I had good reasons, but yes, technically, it is illegal.'

'Look, I'm sympathetic to your situation, but it still doesn't explain your line of thinking regarding the foundation.' I wanted to know *for sure* if what I suspected was true.

'A while back I had a break-in at my house, and as a result some anonymous individual—Leslie Weir I now presume—got hold of my iPad, which had key financial details on it, and subsequently pressured me into backing off about the out-sourcing of the foundation.'

'Okay…this is…bizarre. You have an understandable grudge.'

'That's one way of putting it, I suppose. I was blackmailed and the instruction was unequivocal—make a fuss at the bank, and they call the authorioties. Now I believe beyond reasonable doubt that Kid World Funds is the problem, I want *my* problem to disappear too.'

'You want *money*?'

'What?! I'm no blackmailer. I can sort out my finances, but I need a little time. I have other investments that should come good, and I can fix the tax problem, but I want this Kid World Funds scam sorted out. I'm nearing retirement, and I have an unblemished public record—so I want it to stay that way. What I want is for this outfit to be distanced from the bank, preferably with the money repaid, and any threat to me removed. And I'd like to get that iPad back. Stupid, I know, but it's got stuff on it I really need, and other things—photos for example, that I can't replace. The cover had the Henderson clan crest on it. My wife had it specially embossed when she bought it for me.'

I briefly swallowed, having remained impassive. 'I'm not sure how on earth I can find it but I'll have a look into it. I need one more thing in return from you, however.' I turned to face him, and he raised his bushy eyebrows.

'To keep Carole McLetchie off your back in order to buy you a little time?'

'Exactly. She was even on my case about the police, keen that nothing negative about the bank came of any investigation into Leslie's death. The woman is, as you say …extremely difficult.'

'Correct. Look, there is one last thing. You have a problem here. I probably shouldn't be telling you this.'

'What do you mean?'

'She's going to undertake a *personal* audit of the new arrangements this week. She told me this yesterday.' He interpreted my reaction correctly, as I took in a very deep breath. She'd pulled the carpet from underneath me.

'She promised me more time…the woman is…'

'A bitch? Yes, and she's been called worse. I would watch yourself if I were you.'

'Oh…I don't have anything…to hide…'

Charles raised one eyebrow, and slapped me on the back before leaving. It didn't matter if he believed me or not. His tip-off meant that I had virtually no time to act, but at least I'd been warned. After he left, I texted Elise pleading for her to speak to her ex-husband urgently to see if he could pull me out of the shit.

Chapter 21

Leave no electronic trail, nor the chance to be overheard, Alan said, so I left the building and sat in the Audi in the staff car park and called him straight back. It seemed surreal talking about this issue to someone I'd never met, but I set this aside and scribbled furiously as he informed me of some interesting facts.

The large donations processed by Lexicon Chartered in favour of Kid World Funds had performed some financial gymnastics. The funds had been sub-divided into smaller sums, and had subsequently been routed through five separate bank accounts in the Caribbean. A proportion of the funds amassed had gone to Grand Cayman, and some had briefly rested in the Bahamas. A secondary loop had been created via another bank in the Virgin Islands. Alan knew of all the banks, and had made calls to each of them in order to ascertain tacit details of transactions on specific days. And the crucial thing was that he had been able to identify the final destination.

The Isle of Man.

The island offered easy access for anyone in the British Isles with friendly faces and few real customs problems. It was a destination that also offered the possibility of cash transactions a mere hop, skip and a jump away. This jurisdiction, he explained, was out of his sphere of operation, so the trail, as far as he was concerned, ended there. I jotted down all the details, and thanked him profusely for his help.

I asked that he make one further request of the Antiguan bank, Caribbean

Consolidated International. Would he set up a holding account for me, in an assumed name? He became serious at this point, but I assured him that this would be the most legitimate way to solve a matter of both law and morality. I said he could check with Elise if he wished, but that I needed this done immediately. He reluctantly agreed to do this via a third party but then emphasised this would be the final thing he would do on my behalf as he didn't want to become part of any future investigation. He extracted a promise that his name would remain undisclosed, and that I should not expose Elise in any way. I agreed. Ten minutes later he called to confirm that a new account had been opened in Antigua.

This agreement was firmly in my mind when I called into Elise's office to explain the events, noting that Charles Henderson had also nabbed me.

'Charles Henderson?'

'Yes, I know. I was surprised too, but it's a long story. I have to act now or I'm stuffed. I just want to thank you. If there's any way to repay you…'

'This whole scam thing has kind of hooked me. What am I supposed to do now—go home to my flat and watch TV when all this is going on?' A couple of suits passed us in the corridor, and I hushed my voice.

'Elise, this is dangerous. The less you know the better. If you get dragged into any investigation you could get charged too.' I also briefly thought about Leslie Weir's death but purged my brain of the subject.

'But I'm already involved,' she said softly. 'And surely you don't intend to get caught now?' I couldn't work out if she was genuinely naive, or if she actually had real faith in me.

'There are risks and I'm worried about you. I like you very much, and I don't want to see you in any trouble.'

'Not good enough.' She folded her arms, in a mock huff.

'Okay, but there is something else. Alan asked that I kept you out of it. I promised.'

'Well, that's just tipped the balance in my favour. He has no say in what I do with my life. When are you speaking to Kostas and how do you know that another brain might not help get a result?'

I could see that I wasn't going to win this argument. 'Okay…I'll let you know as soon as I speak to Kostas.'

When Kostas had confided in me previously about his escapade in Athens as a student, he had alluded to an initial carnal high in 'getting away' with computer hacking. Systems had been simpler in these days. When the Lexicon Chartered scam had initially become airborne I had also experienced something similar—minor exhilaration in being an integral element of something clever. Pure hubris. Being ahead of other people who I thought were ignorant. Yet, *I* had been ignorant.

I could understand that Kostas—having consigned his misdemeanour to the past—might rationally tell me to piss off. However, he agreed to see me at his home after work. I told him I was bringing Elise along and he groaned; not because he didn't like her, but rather because he knew that more bodies would simply complicate matters.

Kostas and his wife Elena lived in an imposing semi-detached villa in Bruntsfield, one of those houses that stands testament to the late Victorians—spacious, yet connected so intimately to the neighbours next door. Elena had inherited money from her father which had allowed them to enjoy a mortgage-free existence, retaining property here in Scotland yet also a town house in Athens. Kostas had also confessed to owning a plot of land in Santorini for his retirement dreams. I'd arrived just after dinner time.

The twin nine year-old boys, Nicolai and Alex, were playing football in the back garden with an outside light providing limited vision. No doubt they were considering whether to play for Scotland or Greece when they grew up. They momentarily waved at me through the back window of the kitchen. I introduced Elise to Elena, who ushered us in to their spare living room, seemingly aware of the privacy needed, yet, I suspected, unaware of the exact nature of my visit. We were offered some Greek cake and two strong coffees, before she left us alone.

As succinctly as possible, I made my pitch to Kostas.

'Ally, I've got a wife and kids. If you go to prison, you're not letting anyone down but yourself.' He sat with his arms firmly folded, facing the large mug of coffee.

'Where's your sense of adventure, Kostas?' Elise broke in, and we both looked directly at her. This wasn't actually the way I would have phrased it.

'Adventure?' He smiled sardonically. 'Elise, it's not that I don't enjoy a challenge. It's the odds I'm concerned about.'

'How so?'

'Things have changed. Lots of the systems currently used to deflect hackers have been designed *by* hackers. Poachers turned gamekeepers. These people know how hackers operate because they have used the same bag of tricks themselves. There are lots of little traps. The detection rate has gone up substantially because hackers are often under surveillance from the *start of any* search process. That would mean anyone even attempting to look at a bank's security system would be flagged up immediately. You would need to set up a fake identity, use state of the art software, piggy back onto someone else's device, and then be extremely efficient. And lucky. Oh, and you would probably need to create some kind of decoy to draw attention from the whole process, like a magician.

'So it can definitely be done?' Elise spoke again, smiling. 'Alan has provided the account details.'

Kostas shook his head.o[pe for \kidsHoppe for

'Kostas, I'm desperate, ' I said flatly. 'Carole McLetchie's circling like a hungry vulture. There's going to be an internal audit this week, and possibly an external audit later on. I didn't create Kid World Funds, but it's going to look like I did. Weir is dead, and the money has disappeared. I've been surviving on borrowed time, and this is my last opportunity to get out of this mess.'

He sighed, and took a sip of coffee. 'It might be different if you tackled things from another perspective rather that attempting to electronically scam the offshore bank. If you made, let's say, an apparently legitimate withdrawal.'

'What do you mean? Visit the bank? I know that people can still withdraw large amounts in cash, but it's *their own.* Are you suggesting that I visit the Isle of Man, and assume the identity of the account holder? How would I do that? I don't even know for sure whether the account signatory—or signatories—would be the dead Weir, Doug the invincible, or even Mandy. It could even be that Canavan guy in Ireland for all I know, though he was using an alias too. Even if I assume that it's Doug I don't have any pin numbers or codes. Shit, I can't locate the bastard, even if I do know his real surname.' I ran my fingers through my hair, feeling the tension starting to build. Then Kostas smiled.

'What?' Elise asked.

'I'm thinking of what we just said about piggy-backing on someone else's device. If you did know where Doug was—where he lived, for example—it would be substantially easier to hack into a computer or other device at his home than through a bank. Unlike an attempt made to breach security at an offshore bank—which would be likely to incur a prompt police investigation—breach of Doug's security would hardly amount to a crime. This is dirty money he can't declare. Think about that—you might be able to do something from *his* end. Try something *electronic*. Maybe through his own personal banking account? It's a long shot, but you never know.' Kostas munched some cake, assuming a Hercule Poirot sort of pose.

'So you'd be willing to help me provided that I locate Doug?'

He sighed. 'Maybe.'

'That's fantastic. So I could avoid having to make a trip to the Isle of Man disguised as Doug?' I momentarily smiled, envisaging myself sporting a curly wig and stupid over-sized designer glasses.

'Possibly.'

'But I have no idea of his whereabouts. He could be in Swaziland for all I know.'

'True. But not necessarily.'

'So assuming that I could locate him, how could you electronically access funds?'

'Well, theoretically, it would depend on the type of account and the means of access. Presumably, though, if any electronic withdrawals were made, there would be another trail. You could decide on the means of withdrawal—repatriating money to Lexicon Chartered, for example—if we were successful in accessing the account.'

'I like that word *we* that you've just used. Thank you for that. But how can we find Doug? The trail is cold.'

Kostas stood up, scratching his chin. 'What about that director of the fake bidder company you spoke to? The shady guy who was angry with you on the phone?'

Elise frowned. 'Who's that?' I'd forgotten that she didn't know all the details.

'The guy was registered as a director of the Jerusalem Saviour, one of Doug's fake entities. Duncan Blethan of Blethan Associates. But he cut me off when I called him, because, surprise, surprise, he too was a crook and could spot spin a mile off.'

'Okay. Let's try a little digging. Elise, can you go through to the lounge and ask Elena to bring in my laptop? Let's see what we can find out about this guy.'

Two minutes later we were into the Blethan Associates website, though nothing unusual was evident. I wondered if there was anything financial that might add leverage for us in any potential conversation about Doug, and Kostas then produced a clever twist—why not cross reference them against a credit rating agency. This proved interesting. For a trivial fee we were able to discover that this company had indeed had some financial problems, and resultantly, a poor credit rating. We then searched for the media stories I'd found before I'd spoken to Blethan the first time. One article explained that Blethan had been in court on fraud charges, but that he had escaped a sentence on a technicality. An individual from the Inland Revenue had been quoted saying that there were other forthcoming issues that might arise, but that he was unable to discuss any details due to client confidentiality. Ironically, it was a Greek name—Georgios Kesopoulou.

Elise looked at Kostas, who flipped his eyes toward the ceiling in a 'what now' mannerism.

'You could help,' she grinned.

'How?'

'If Ally spoke to Blethan already—he'd be suspicious if another Scottish guy starts asking questions. But, hey, there is a fighting chance that,' she checked the name, '*Georgios Kesopoulou* might be a first generation Greek. You could pretend to be him.'

Kostas momentarily shook his head, but we both stared at him. 'Okay! What do you want me to say?'

I stood up and walked around the room, chewing on the side of my index finger.

'How about this: You are Georgios Kesopoulou from the Inland Revenue. He will remember you from his court appearance case? The Inland Revenue played fair, but of course Blethan won the case on a technicality. There are however, other remaining potential charges against Blethan Associates that you cannot discuss over the phone. Off the record, however, you wish to make him a once only offer that will be seen *very favourably* in the eyes of the Inland Revenue. Give us a location or contact number for Doug Mundel. That's it.'

I sat down, as if this was the answer to everything. Kostas blinked, before saying, 'And if he knows instantly that I am not the aforesaid Georgios Kesopoulou?'

'Put the phone down. It doesn't matter.'

Kostas slowly picked up his phone, shaking his head. He dialled the same mobile number as I'd called previously. There was short delay before he nodded to me. Blethan had obviously answered. This time Kostas stood up, facing away from me, as if in character. He went through the spiel. Luckily, Georgios Kesopoulou must have had a broadly similar accent. There were some gaps in the conversation, and Kostas added some decoy bullshit about legislation applying to Blethan's case—the Bribery Act—and there was further silence. Then, suddenly, Kostas motioned for me pass the pen that I held, quickly scribbling down some notes. He then quickly ended the call by saying that the value of the call to Blethan was strictly on the basis that he discussed this with no one, least of all Mr Mundel.

'You've got it?'

'I have indeed.'

'*Fantastic*!' I said, as I slapped him on the shoulder and kissed Elise on the lips. She gave me a direct look…that was the first time I had done that.

Kostas held up the piece of paper, as if suddenly inspired by the brilliance of his own deceit. 'Blethan spoke to Doug Mundel only this week, so this is *live*. We have Doug's mobile number. Blethan doesn't know where he is but I can maybe find the location. Hang on.' Kostas tapped away on his laptop for a few seconds. 'There is a police website which can identify a registered address if you plug in a mobile number. I have an access code for it somewhere that a friend...eh, in the police...gave me. Needless to say, don't mention this to anyone...'

Elise and I shook our heads. We waited about thirty or forty seconds. 'The phone's registered to an address in Glasgow. He might not be that far away after all.'

'Where in Glasgow?'

He looked at the piece of paper. 'Cleveden Drive, postcode G12.'

'West End. Know it well. Dated a girl who lived round the corner for a few months when I was a student.' Elise raised her eyebrows at this revelation, but I just smiled in response.

'Strike when the iron's hot?' I said, hoping for an affirmative response.

'What?' Kostas asked.

'We could go right now.'

'You want to go to Glasgow—now?'

'Actually, I'd like to visit the bastard right this instant kill him, but that would be daft. What if Blethan sleeps on this and speaks to the Inland Revenue tomorrow? Or he might warn Doug. Could we scam details from outside his house, whether he's there or not? Dependent on wireless internet? Though I'm not entirely sure how you can do that.'

'Don't ask too much about that. I do have...some capability. But you actually want to go there tonight?'

'It would only take an hour at this time of the evening to get over there.'

Elise then touched us both on the shoulder. 'I've always dreamed of a night out in Glasgow...with two guys. I'll check the house on Streetwise.'

Kostas contemplated the suggestion and then, as if fearing that I would lay on the emotional blackmail again, he shook his head and smiled. He had a quick word with Elena. She appeared troubled that we were leaving unexpectedly on a trip across the country, but acquiesced when he said he'd make it up to her. Another favour owed. Kostas picked up his phone, his laptop and another little black gadget which I'd never seen before. It was the size of a cigarette packet.

'Let me first get the Lexicon Chartered account details too, which are on my old laptop in the car. We'll need to take your car though because if he's there he could recognise mine.' I took a couple of minutes to access all the details I thought we might need, and then the three of us left in Kostas's five series BMW.

Within fifteen minutes we hit the M8 motorway, the main artery connecting Scotland's two major cities. After a few minutes on the motorway, Kostas broke the silence.

'I hope that this journey is worth it, Ally. But you do realise something?'

'What?' I glanced at him.

'This might simply be a mirage.'

'You have a point.'

'And…Mandy,' he said quietly as he carefully overtook a juggernaut which was generating significant side spray. 'Yes, Mandy. She might even be…in residence.'

'I suppose…'

'Are you prepared for that?'

'No. But what option do I have? We're pretty much winging it as it is.'

Elise spoke from the rear seat. 'I'd quite like to see what she looks like, actually.' Kostas suddenly laughed out loud, and eventually I joined in, some of the stress dissipating.

'There is something more serious,' Kostas then said in a quieter tone, clearing his throat. He tapped the dashboard to emphasise whatever point he was about to make. 'We may be visiting the home of a murderer. This guy might have killed Leslie Weir.'

'Do you think that, Ally?' Elise asked me.

I hesitated, having tried very hard to block this out. 'Shit, guys, I've been trying to forget about it. The police haven't been on my case for what, five minutes, so maybe the thing has cooled off. Maybe one of Weir's neighbours did him in. You know, I wouldn't blame them. The man was a menace.' Neither of them laughed this time, yet neither did they disagree.

We reached our exit junction sooner than expected, allowing us easy access onto Great Western Road, which links the city centre to the West End.

Cleveden Drive was a pleasant, leafy place, populated with old sandstone villas and semis built more than a century before. This was an expensive address. Maybe he'd just emptied the Isle of Man account.

The house—Rowanlea—was detached. An outside light partially lit the driveway, but it was difficult to determine if there was anyone inside. A car was parked in the driveway: Doug's Mercedes. This was the right place. We parked outside in the street, directly behind a white van. If Doug appeared from the house, he wouldn't immediately see us because there were large oak trees in the front garden.

'That's his car. We have to assume he's there. Are we close enough to be in range for Wi-Fi?'

'Should be,' Kostas said. 'It's good that it's a detached house. If we had a block of flats we would possibly have had problems,' Kostas explained, as he began to set up his laptop and connect the little device he had brought along. I asked what it was.

'The wonders of technology. Let's say that it should be able to circumnavigate wireless security and get into any live device in there, unconnected to us.' As he tapped away at his laptop I peered through the trees at the front of the garden. Was Mandy in there right now? My pulse suddenly quickened.

Kostas looked round directly at me. 'I've got a signal. There's a live Wi-Fi connection, as you might expect. Now, let's see what we can do.' He mucked about for a minute or two, before grinning. 'We're in. I love this sort of app. State of the art. I could use it to see browsing history and what domestic bank he uses.'

'How do you have this?'

'Don't ask.'

I watched as Kostas applied the app. He said this software could also help bypass the latest biometric security measures, and within two minutes he had obtained access to Doug's email account. Kostas then shook his head, before scanning and browsing to search for any references to personal banking.

'He's got an HSBC account. Let's see.' Again, Kostas was quickly able to secure the password for Doug's bank account.

'If this software was available to the public, there would be mayhem,' Elise observed. There were many transactions listed, but nothing recent that indicated withdrawals from an account in the Isle of Man. Kostas continued to search in a reverse chronological order, finally going back over a year.

'I don't know. Perhaps he has no electronic connectivity from the HSBC account to that Isle of Man account. Keeps everything separate. Maybe funds are building up there nicely, and he simply visits in person if and when he needs cash. It's cumbersome, but more secure for him,' I said, scratching my head. 'What are the larger transactions, in or out? Is there anything there, over a thousand but fewer than ten thousand?'

Kostas scanned again, going back over a year and a half. And then something on the screen jumped out at me. It was a payment *out* of his HSBC account for exactly five thousand pounds, but an irregular one.

'Hold on Kostas. *That one.*' I pointed at the transaction on the screen, and quickly checked the reference, and it matched the account number in the Isle of Man. 'That's it! Look, he's made exactly one payment *out* of his domestic account about 18 months ago. This makes sense. Something has come back to me. I think that part of the new money laundering rules mean that citizens here must make opening payments *electronically* into certain new offshore accounts. Doug must have been *forced* to open the account using funds from his HSBC account. Thereafter he could probably do as he liked, but we have a link. It's right there in his personal account history. The banking regulators have actually done us a favour!'

Elise then spoke softly. 'The question is, Kostas: can we move money *out* of Doug's offshore account?'

'Possibly,' he said. 'You say he's a cocky bastard? He's obviously been confident of not being caught by leaving this electronic loophole from his domestic account. He's assumed that no one was going to look at the offshore account from this side.'

'Either that, or he wanted the option to access funds quickly without having to go in person to the Isle of Man. Maybe he felt that this was a risk worth taking.'

'But if we were able to transfer money electronically from the Isle of Man account to this one, we'd need to send it *from* that account—we couldn't simply debit it from Doug's HSBC account?' Elise asked.

Kostas shook his head. 'You're right. Having Doug's domestic bank account and a link is a help, but we'd still need to hack into the Isle of Man account to send the funds here, which is exactly what we wanted to avoid trying in the first place. We've not had time to think this through. Shit.'

I slapped the dashboard.

'Calm down, Ally. This is my car. Let's have another look to see if there is a way of entering his offshore account legitimately.' He scanned the emails again, but there seemed no further links. Obviously Doug had avoided electronic connectivity with the offshore account in all but the opening transfer.

I sighed. 'Maybe if we had his laptop or phone—passwords. Would that help?' I suggested.

'You mean by breaking in?' Kostas asked.

'Well, I am desperate. If there is no biometric security on the offshore account—but passwords and numbers—maybe he's got that hidden inside his house. And lots of people keep their passwords written down. Especially those that they have to change or they don't remember.'

Elise then interjected. 'And how would you intend to do that if he's in the house? It does look as if he's in there.' We all looked at the house; there were a number of lights on. And again the Mercedes was there in the drive.

Kostas turned in his seat to stare at me. 'What do you suggest, Ally? You did get yourself into this mess with some degree of complexity, I might add, so surely you can think of some kind of solution?' The sarcasm seeped out.

Elise suddenly placed one hand on each of our shoulders. 'I bet you're glad that you let me come along on the trip.' We both turned to see the smile that was expanding across her face.

'It's obvious, guys. I will be a decoy.'

Chapter 22

'Elise, *no*. If anyone's going to do anything, it should be me.' How could I let Elise take any risk in this situation?

'But Ally, don't you see? Doug doesn't know me, so I am the best person to distract him. Assuming he's there.'

'Are you sure that he didn't see you at the bank the day he spilled the coffee?' I asked.

'I don't think so. That only lasted for about ten seconds and it was ages ago, when he was distracted by the pain of a boiling substance pouring over his crotch.'

'I wish I'd seen that,' I said.

'Even though I don't know the guy, I think I hate him' Elise said. 'But I'm confident that he won't recognise me.'

'I think Kostas would need to make himself absent, just in case.'

Kostas and I looked at each other. 'This is stupid, Ally,' he said bluntly.

'Oh for God's sake,' Elise blurted. 'You're a pair of big jessies! Isn't that what the Scots call a chicken? Do you have me as Penelope Pitstop or something? I may have the accent, but *come on*.'

'Okay…you're some girl, Elise. But how would you distract him for long enough? I'd need at least ten minutes to scout about. And what if there are other people in there—like Mandy?'

'I told you…I'd like to meet her…'

'Oh for God's sake, Elise,' Kostas said.

'I'm *joking*, Kostas. Look, how about this? We drive a bit round the corner. I go up and knock on the front door, pretending that I'm a tourist in Scotland. That I've driven from Stirling, and have a flat tyre—we can deflate a tyre?'

'Yes. And I have a pump that plugs into the cigarette lighter. I suppose I *could* get it out of the boot.' Kostas joked, waiting to hear what might become of his car.

'Well, assuming he's there, I'll ask him for a favour—that I have a flat tyre and a pump but that I don't know how to use it. If he agrees to help, then Kostas can call the house phone number which we have. If there's anyone there they would probably answer, so if there's no answer then there's an opportunity.'

'Assuming he doesn't lock his door behind him if he does agree to help,' I said. 'Let's leave the car here. That way you can say you're just parked in front of his house. He'd be less likely to lock up if that's the case.'

'And where am I going to be stationed during this exercise?' Kostas held out his hands.

'Hiding in those bushes at the side of the house.' I pointed at the bushes.

'This is ridiculous,' he replied.

'It is. So let's vote. Those in favour?' Elise and I raised our hands immediately, smiling at Kostas.

'The Greeks invented democracy, Kostas, didn't they?' she said, in a matter of fact manner. He grimaced before opening the door.

'I hope that you know what you're doing,' he replied, handing me a torch that he'd taken from the glove compartment.

We shifted the car a little, checking that no one was about to appear from the house. It then took about forty seconds to deflate a rear tyre, before Kostas and I shuffled to the side of the gravel covered driveway, behind the bushes. There were no obvious external security measures, so we manoeuvred as close to the house as possible without being immediately visible from the front porch. Elise then marched up the driveway, barely glancing in our direction as she approached the doorway. Having evidently pressed the buzzer—we couldn't see from our vantage point—she stood, hands on hips, awaiting a response.

Time seemed to stand still during those few seconds, before I recognised the unmistakable voice of Doug Mundel. Part of me wanted to run over and smash his head in, but I was in enough trouble already.

Elise pointed in the direction of the car, and there was a small delay. Kostas gawped at me as if to point out that our ploy had failed, but then Doug reappeared wearing a jacket and carrying a torch. He closed the front door but did not appear to lock it, and then he followed Elise down the driveway towards the car.

I grabbed Kostas's arm, and motioned for him to phone the house. He gave a 'thumbs up' to indicate that the phone was ringing—in fact, we could hear the tone from outside the house. After about fifteen seconds an answer machine kicked in. No one else in?

I crept towards the house, attempting to minimise the crunch of gravel beneath my shoes, though I could have sworn that the thump of my heartbeat seemed louder. An outside light had already been switched on so no further sensor was evident. I tentatively peered into the porch before making my final move to touch the front door handle. Once inside, I carefully closed the door behind me. The door contained a stained glass panel, alerting me to the prospect that Doug might still spot me from outside, so I side stepped into a front lounge lit only by a lamp. The place was beautifully decorated. A sixth sense, perhaps, confirmed to me that no one else was present.

Darting between ground floor rooms there appeared no obvious office or den; the objective being to locate the kind of hub where people leave pending projects, financial details and generally unfinished business. And I had unfinished business. As I quickly moved to the second floor, I experienced the sudden force that adrenalin brings, propelling me up three steps at a time. I kicked a small hall landing table over in the rush, but immediately replaced it.

Although the hall landing light was on, the four second floor rooms remained in darkness. Three were bedrooms. A lightning quick scan with the torch revealed nothing of note, though I did spot a lady's handbag in what appeared to be the master bedroom. Mandy's? I considered having a rummage—which would remove beyond doubt Mandy's putative duplicity;

yet something stopped me. I'm not sure if it was latent embarrassment, or fear of being diverted and caught, but I left the bag alone. The fourth room appeared to be Doug's office. Two couches mirrored each other. The torch allowed some light, and I kept the beam low as the room was situated towards to front of the house. Then I slowly pulled back one full length velvet curtain to reveal the street outside. Glancing out of the window, through the trees, I could just make out Elise with Doug—he had the air pump in his hands, so the ruse had worked so far.

At the side of the room stood a solid-wood computer cabinet. Inside was the wireless kit for the house, and an empty space existed where a laptop may have sat on occasion. Various papers were stacked on the desk element of the cabinet, plus various other bits and bobs, including another torch. Clearly, Doug had not gone totally paperless. As quickly as possible, I scanned the papers. Nothing appeared to be of interest. The side doors of the cabinet contained *Post-It* notes, with various scribbles that were difficult to make out in the light. Then there were two desk drawers, one locked, and one unlocked. The open drawer contained two pen drives. Given Kostas hadn't mentioned hacking into the cloud, should I just take the lot? Would these provide the secret of Doug's fortune, or simply a series of bills and holiday photographs? I hesitated. Then I shone the torch into the back of the drawer, where a small key was illuminated. I was too nervous to smile as the key simply provided access to the locked drawer. Some security measure that. In this drawer were other keys. God knows what they opened.

Where was his laptop or tablet? I hadn't really checked much downstairs as instinct had steered me towards a home office, yet no computer had been evident in this location.

Then I heard the voices at the front door.

Doug…*and* Elise. What was she doing in the house?

I switched off the torch. I couldn't make out what Doug was saying, but Elise coughed very loudly, evidently in a warning to me. Then I heard the footsteps downstairs, before a change in direction of the sound—*onto* the stairs. I slithered along the floor toward the bay window, trying desperately not to press on any old creaky floorboards. I shuffled behind the velvet curtains about two seconds before Doug marched into the room, switching on the main room light. Instinctively, I measured my breathing.

I waited.

'There's the bloody thing!' he eventually said, under his breath, before leaving the room and thumping back downstairs. He left the main light on. I waited until the front door had closed again to confirm that he had in fact taken the torch. Suddenly, I was relieved not to have removed all his stuff—there would be no way he could have missed such a theft.

Then a thought occurred to me. I looked again at the *Post-It* notes inside the cabinet doors, which were now properly illuminated by the main light. One or two of the notes obscured others. As I inspected those underneath more closely, I noticed a series of asterisks interspersed with letters and digits within one note. Some of the characters had been scored out, but there appeared to be a sequence of some sort. Pin numbers? Passwords? Shining the torch with one hand, I took a photo of the notes with my phone, now possible with the full main light. I also noticed various pieces of correspondence, and photographed one form bearing Doug's signature, just in case it proved handy.

There was a built-in cupboard in the room, so I quickly opened it and shone the torch light toward what appeared to be a pile of junk. Then, underneath some cardboard folders, I spotted a black iPad cover. Could this be Doug's? Would he keep an iPad in a cupboard? I opened the cover, and as I brought it out I noticed a bold crest on it. One I realised had been commissioned by Charles Henderson's wife.

I then replaced the cover where I had found it under the folders, but grabbed Henderson's iPad itself before literally leaping downstairs. But as I swung round into the hallway, car headlights appeared in the driveway. Shit, someone *else* had arrived. I hit the floor. Afraid of being spotted through the stained glass window in the front door, I jiggled on my knees toward the kitchen. I couldn't see through walls, but within seconds I recognised the solid click of high heels emanating from the porch, and then the door opened. For a split second I also spotted a laptop placed on a table in an adjacent dining room, but I didn't dare risk returning for it.

The footsteps stopped, before seemingly being redirected back toward the front door. Perhaps *Mandy* had spotted Doug outside. I had no exit strategy, so I shuffled in semi-dark toward the back of the large dining kitchen, where a rear porch was revealed. I tripped on a mat that covered the floor, and when I placed my hands down to smooth it over I caught something sharp underneath—a handle for an old trapdoor of some kind. I didn't cut myself or I would almost certainly have left blood, but I gripped the back door: it was locked, with no key in the lock. Then the high heels clicked in the hall again. I switched on the torch, desperately looking for a rear door key. I shone the light about, until I focused on a series of plant pots on the window ledge, each resting on saucers. I cautiously felt under each plant pot. Under the fourth or fifth pot I found a key. I slipped it into the lock, which it actually fitted. Lucky break. A slow, lightly scraping motion then released the two deadbolts, allowing me to ease the door open, before slithering out. As I edged the door closed behind me, the cool evening air did little to quell the sweat that had enveloped my body, a body which suddenly felt very weak.

Creeping into the bushes at the left side of the house, I realised that the back door was now left open behind me. Would they notice? Would it matter?

I remained in the bushes for about two minutes more as I could still hear voices from the street. Having escaped from the house undetected, I was reluctant to even look inside to see if those female footsteps had belonged to Mandy. Part of me still didn't want to know. Then I heard louder voices from Cleveden Drive, followed by the firing up of a car engine. Doug had actually done a good deed. Staggering.

Through the leaves, I witnessed him waving at Elise as she drove off round the corner. The front door of the house thumped loudly, signalling the opportunity of an exit for me through the adjoining neighbour's garden. A quick check in either direction showed no passing witnesses who might report me. I noticed that the vehicle that had arrived was some sort of big SUV, black in colour. Then, I simply walked with my head down round the corner until I reached Kostas and Elise.

'What took you…?' Kostas asked.

'I hope you weren't looking in Mandy's underwear drawer,' Elise suggested.

I glared at her, before seeing the funny side of the remark. 'I was hiding behind a pair of curtains when Doug came in for that torch. That was close.' I breathed out heavily, echoing post break-in relief.

'Doug's quite cute, actually,' Elise then said, raising her voice in mock praise.

'Aye, right. Elise. I wonder if it actually was Mandy in the SUV.'

'I couldn't see. She had her back turned when I looked round. Did you see her, Kostas?

'No. More importantly, what's that?' Kostas asked, pointing to the bulge under my jacket. 'His laptop?' He smiled.

'Actually, it's Charles Henderson's iPad, Kostas. I found it under a pile of stuff in a cupboard.'

'What? What's the point of that? We went through all that for Henderson's iPad?' He frowned at me, shaking his head as if I were the world's greatest moron.

'Look, I didn't see Doug's laptop until it was too late, downstairs. And he might have missed it right away, which would have been no use. Anyway, Kostas, I had hardly any time. How was I supposed to know Doug would march straight back in?'

'Don't blame me,' said Elise. 'I didn't know if Kostas had a torch in the trunk or I could have used that one, but I was scared to look in case there was something else there that gave us away.'

Kostas nodded. 'Fair enough. There's actually a Scottish Chartered sports bag in there. He *would* have spotted that straight away. Might have raised questions. So Henderson's iPad is all that you could find?'

'No. I have these photos.' I quickly accessed the pictures on my phone, maximising the image so we could just make out Doug's scribbles. 'There were *Post-It* notes on the doors of the computer cabinet. I missed them at first, but then when Doug left the light on after he came in I had a closer look. I might be wrong, but there's some sort of codes here.'

'Passwords?' Kostas asked.

'Possibly. I know that people try to disguise that sort of thing if they write it down. You know, if you have to change passwords regularly, there's often a link between each of them. Some sort of sequence. And people are often reluctant to keep passwords on their person—wallets or whatever—in case they lose them. So inside the home is the most secure place.'

'Maybe you're right. Let me see,' Kostas said, peering at the digits and letters on the screen. 'Ally, what's that account number in the Isle of Man bank again?'

I accessed the account number. '211266780.' Kostas scrolled down the enlarged photo, scanning slowly given the constraint of viewing on a phone. 'Do any of these numbers appear on there?' I asked.

'One or two. Some letters and digits are crossed out in places, except at the bottom. I can't see an immediate sequence.' He scratched his chin.

'But then, maybe he memorised the account number, as that would be permanent. Passwords are different.'

'*If* this is indeed the password to that account.'

'Let me see,' Elise took the phone, scrolling down the photo. Why don't we concentrate of the bottom one? That would likely be the most recent. That looks like a 'J' to me.' I nodded. Kostas looked up, unconvinced, before Elise continued. 'Then there are three asterisks, followed by what looks like the letter 's', then three further asterisks, followed by the digit 7. It's a capital J. Proper noun?' She stared at the scribble. 'This Doug, he's not religious, is he?'

'I doubt it.'

'*Jerusalem*. See?' She filled in the asterisks. 'Jerusalem7?'

'Jerusalem Saviour. Jesus. This was the title of one of those bogus companies he set up. That could be it.' I ruffled Elise's hair, causing Kostas to shake his head once again.

'So what now?' she asked.

'Intercourse?' Kostas suggested.

'Come on Kostas, try to be more constructive. This might be the key. Let's try the Isle of Man Bank's site. Who knows?' Elise said enthusiastically.

I confirmed the bank name and details to Kostas, who quickly accessed the website.

'Supposing we actually get in, where do you want to transfer money to?'

'Elise's ex has set up a holding account for me in Antigua. The account is with the same bank as Lexicon Chartered, under the name of Kid World Funds. I was going to return the money to Scottish Chartered, it would be more convincing if it was sent from the same bank—Caribbean Consolidated International. I hadn't figured how I would get the money to them, but as you say, there may be an electronic means.'

Kostas viewed me mock-suspiciously. 'You *are* going to return the money?'

'Of course.'

'Okay.'

'The thing is, as we did not have access to this offshore account directly, we don't know how much is in there,' I said.

'So exactly how much are you trying to transfer? How much were the total donations to this Kid World Funds lot?'

'It's over six million. Plus the 10 K he owes me…'

'And my fee,' Kostas said.

'And something toward my next holiday to Tahiti,' Elise noted.

'Your wishes are my commands, guys. But you do have a point, Kostas. We're going in here blind. Who knows how much he's got in there?'

The possibility hung in the air as Kostas proceeded to enter the account number, and then the password Jerusalem7. There was a slight delay on the site as the details were initially processed.

'Wow. Looks like the correct password.'

'Hold on,' said Kostas. 'Date of birth. We need that too.' He held out his hands knowing that this would be a guess in 365. 'This is a wild goose chase, Ally. And the goose is chasing a needle in a haystack.

'Fourth of September, and I know what year too.'

'Really? How do you know that?'

I explained. Kostas then typed in the date and we watched as the timer edged toward its conclusion.

'We're in.' He grinned.

'*Fantastic.*' I said, gripping him on the shoulder. 'Quick. What's the balance?'

He clicked the relevant box, and all three of us gasped simultaneously.

Zero.

Chapter 23

The journey back to Edinburgh was a sombre affair. A brief assessment of Doug's offshore bank account had revealed a desperately frustrating near miss. A matter of four days previously, a massive withdrawal had been made. Over *seven million* had been removed from the account. In cash. So much for an electronic world. Presumably Doug had made the trip to the Isle of Man and literally emptied the account. Had Weir been given a slice, or cut out? Where the money had gone was anyone's guess. Maybe Doug had taken cold feet about the security of the offshore account. Maybe he was planning to leave the country, or launder the proceeds. Whatever the reason, the timing did not help me one iota. Both Elise and Kostas told me to accept it; that we had tried our best given the impossible constraints, and that I should stop beating myself up about it all. I even suggested that we take the nearest exit off the motorway and drive straight back to Doug's house so I could have it out with him, or at least land one on him. Both Elise and Kostas refused to go, insisting that any confrontation would nullify any advantage I might still have over Doug, or see me charged by the cops. And given their questions about Leslie Weir's death, this was the last thing I needed. I arrived home dejected.

First thing the next morning I opened an email demanding that I see Carole McLetchie. Her secretary instructed me to wait for her in her office, as she was on a conference call next door. The dog in the photo scowled at me once again until I eventually broke eye contact. When she arrived, wearing a platinum power suit, she buzzed her secretary requesting that we were not disturbed. Not a good sign. She took her seat in one swift motion.

'The first thing I wish to say, Ally, is that this meeting is off the record. I am pretty sure that this would be in your favour, but if you wish to have representation or minutes taken, you can do so,' she said, staring at me for any reaction. From her brief statement, it seemed like some kind of disciplinary hearing. I erred on the side of nonchalance.

'No, Carole. That's fine. What's the, eh, issue?' I clasped my hands in front of me, only barely realising the prayer-like appeal I was making.

'I'm going to be blunt.'

'Okay…'

'The police have been in touch. Well, more accurately, they have responded to a query that I made.'

'About…Leslie's death?'

'Yes. And the good news, from the bank's perspective, is that they are dropping their inquiry into the possibility of a connection to Leslie's work.'

Suddenly I felt much, much better. A massive wave of relief swept over me, because this had eaten away at me. 'That's great!'

'However,' she then said, 'that's not the point.' Perhaps I had misinterpreted her initial words in my mild euphoria.

'But this is great news! I mean, the bank *wouldn't have been* connected, of course,' I replied, though she simply continued to stare.

'Your involvement will not now be required, Ally. There are issues which the police may not have proof…though let's say *I* have.'

I swallowed, unsure what to say. 'I don't know what you mean.'

'I'm sure you do, *Ally*.' This time she used my name with a degree of venom. 'So I will be clear. The bank is now in a position to let you go.' She held my gaze as I took in what she'd just said. Let me go?

'*Let me go*? You're…you're firing me?'

'It would be much better if you simply resigned. But if you refuse, yes, I will fire you.'

'I have no choice?'

'No choice.'

'So do I get the courtesy of an explanation? I've got a long track record here. There's employment law—'

'Oh *spare* me the drama.' She leaned forward in her chair. 'Do you realise the potential embarrassment that you could cause in this institution? Have you any understanding of the consequences of your poor and reckless decision-making for the standing and reputation of this bank? We survived the banking crisis because we were more cautious than others, risk averse. A conservative, safe, institution. Over a hundred years of solid financial management is at stake here. But we're only as good as the people we employ, and we cannot afford to employ those who jeopardise the image of the corporation. *Losers*.'

'Losers?' I let the words hang, not knowing *what exactly she knew*. Perhaps I would incriminate myself by saying too much. I hesitated, and those few seconds spoke volumes.

'Need I remind you that I am the Director of *Compliance*?'

'If…it's to do with the new foundation? There are reasons for various… decisions…'

'Cut the bullshit, Ally. You are a *very lucky young man*. In any other circumstance you would be prosecuted and jailed, but I am going to make you an offer. Go quietly, by signing a resignation letter and a confidentiality clause, and you will be *permitted* to leave the bank with six month's salary and your existing pension intact. This is *exceptionally* generous in the circumstances. That way, the current situation can be managed by people who can avoid damage to the bank's reputation. Professionals who know what they are doing.'

'And who's that going to be?' This basic question was all I could say.

'None of your business, really. But I will no doubt have to sort out your mess first. You will say *nothing* to any other member of staff, or any external contact. Not even your lawyer. The police are now off the case as far as we are concerned, which is very fortunate for you. You must understand the consequences of any breach of this agreement. Officially, you will be pursuing new opportunities, and we will brief the media and various stakeholders to that effect. For your convenience, I have drafted a letter of resignation on your behalf, and I have a termination agreement here also, which I want you to sign right now. It includes a very strict confidentiality clause. This is non-negotiable, and the offer will be withdrawn immediately if you refuse to sign it.'

She pushed the documents toward me in a sharp gesture, and slapped a fountain pen on the table. I gazed at the print, which seemed to drift upon the page. So this was what it felt like to be fired?

Weird. Surreal. Beyond words...but maybe a huge relief...

I glanced at her briefly, and found my hand reaching towards the pen. Barely able to compute the words typed before me, I signed both documents. The signatures were hardly my best, nothing like those I'd practiced as a teenager in preparation for that professional football career which didn't materialise.

But they *were* my signatures, and I had duly resigned from my job.

'Your desk has already been cleared. You can pick up your things from the goods entrance on the ground floor, east.' She held the door open as I stood up. 'And remember what I said. If you wish to avoid prosecution, keep your mouth completely shut. *In perpetuity*.'

I noticed two security guards standing outside the door.That was quick. I felt oddly removed, as it if were happening to someone else. The slow walk to the stairs and the embarrassing wait for the elevator created a strange numbness. Carole McLetchie had managed to fire me with barely a mention of Weir's death and Lexicon Chartered, and no mention at all of Kid World Funds or the missing millions. Too embarrassing for the bank to even discuss, and crucial enough for me to be silenced. No opportunity to say farewell to a single colleague, probably to stifle any immediate—if irrational—desire I might have to spill the beans.

But that wasn't going to happen, was it?

The security personnel made me sign for my personal belongings that were presented to me in a plastic bag, including one of those bright pink rubber corporate stress-busters that I could have pulled apart. I was forced to return my car park entry fob and security pass. I was on nodding terms with one of the guards, who pursed his lips when I looked directly at him, obviously aware that I had fucked up in some way, but uncertain as to the specific reasons. No doubt he'd figure 'money'.

Money is all that matters at a bank, right?

For some strange reason I suddenly felt very chilled as I drove out of the Dosh Dome for the final time. Perhaps it was relief that the whole ordeal was over, and that I might try to forget about Weir, the police, and Doug. At least they couldn't take the car from me as the Audi, however old, was mine. I picked up a sandwich at a local deli and found myself driving out of the city, heading east. Forty minutes later I stopped at the little car park close to Dirleton Beach in East Lothian—a place I'd visited with Mandy a couple of times in the past. I wandered past the kids' rustic playground and through the sand dunes that were partially covered by long grass, before planking my backside in the sand, viewing the Forth estuary and the Bass Rock to my immediate right. The Fife coast was clearly visible to the north, and a few ships meandered in the distance. One dog-walker had wandered off round the corner on the North Berwick side, so I sat alone in the salty air.

I gazed into the water.

The mesmeric tide drew back and forth, a platinum grey. A predictable, unrelenting force, out of my control. 'Go with the tide', an ancient expression advised. There are occasions to stand up and fight, though there are other times where we must accept defeat, those unwinnable battles against the tide. Ask Canute. Yet, what differentiates the two? How can some people end up as winners, taking all, using the ebb and flow of the tide in their favour against others? By rights, I should have driven straight to Cleveden Drive in Glasgow and murdered Doug. Weir was dead, so why not get rid of the other main prick in the story. I had chickened out of any form of confrontation with the bastard the night before as I had stupidly believed that we'd get the money, and repay the bank. What timing! Had I ascertained Doug's whereabouts a week earlier then we could have moved the money and saved my job, and reputation.

The sand seemed beautifully uniform, disturbed by a solitary small grey rock which protruded from the smoothness before me, echoing the bluntness of the Bass Rock out at sea. A single stone unturned.

I stretched a foot outwards, and knocked the rock over before smiling to myself. On the last occasion I'd visited this place with Mandy, I had been romantically content, and financially secure. Not rich, but very comfortable if a little bored. Yet it hadn't been enough for me. Greed had entered the equation, one of the human emotions that social scientists definitely cannot quantify. I had succumbed to deadly sins, been humiliated by my girlfriend, and lost my career. And I still had no guarantee that the police wouldn't return to haunt me later on if they found grounds for investigation. What a fucking mess.

The rock I had overturned must have been metamorphic, as its composition appeared quite different underneath. Normally I would leave no stone unturned, and maybe that's why I had kicked it over. Curiosity, frustration, whatever.

Latent anger?

Then I considered Mandy. *She* was actually the last stone unturned. Come to think of it, I had studiously avoided the thought, concentrating my efforts tracking Doug Mundel. Yet Mandy had been implicated. Laura had found the data stick in their flat: that was a fact. Where was she? Glasgow? Yet, somehow I'd felt that it hadn't been her last night. Had she helped Doug to empty the millions from that offshore account, or had she just disappeared? Perhaps she had returned to the Czech Republic. Or maybe I could find her too and let my temper take the initiative. Frustration burned within me. Who could I try? Laura?

Laura's number was still stored on my phone, so I dialled it and she picked up after a few seconds.

'Hi Laura. It's Ally Forbes. Mandy's ex.'

'Hello.' She sounded tired.

'I was wondering if you'd ever heard from Mandy?' A brief silence ensued; a momentary, yet discernible gap.

'Laura? Are you still there?'

'Yes. Sorry. What were you saying?'

'I asked if you'd ever heard from Mandy? You know, has she ever been in touch?'

'Mandy? Mmm. Things move on Ally. You're not still harbouring thoughts of getting back together?' Something in Laura's voice didn't ring entirely true.

'No, not at all, Laura. I still have a couple of items belonging to her, and I just wanted to return them. You're certain you haven't heard from her?'

'Would it matter? It's all history now, anyway.'

'Laura, are you being evasive with me?'

'Why would I do that?'

'I don't know. But you sound as if you know something. Have you seen her?'

'Look Ally, you'd be best to forget all about Mandy.'

'Why is that?'

'Look, I can't really speak right now.'

'Laura, I went through a hell of lot of trouble at the time we split up. I got fired this morning, for Christ's sake. Actually, you're the first person I have told. Mandy is, let's say, indirectly to blame for certain events. You gave me a data stick that implicated Mandy in something, so you're partly involved too.' I felt a little guilty about saying this, as Laura had actually helped me, but what the hell.

'I'm not involved in any of whatever you are talking about. And I don't wish to be. Now, if you don't mind—'

'Laura, *please*. Have you seen Mandy? What do you know?'

Again, a brief silence.

'Mandy is not what you might think, Ally. She may have made mistakes, but it's not what you think.'

'Really? Is she shacking up with a guy called Doug in Glasgow?'

'Definitely not.'

'Oh…right. So you *have* seen her.'

'I shouldn't be telling you anything.'

'Where is she?'

'She's still…in Scotland. Look, if I tell you where she is, you have to promise me that you don't shop her. She's been through enough.'

'Shop her? I've been through plenty too, Laura.'

'I think that she's been through a lot more than you.'

'Why? Where is she?'

She sighed. 'She's in a small apartment. In St Andrews. Hold on a moment.' I waited for half a minute or so. 'Tom Morris Drive. Number 16H. Though she'll probably tell you where to go if you show up.'

The next two calls were brief, but necessary. I got hold of Kostas right away. He'd already heard about my dismissal and the rumours were rife. No one knew the real reason but people had jumped to conclusions of theft. It was a bank, after all. I thanked him for all his assistance and said I'd get back in touch once I'd dealt with some business. The second call was to Elise. She hadn't heard as she'd been at a corporate event. She was sympathetic, yet realistic as she suggested that it could turn out to be a good thing. A fresh start. She even agreed to see me at the weekend. This perked me up as I felt I had the distinct brand of 'loser' forged across my forehead at this point.

The decision to pay a visit to St Andrews came easily, however. I had nothing constructive to do with my day, so why not do something destructive? If she wasn't there I might as well camp outside until she returned.

I took the city by-pass before veering north to cross the Forth. There were heavy queues leading onto the bridge, but eventually the traffic eased as I arrived in the Kingdom of Fife. Pleasant countryside with patchwork fields drifted past as I headed east towards Glenrothes, and Cupar, before arriving in St Andrews about two o'clock in the afternoon.

It had been a while since I'd been in the little university town. I'd played the Old Course a couple of times at corporate golfing events, though such experiences now suddenly felt as historical as the town itself. Golf had never really been my sport, just a corporate necessity in specific circumstances where you were expected to lose to the big cheeses anyway. I checked the satellite navigation system to locate Tom Morris Drive. The street was mixed residential and business, with a number of older flatted properties of blonde sandstone. I parked the Audi on the street a couple of hundred yards from number 16.

Controlled entry proved no barrier, as I tried a neighbour on the ground floor and explained that I needed to post an item through a neighbour's post box internally. The apartment was on the top floor.

Upstairs, the name *Brown* appeared on the solid wooden door. Brown? Was she flat-sharing or had she simply changed her identity? And did I know who she really was anyway?

I knocked, loudly.

Chapter 24

For a moment, there appeared to be no response. But then I heard the muffled noise of a door opening internally followed by footsteps on a wooden floor. There was no peephole, so who ever was inside wouldn't be able to tell who was outside. I knocked again.

'Who is it?' Mandy's distinct accent cut through the solid wood between us.

'I have something to deliver.' I spoke with a fake Fife brogue.

'Can you place it through the letter box?' she replied.

'It won't fit.'

The jingle of keys was followed by solid clunk as the door was edged open. Suddenly, Mandy recoiled back as our eyes met over the security chain partially securing the door. I instinctively wedged my left foot in the available space.

She held her hand firmly against the door, our eyes locked.

'*What are you doing here*?!' Her voice echoed in the hallway; a sharp, shocked, whisper.

'Let me in and I'll tell you.'

'I'll call the police!' She pushed the door hard against my shoe, but the door did not budge.

'No perhaps *I will*, Mandy. Or should I use your real name?' I used the bluff without thinking, and the pressure against my shoe subsided a little.

'So Laura must have blabbed. I can't talk to you,' she said bluntly. 'What do you want? You have no business being here.'

'Yes I do. I need an *explanation*. That's what I want. Then and only then I will leave.'

'Why should I believe you?'

'You have no option. If you don't let me in, I will shop you.'

There was a momentary hesitation and then the door slowly opened. She had changed her appearance. Blonde now, with a short bobbed style. Still striking, yet different.

I stepped inside. 'You look different,' I said, standing back.

'You don't.'

'Yeah, well there you go. A coffee would be nice.' Somehow, most of the latent anger I had felt at Dirleton beach suddenly dissipated.

The lounge was fairly chic, with modern fabrics in autumn colours coupled with some designer furniture. I sat on a leather armchair situated beside a large bay window, shaking my head. Mandy then returned with a mug of coffee. Black. She remembered of course.

'Nice pad. You've done okay. *Miss Brown*, is it now? Or *Mrs* Brown? Is the Mandy part even correct?'

'Mandy is who I am, who I became many years ago. My real surname does not matter.' She ran her fingers through the new blonde locks. 'You don't understand. I'm not sure what you *think* you know, but you do not really know anything about me, or my circumstances.'

'Well, funnily enough, that's why I'm here. Because you don't know about mine either. I lost my career this morning. *Fired*. I've also lost ten grand, *and* my reputation due to you and Doug Mundel.' I let the words hang, showing that I knew Doug's real identity.

She stood up, arms folded. 'You make an assumption. You may have been manipulated, but you're not the only one.'

'Really? My heart goes out for you. Why did you do it to me? Put me through all that shit? I actually really liked you.'

'None of it was my idea. I am not who you think I am.'

'You're right there. So who are you then?'

'I am a Chechen national.'

'Chechen? Russian? Not Czech?'

'I am *not Russian*. I am Chechen.'

'But you can obviously speak Czech…and no one doubted your *Czech* accent.'

'No shit, Sherlock. I spent some time in Prague.'

'So that's another thing you lied about.'

'I had no choice. As I said, you really don't understand.' As her words trailed off I held my hands up, awaiting an explanation. She sat down again, hands under her knees.

'Ally, you had an ideal childhood, growing up in a nice place, with loving parents. Have you any idea what it's like to grow up in a war zone? Your 13 year old brother murdered when you were 12 years old? Having no prospects? Some people need to forget their past and invent a new one.' She folded her arms as I stared at her—surely this wasn't more bluster?

'Is this the truth? You never told me any of this.'

'I couldn't tell *anyone*. And I swear that's the truth.' She looked directly at me. 'I'm sorry that you've been a victim, but it is minor compared to what some people go through. My entire life has been a mess, not of my making.'

'But it doesn't explain why you did to me what you did. I assume that you were sleeping with Doug Mundel the whole time that scam was going on.' I gazed into her eyes for signs of evasion.

'I never slept with him.'

'Really'

'Yes.'

'How come a data stick with the plan for my identification and manipulation was found in your flat, then?'

'So Laura found that data stick and gave it to you?'

'She did. Some time back.'

'I wondered where it had gone. Laura didn't know my real circumstances either, at that point. She obviously told you where I was, though. I contacted her to apologise recently. Ironically, that data stick was supposed to be my insurance. It was the only direct evidence I had on Doug. I took off in such a hurry that I left it behind.'

'So you are an unwitting accomplice too? You expect me to believe that?'

'Look, Ally. I did not set it up. Doug did. *He* targeted you. He is a manipulative bastard. He's done it before to others. He picks on vulnerable, naive people and uses their emotions against them. In my case fear, and in your case, greed.'

'Greed?'

'Yes. You could have turned him down. You made the decision yourself.'

'With your help.'

'That's a matter of opinion. But my main emotion was fear. Don't you understand? Have you ever seen Chechnya on the TV news? If I'd refused to help Doug, I would have been deported and possibly killed. Doug knows the Russian gangsters in London. He may be a white collar criminal, but he has connections. I couldn't take the chance because there was a carrot but also a stick. What he offered me when I met him in London was a fresh start. A fake passport. I got a little money to help set up on my own, and the promise of some more. I am no different to you in that respect. I believed that I could have a fresh start out of all this. But then the blackmail began. Threats of putting the Russian mafia on my back, reporting me to the immigration people.'

'So you never got the fifty thousand?'

'What do you think? I was much more worried about my safety, but no, I never got a penny. And I had come to understand that he was a nasty asshole who would probably shop me at any convenient time—and my family back home—so I took off.'

'And this Russian mafia lot?'

'These people are like wild animals. They take what they want, and have no respect for human life. When I met Doug in London, he'd done a dodgy deal with them. There was some kind of dispute over money—there always is with these types—and he never paid them. He can't show his face back there or he's in real trouble. That's part of the reason for his change of identity. If they found out where he was, he'd be killed.'

I considered this fact. Doug had over seven million, probably in cash, yet he might be in danger from hoodlums who didn't know his whereabouts?

'So what about us? That was some act you put on. At least from my perspective.'

Mandy averted her eyes. 'I am not a prostitute, if that's what you think. If I had been asked to go out with someone awful, I would have refused. I only did it on the basis that I could meet you first.'

'The first night we met was a set up to see if you could go through with it?'

'Yes.'

'Bloody hell. So you had no feelings for me whatsoever? Is that it?'

'Ally, I did like you or I wouldn't have gone through with it. I didn't know all the details of what he might do. But you *did* become a willing participant in a major scam against your employer. You have to remember that too. And once the whole thing was set up and I realised *my* mistake, if I'd admitted that our relationship had been based on lies how would you have reacted? Doug *forced* me to get involved. Even that apparently chance meeting I had with you and Doug in the White Hart bar? I was forced into that too, to stop you demanding money. To put you off the scent. I got nothing either for all that bullshit, just threats.'

She viewed me directly, and I could interpret no deception.

'I'm sorry about your brother,' I said. She smiled sadly in response. 'How did you end up here in St Andrews?'

'I couldn't go back to London. It seems odd, with London being such a large city, but I couldn't have relaxed there with the proximity to the people who Doug knew. There is no Russian mafia in St Andrews, thankfully. A contact I had through work owns this flat, and she's in Australia, so I offered to house sit for a small rent. Provided I am left alone, I can make a fresh start. I've done it before in harder circumstances. What about you?'

'I'm left with a feeling of total ineptitude…and uselessness…and most of all, powerlessness. Okay, there's relief. The police seem to have moved on in the case about Leslie Weir's death.'

Mandy slowly nodded. 'When I found out about that, it really frightened me. Maybe you can see why I reacted the way I did before that? I knew that you couldn't stand Weir and when you discovered that he was involved with the scheme, it became more difficult. I had only realised that he was involved after some time, not from the beginning. I still don't know how they split it all up.'

'Weir's whole "I want in" thing was just a ruse.'

'Doug said that if Weir hadn't threatened to blackmail you—and in a believable way that you would fall for—you would just have resigned. He said that would be the only way to stop you. They were just acting.'

'Yeah, that's what I figured. Insurance.'

'I'm afraid so. The whole idea had to look like it was your baby in case it imploded at some stage. Look Ally, I'm sorry. This is all shit. Trust me, I know because it was shit for me too.'

'But you were acting too.' I sighed.

'I wanted out. I couldn't play the game anymore, so I engineered our split. It looks deceitful, but because of my family I had little choice in my involvement—until it became too much. My family have now had to hide back home. Doug is a total fake, in every sense of the word. Fake statements, fake name, fake driver's licence, the lot. He owns nothing in his own name in case he's caught, and rents everything under fake names, even that Mercedes.'

'He even used my name for his fake office rental.'

'Did he? Weir and him were two of a kind, just liars,' Mandy said. I nodded as she continued. 'But there was someone else too. Someone else in the loop.' She looked at me, about to speak, before choosing not to do so.

'What?'

'It's probably nothing, but there was this woman, and I thought she was possibly involved. Sometimes you just have a hunch. He knew a bit about the bank, and he also fancied himself a lot as a ladies' guy.'

I let this sink in. I hadn't thought of such a possibility. Was Mandy just spinning a line? Could this be true? Doug did have contacts at the bank, and had turned up in person on more than one occasion. I only knew that he had met Weir, not anyone else.

'So who might that have been?'

'I don't know. But the one person who looked obvious was Weir's wife.'

'*Lucy Weir*?' The hair tingled on the back of my neck.

'She might have had a lot to gain by his death.'

'You know, I didn't think she'd be the type, but now you mention it, she did ask me a lot of questions about the police investigation. Shit.'

'I saw a woman driving off one time as I arrived to meet Doug the day when all this began. We were in a car park in the city centre but I didn't see her face. When I asked him who she was, he was awkward. Call it female intuition, but there was something more to it, more personal. I can tell you that she was driving a black SUV.'

I considered her words. So this was the same woman who had arrived the previous night at Doug's home. I decided not to mention my trip to Doug's new home in Glasgow.

'That's very interesting. I'd like to find out what car Lucy Weir drives. Maybe she has been with Doug, and Weir discovered the affair, and then the scam. It's certainly possible. But as someone with no career prospects, what I would really like to know is where all the money's gone.'

'It won't be in a bank account, I'll tell you that. Doug said to me more than once that he didn't trust banks.' We both smiled at the irony.

'So where would he put his money?'

'He never said directly. But I do remember him saying that people were safer putting their cash under the floorboards. Maybe he was joking or maybe he has a stash wherever he lives now. Who knows? I don't care. I never want to see the man again in my life. But it looks like you still want to get even.'

I stood up, nodding.

'I'm sorry this all happened, Ally.'

'So am I.'

'Perhaps if we had met under…different circumstances…we could have made a go of it.'

I considered the retrospective fatalism that this represented as I walked toward the door. I turned back to face her at the front door, and she looked up towards me and kissed me on the cheek.

'Here's my mobile number.' I took it. 'I might have the number for a short while, but then I might have to disappear again, maybe for good. Be careful,

Ally, whatever you decide to do. Doug is capable of nasty things. You'd probably be better letting it go and aiming for a fresh start yourself.'

Perhaps Mandy was right. In the words of Paul McCartney, maybe I should simply *let it be.* The traffic provided ample time to consider apparent options, and when I reached the city boundary, I headed for the south side. Curiosity led me to the Weir residence in Morningside. Lucy Weir might be in residence, or perhaps she'd left the country. Or was she now shacked up in Kelvinside in Glasgow? As I passed the house there it was: a black Toyota Land Cruiser sitting proudly in the garden.

I pulled into the side. Improbability relinquished ground to possibility as I recounted events. How did Weir acquire information about the scam? Weir and Doug had both denied involvement with one another; so there had to be an initial connection somewhere. Maybe Lucy Weir was lying low for a while before she and Doug took off together. Christ, she had no taste in men; first Leslie Weir, now Doug Mundel.

I considered entering the house and challenging her, just to see what she'd say. Maybe the money was hidden in here? Yet I figured that Doug would be the sort of person to trust nobody, principally as he was a thief himself and would assume all others were liars too. And what had Mandy said? Doug *didn't trust banks.* Obviously he had been forced to use the two offshore accounts for laundering purposes, and he'd made recent huge cash withdrawal. Mandy had even mentioned that he'd noted the term 'under the floorboards'.

Under the floorboards.

At Doug's house, there *had* been some kind of trapdoor close to the back porch door. I remembered that I'd tripped over the mat on the floor in my haste to exit the house, and my foot had caught on some kind of handle. Could he have a safe or something in there? I wished that I'd kept the key for Doug's back door when I'd been there, though a missing key would probably have led to greater suspicion and precipitated a change of locks. As it stood, Doug had probably not changed the locks. But the question was, might he actually have millions stashed under the floorboards?

There could easily be another hiding place in the house that I might not find, or the cash was simply somewhere else. There had to be another solution, so I headed home to think things through.

Having poured a generous measure of Glenlivet, I crashed on the sofa and almost instantly my phone buzzed. Kostas. He explained that the official line at the bank was that the new foundation set up just hadn't worked. There were opposing viewpoints on my demise, with some expressing sympathy and others delighted that I'd gotten what I deserved. What goes around?

One important point then struck me: as it stood the bank hadn't actually lost anything so far. So who were the losers? The only conclusion I could arrive at was that apart from Leslie Weir, the main loser was in fact me. Having been instrumental in setting up the new foundation to save the bank a packet, I'd been the fall guy. Doug was a millionaire winner, walking off with a cash prize at the expense of everyone else. It was also evident that Carole McLetchie had intervened in some way, protecting the bank's interests. Charles Henderson had told me that she'd brought forward her review, and acted in character by delving into the foundation's expenditure. Yet something here didn't ring true. As far as I could interpret things, she was complicit in the cover up even though she'd failed to mention any *specific* impropriety on my part when I'd been fired. It had all been vague. Threatening, but vague.

Three large drams later and the bitterness began to exude from my pores again. *Do something, Ally.* Alcohol can often impinge on a key decision making process, yet sometimes it can add clarity, or at least foster motivation and drive. As a mood enhancer, it suddenly galvanised my thoughts. Was I going to let Doug Mundel *off* with all this? The bastard could be sitting with millions in cash at his house, and I didn't have the courage to repatriate it? How *pathetic.*

I paced round the flat, and then it came to me. What does Doug fear? Not me. Not Mandy. Not even Scottish Chartered Bank. But Mandy had told me something important.

He feared a bunch of Russian thugs in London.

Of course, I had omitted to tell her that I knew where Doug was actually living, partly out of embarrassment at having failed to make anything of the break-in. But what if that changed? What if I were to tell Mandy that I knew *exactly* where Doug lived? And what if she were to inform the Russians where he lived?

But then I considered an altogether different move. I put down the glass of whisky and went to the large cupboard in the hallway. There was a cardboard box on the top shelf. I shuffled some old catalogues out of the way and found the box. I checked inside, and some of the contents were as I recalled: a black polo-neck, a balaclava and a fake handgun. I'd held a fancy dress party at the flat a couple of years before and one of the guys from the bank had come as a paramilitary figure; not a politically correct choice, but a memorable one. His girlfriend had turned up later on and insisted that he remove the outfit, and it had been left in my flat.

The type of shit that you don't throw out and for which you will never find a use.

I grinned, partly courtesy of the Glenlivet, but partly as I figured that I might just have a means of sending a bug right up Doug's arse. Why try to break into his home again to locate his safe hiding spot, when all I needed to do was let him access it himself? Let *him* remove the money, wherever it was hidden. And I knew of the very person who could make such a threat seem real: Mandy. He knew that *she* knew of this Russian grudge. That might be motivation enough.

I phoned her and explained that I would be calling again in about an hour and a half as I had to ensure that Doug was home before I acted. Mandy, slightly surprised by the call, and confused by the subterfuge, agreed to take another call from me when I said it would be worth her while.

A drunk-driving charge didn't cross my mind. I'd just been fired and knew where a shit load of money was possibly located—money that could not be reported to the police as stolen. I checked that I had Mandy's number, and also Doug's number, and I put on the only hooded top I possessed and threw the balaclava and fake handgun in the back seat of the Audi. Dusk had been replaced by a full moon, which did nothing to reduce my motivation as I headed to Glasgow.

Chapter 25

When I arrived in Kelvinside for the second time I found a space three streets away from Cleveden Drive on Kirklee Road, near the Botanic gardens. It was now after 11 o'clock at night, and the pavements were quiet for a Thursday night. The wind had increased, with the moon intermittently obscured by clouds.

'What's this all about, Ally? It's late.' Mandy's voice betrayed wariness down the line.

'I'm parked about a quarter of a mile from where Doug lives.' I spoke softly, awaiting her reaction.

'You've tracked him down? What, since this afternoon?'

I took a second to answer, before choosing to be candid. 'Mandy, I knew where Doug lived before I spoke to you today. I chose not to tell you, as once I had heard the truth about your relationship with him I feared that it would simply open another can of worms.' There was a brief silence.

'I'm not sure what to say. What's the point in phoning me to tell me this now? You want something from me, I take it?'

'Yes, I do. I want to scare the shit out of him, and maybe shake some money out of him too. I also happen to have his phone number.'

'You want *me* to call him, don't you?'

'Yes.'

'And what am I supposed to say? Am I to make a threat?' I could detect the scepticism in her voice.

'More subtle than that. I want you to *warn* him.'

'Warn him? What do you mean?'

'Tell him that you know where he lives.' I told her the address before continuing. 'Refuse to say how you know, but tell him that due to circumstances beyond your control, you've been speaking to certain Russian nationals in London within the past half hour. To get yourself off the hook, you've been forced to give him away. You didn't want to do it but you had no choice. They know *where* he is *and* his real name. You know how ruthless they are, so, despite what you think about him, you felt you had to warn him.'

'This is crazy, Ally. What do you expect him to do? Do you think he'd actually believe that?'

'It's about the balance of probability. If he's hiding a fortune in his house I would expect him to pack up and leave. You said that these guys are nutters. Would you hang around for a visit in the middle of the night or leave your loot unaccompanied? I'd be off in an instant somewhere safe.'

'So you're going to jump out and grab anything he has?'

'Something like that.'

'It's a real long shot, but maybe it's worth a try. It would be nice to get revenge, I must admit.'

'You said you were a victim too, and that you'd never really had a break. I've thought about it and I've forgiven you for…for *us*. The bank may need to be paid back, of course. I haven't thought it through yet. But I do know that if all the money that was in an off-shore account Doug had is at his home, it's a huge sum.'

'When you came by this afternoon you knew more than you let on.'

'That's true. Can you blame me for being cautious? I needed to meet you in person to know the truth. But now I see a way forward. There's nothing to lose.'

'Okay, I'll do it.'

'Thank you. I'm going to drive by to see if he's in. Give me a minute and I'll call back. If there's no one in, this will have to wait, but if he's there I want to strike right away.'

I took a left at the end of Kirklee Road, and drove towards Cleveden Drive.

One slow pass of Doug's home revealed his Mercedes in the garden and several lights on in the house. A strange sense of déjà vu crept over me. A brief return to another side lane three streets away enabled a return call to Mandy. I explained that she needed to find a phone unconnected to her—just in case—to avoid any direct connection with Doug. Mandy said that there was a public phone in a hotel near where she lived. She took a note of the address and the number and then we agreed the script. I was to await one further call confirming that she had made contact, so I drove to a position in the street where I could see Doug's house, and waited. About six or seven minutes later my phone buzzed.

'Well, that was a short conversation. He told me to fuck off, that he was scared of no one. We'll see about that…I'd get in there *quick*, as I don't think he's that brave. And Ally, *don't hang around*, promise me? Give it a go, but *make it quick*.'

I didn't really know exactly what she meant by the latter comment, so I took a deep breath and made my way towards Doug's home with the balaclava and fake gun stuffed in my jacket pocket. Tonight, I was on my own—no Kostas or Elise to offer decoys. I passed one dog walker at the end of the drive, and once he'd disappeared round the corner the coast was clear. A slight breeze stirred the bushes, partially masking my footsteps as I took the same position that Kostas had occupied the previous evening.

Then I heard the banging.

At first it sounded isolated, but then it became a series of loud thumps. Was he knocking down a wall? I made my way towards the house to peer in the dining room window, but the noise appeared to be coming from the other side of the property—from the back porch I'd escaped from the previous evening. I shuffled round the back towards the noise. Cautiously, I climbed onto a bench and peered in the back window of the kitchen through the gap between the blind and the window frame. I bit my bottom lip: Doug was hammering a large chisel into the floor in the back porch. What had appeared to be that same trapdoor must have jammed—or did he simply not have means of entry? My mind raced, riveted at the scene in front of me. Lucy Weir must definitely have been out of the house, for surely she would have been assisting? Suddenly, the banging ceased, and although my view was partially obscured by the door into the porch from the kitchen, I could see Doug opening a trapdoor before stepping below the floor.

Some further subterranean thumps followed, and then a sudden movement within the back porch. I cranked my head to squint inside.

My heartbeat leapt: four black attaché cases had been thrust into the doorway between the porch and the kitchen.

This was my chance. I grabbed the balaclava from my pocket, thrusting it over my head, and then firmly gripped the fake handgun in my right hand. I peered inside again, realising that Doug had moved out of the kitchen. The cases were there in plain view. If I could only break the back porch window, they'd be within reach. Crouching, I made my way round towards back porch door.

I tried the handle: locked.

Then for a few seconds I looked around for a loose rock that might be big enough to smash the glass. I leant over to a rose bed adjacent to the porch, momentarily noticing a sharp sound directly behind me.

Then, a split second later, I blacked out.

I had no idea how long I had been unconscious. The searing pain enveloped my entire head and neck. I could barely move because I was crushed in some sort of small, enclosed space. There was only darkness. I could taste blood, and one nostril was blocked. My thigh felt numb. Where the hell was I? Although one ear was squashed against something cold and metallic, I could vaguely hear ambient sounds from outside somewhere. What did that mean? I struggled to move my arms, though I could feel something warmer with my fingers, fabric of some kind. I rubbed the material and detected a plastic odour. It smelled like the interior of a car. Shit, I was lodged in the boot of a car.

I inhaled and exhaled strongly, beginning to panic.

Don't panic, Ally.

I remembered having been locked in a car boot years before, the victim of a prank by fellow students, and though I'd only been there for fifteen minutes the claustrophobic pressure had led to panic and a dislocated shoulder.

As I tried to move my head again I felt the cold metallic thing again, and as it moved against my cheek I could smell mud. A spade? Shit, is this what he hit me with. Why was it the boot?

I thrust my body against the back seat of the car, but nothing would budge. What should I do? Scream for help? Who exactly would hear me? Doug? Why had he put me in a car boot and how long had I been there? Shit, my head hurt. I struggled to move my arm to see if I could activate the light on my wristwatch. However, the movement proved impossible in the constrained space. I pushed the watch against the floor of the boot, and pushed my head downwards. The light had indeed activated, but I couldn't see the time. I cranked my head again and just caught something. What was that? 23.40? That meant I'd probably only been in the car for about half an hour. I tried to shuffle again, but found no means of unlocking myself.

I suddenly gulped. What if Doug had taken off but left me here? He could be on his way to an airport or down the M74 to England and no one would have a bloody clue where I was. *Fuck.* My mind raced, fearing the horrible possibility of a slow, agonising death.

Then I heard footsteps on gravel. A phone rang, and one voice answered: Doug. The pain made it difficult to hear properly, as there were concurrent footsteps and muffled noises, but something filtered in. Was the car still parked in his driveway? There were gaps in the conversation on the phone. What was that he was saying? Something about money.

Then I heard the word 'dead'. Who? Me? I struggled to follow the conversation, but then the he must have moved closer, and the content became clearer.

'I'm saying absolutely nothing on the phone…no…when I see you…I've a couple of things to sort out…yes…I've got the…you know what…this place isn't secure anymore… the ticket…it's nearly twelve…half an hour tops at this time of night…no. I'll take this…*thing*…somewhere it won't be found. I've something to get rid of on route to yours. I just need to get my passport.' Then more footsteps followed, moving away from the car.

Shit.

He must have thought I was already dead, and was going to dispose of me on the way to Lucy Weir's home. But he was keeping any talk of my identity quiet on the phone. The pain felt horrible, but I was, actually, *alive*. Doug must have thumped me so strongly and with such instant results, that he had believed me dead.

And if he figured that I was already dead meat, then perhaps I had the element of surprise when he finally opened the boot. *If* he opened the boot. And *if* I could actually move after being crushed in this position. I pushed with all my strength against the back seat once again, hoping for some kind of leverage, but there was little to no movement. Assuming I was in Doug's Mercedes, I couldn't see there being loose seats. Solid, German engineering—when you wanted it least.

Then something odd happened.

The low reverberation of the engine of another vehicle became evident from a distance. It sounded like an SUV of some kind, powerful. It approached slowly, and I expected it to disappear along the street. Yet, as it came closer, it turned. The vehicle crunched its way stealthily towards the car, the engine coughing to a stop in the garden. Someone *else* had arrived. My first guess was that Lucy Weir had arrived, on cue. But then two doors opened, almost silently in quick succession, and then closed quietly, followed by whispered voices in foreign accents. What sounded like two sets of footsteps then followed, moving away from the car.

I heard faintly what appeared to be the sound of breaking glass, albeit muffled—as if someone had dampened the sound deliberately. There followed a series of thumps, and then for a moment, silence. I waited, my head throbbing. Then, suddenly, the front door of the house slammed and this was followed by rapid steps on the gravel as someone ran towards the car. A door was thrust open and then I heard shouts from the house before the engine fired up.

Doug was in the car. I heard him shout '*bastard, bastard!*' before the car swerved out of the garden, spinning violently as it cornered out on to the street. I was thrust against the door of the boot, my head thumping off the interior of the lock. I gasped under my breath, desperate to avoid being detected alive. The car accelerated wildly.

'Change…*change fucking lights change!*' Doug cursed, then shouted 'Ah, fuck it!' before accelerating again, the forward momentum forcing my body against the back door again. I tried to gain purchase against the side of the boot, but there was nothing to grab on to. Two horns howled in quick succession as the Mercedes twisted and turned through the streets, braking violently one moment, before thrusting forward the next. I was thrown from side to side, the raw guts of the engine mirroring Doug's angry dialogue. He swore repeatedly at those clearly in pursuit.

Then we hit a straight piece of road, presumably dual carriageway or motorway, and the car really took off. It must have been after midnight at this point, with limited traffic probably facilitating the speed of the car. God knows what speed Doug reached, as the forward momentum and engine pitch reached a crescendo. Doug was clearly weaving in and out of lanes at high speed, with every turn leaving me cold and scared. For some time, we went at excessive speed, before he hit the brakes fiercely once again, shoving me forward.

'Fucking cones!' Doug shouted. '*Fucking road works*! Get off my fucking tail you commie bastards.'

My heart was racing at this point. Commies? *Russians*?

Mandy must have called them after all. No wonder she said not to hang around. It was a coded warning, but she could have been more explicit—she owed me that much. Maybe she'd changed her mind after speaking to me. And where did they come from? Not London, certainly. These guys must have been somewhere close. Maybe the guys in London had ordered a direct hit on Doug.

Shit, if they opened fire on the car I'd get blown away in the boot.

Suddenly, there was a sequence of thumps as the car swerved ferociously to stay on the road. Another horn sounded, accompanied by an elongated howl which came startlingly close.

'Get out of the fucking way!' Doug screamed, before the he jammed on the anchors, skidding in the process. Then he thrust the car into reverse, before desperately speeding forwards over some kind of obstacle. The car must have jumped a pavement or such like, as I thumped my head on the ceiling of the boot, desperately gritting my teeth to muffle the sound of my response. More horns sounded as we changed direction. Then the road suddenly became rougher, a track of some kind, with bumps and potholes throwing me from left to right as the car raced along the uneven surface.

A sudden change of pitch in the engine revealed another vehicle accelerating behind us: Doug had not lost the tail.

Then, there was a sudden explosion; and the instantaneous sound of glass shattering. A *gunshot?* We swerved violently once again, as the vehicle behind touched the bumper of the car, thrusting me against the metal surface again, bashing my cheek. I could feel the blood run down my face. The car boot lock had become partly dislodged, and the door juddered forcefully; the cold exterior air filling the cavity and the courtesy light suddenly engaging.

Then, strangely the car appeared to decelerate.

What followed next lasted for only two or three seconds. It's the type of thing that we experience in dreams: the feeling of flying, yet different and difficult to define. The Mercedes had literally taken off. But we were not flying at all.

We were falling.

For a brief moment time seemed to freeze. Then, impact.

The intense resonance of the car landing penetrated my entire body; an initial, deafening thump followed by a more muted, fluid surge. *Water.* A hot pain seared though my head and neck contrasting with freezing water that gushed into the car boot through the partially opened boot lock. I tried to reduce the flow of water by closing the door, but the flow continued unabated.

Fuck, we were sinking.

I thumped the boot. *'Doug? Doug! For God's sake, let me out. Please…please.'*

There was no response. Was he dead? Only the overwhelming pain of the freezing water enveloping my body rivalled the mental panic I felt. Desperately, I grabbed at the partly open boot door. The courtesy light was still operating, allowing me to see a little. I thrust my body against the door with all the force my being could muster, but it wouldn't budge. Within seconds, the water was now almost two thirds of the way up the available space. I tried again, holding my breath to dive below the surface in order to get closer to the lock. If I could only get my hand in, I might be able to find the catch.

There was no leverage.

The last few inches of airspace were disappearing before my eyes. Then the interior courtesy light went out as the water level rose, and I could see nothing, but feel everything. The ache, the cold, the dark, and the hell.

I gulped a full breath of air—the fullest breath I could possibly take in—as the water filled the available space.

Then, bizarrely, under the water, the interior light came on again in unison with the rear lights, the dregs of electricity somehow managing to illuminate the dark. I opened my eyes, and right before me at the side of the boot was a slight opening, where the metal had been twisted by contact with the other vehicle. My hand reached out and pushed, and my knee thrust forward.

I squeezed my left hand through the aperture, forcing my forearm outwards, up to my elbow. The pain in my head was now intense, but I desperately held my breath knowing that the second I exhaled, my lungs would explode. Frantically, I managed to jam my arm upwards to the rear of the car, grasping towards the exterior of the lock.

I felt the catch with my frozen middle finger, and pushed.

Nothing.

I pushed again, and this time I felt some kind of movement. Then, I felt something sharp against my calf: the spade which had been lodged in the boot behind me. It must have been loosened in the crash. I thrust upwards with my knees, pushing the blade towards the gap with all my remaining strength, and suddenly the car boot jerked in a spasm, releasing me outwards.

My body caught part of the electro-hydraulic mechanism, which must have opened the soft top of the car. Hundreds of air bubbles burst out of the Mercedes, partly illuminated by the interior lights of the car as they cascaded up through the water.

As I twisted my foot frenziedly to release it, something gripped my lower calf, forcing me downwards. I kicked out again, trying to force my leg upwards through the water. Then the grip became tighter and I bent my knees, I realised that I was being drowned by Doug. The remaining light revealed that he was trapped in the car's soft top mechanism, madly trying to use me to leverage himself out.

But he had made a fatal error, using only one arm to grab me. The other arm held an attaché case. As the lights from the interior of the car again faded, I witnessed the anguish on his face as his grip loosened, and he released the case, and me. My final view of Doug Mundel depicted the fear and desperation in his eyes being replaced by something else: the sudden, placid release of death.

As I kicked free, for about seven or eight seconds my body arched upwards, until I could retain my breath no longer. My lips began to part, air being released slowly, before the unavoidable onslaught from my lungs. The air was replaced by freezing water, an intense pain burning through my throat, neck and eyes.

And then there was light.

Is this death? I reached outwards toward the light, but there was no powerful, benign force beckoning me to another dimension. Rather, I experienced a horrible, searing pain as I emerged above the surface, gasping horribly as water was expelled powerfully through my nose and mouth. My arms and legs floundered madly as I realised that I'd broken to the surface and the bright light had been gifted by the moon.

Then I retched, desperate for life, coughing up a mixture of water and air.

As suddenly as the moon's reflected light had appeared, it disappeared, the breeze rapidly moving clouds in its path. I could barely see anything as I splashed about, and I scarcely had the strength to remain afloat. Then my arms hit something floating on the surface: attaché cases, clipped together. I grasped for a handle to obtain some buoyancy before draping my arms over the cases.

Where was this place? Certainly, I was located in freezing, fresh water, not the sea. Was this an inland loch of some sort? The water was a little choppy, but I desperately paddled with the wind, hoping to reach ground somewhere before hypothermia set in.

I could vaguely make out dark shapes on one side due to the intermittent light, so I paddled towards these dark shapes, the pain in my neck stinging strongly as I moved my arms outwards.

As I got closer to the edge, I realised that the dark shapes were rocks. Indeed, what looked like cliffs towered over the water. Suddenly, things became more lucid. It appeared as if the Mercedes had crashed into an old, flooded quarry. Exhausted, I felt my feet hit something solid underneath, my numb legs barely able to move, but waves of relief were infiltrating my body. I grasped the rock before me, gasping for breath.

Then I heard voices from above. Foreign accents. *Russian accents.* Shit, they were here. I lay motionless—partly though exhaustion, yet more through fear—and I clung to a rock that was partly submerged, attempting to remain as silent as was feasible. Another huge rock obscured the voices as they approached. I could smell cigarette smoke, and the voices moved closer, downwards. Then, light from a torch beam drifted out across the water, sweeping from side to side. There was no doubt that they would kill me if I were spotted, irrespective if I were Doug, or Ally Forbes. Yet, as the light swept over my head, I detected a calm element in the voices—complacency, almost—that transcended the lingo. If they had stopped for a cigarette, then they must have believed the job to be complete.

I waited, for what seemed like an eternity, until the voices had subsided, and the sound of a four by four vehicle struck up in the distance. Frozen and battered, I pulled myself out of the chilly water onto a rough track at the side of the quarry, the wispy clouds once again drifting away to reveal the full moon. The erstwhile disappearance of the moon and the simultaneous reappearance of the attaché cases on the surface of the water had probably saved my life.

An arduous hour's walk found me on the outskirts of Broxburn in West Lothian. Doug had driven further east than I thought. Despite the weight, never once did I let my grip loosen on those four, large cases. Exhausted, I pulled up the hooded top to obscure the bruising on my face and followed the street lights onto the main drag, before flagging down a local taxi that passed. The driver grunted that he wasn't supposed to pick up on the street, and he wanted evidence of the fare, so I pulled out some wet, crumpled bank notes in my pocket, and twenty minutes later I found myself home in my flat in Stockbridge.

Despite my exhaustion and pain, a further brutal twenty minutes with an old hacksaw on the first case witnessed the appearance of more money than I had ever seen in my life.

Sheer excitement accelerated the destruction of the locks on the other three cases. Bricks of compressed bank notes were present, including high denomination Singapore bank notes. These were *$10,000* notes. A quick check online search revealed that each note was currently worth a staggering four and a half thousand in pounds, and they were among the highest denomination notes available anywhere in the world.

A synthesis of awe and fear gripped me, as I fumbled the notes, attempting to make a rough calculation. Notwithstanding the possibility that a very well prepared Doug may have siphoned off some of what he'd withdrawn, it appeared that after applying a conservative exchange rate, there was still over seven million pounds in sterling on my lounge floor.

Faced with such a mesmerising bundle of wealth, one central question replaced all other thoughts: should I simply keep the lot?

Chapter 26

'What *on earth* happened to you?' Elise asked, frowning deeply as she gave me an extremely cautious hug. Her concern reflected not only the facial bruising and cuts, but also the neck brace that I had acquired from a morning trip to Accident and Emergency.

'Cut myself shaving.'

'This Scottish male bravado thing is *pathetic*. Tell me what happened.' She folded her arms and sat back in an arm chair in my lounge.

I assured her that I would give a full of explanation once Kostas arrived. I'd insisted that they both came to Stockbridge after work had finished. Elise reluctantly agreed to wait for Kostas, and made some coffee, which allowed me to reflect on events, and numbers. Strong pain killers and half a night's sleep had produced barely enough energy to make a precise count by early afternoon. The shock of the car chase and Doug's death had then been mirrored by fear of harbouring so much cash in my flat.

What puzzled me was whether Mandy had told the Russians about the possibility of the money being in Doug's home. A minor doubt had entered my mind when I'd surfaced in the morning. Clearly, Mandy had alerted the Russians, but her tacit warning to me made it ambiguous whether these thugs had been there to repatriate the money, or simply to snuff Doug out as a professional hit. My concern was very real. If Mandy had been involved, these guys might turn up at my flat, especially if they had returned to Doug's home to ransack the place. Mandy had appeared truthful though, in as much as any truth was genuinely likely from any of the participants in this whole farce. Perhaps she'd simply been hell-bent on revenge. Then again, these thugs had driven *away* from the quarry, so they'd almost certainly been unaware of the contents of the sunken Mercedes. And as for Doug, he'd not only tried to kill me in his back garden with a spade, he'd almost drowned me in the freezing water. So fuck him.

Kostas arrived, and before I could speak, Elise piped up that whatever I was going to discuss was just smoke and mirrors, and that they'd been invited for a murder mystery evening.

'What the hell happened to your face?' Kostas asked, but I placed a finger vertically on my lips, and he shrugged. They both sat down, and I brought out the 'sawn-off' cases, telling them to take a deep breath.

Then I displayed the contents.

'*Wow!'* Elise spoke first, fingering the money. 'They're dinky! This has been worth the wait. You know, Ally, I've *always* liked you.' She grinned and put an arm round my shoulder. I looked at Kostas, who was shaking his head, but then he whistled softly.

'You went back, didn't you? To his house?'

'Yip.'

'How much?'

'Over seven million worth...give or take any errors by someone who has been whacked on the head with a spade, left for dead in a car boot, chased at speed by Russian gangsters, and then nearly drowned.'

'*Jesus*,' Kostas said.

Elise just stared at the cash, before examining some of the Singapore high value notes.

Then I relayed the rest of the story. Finding Mandy shored up in St Andrews, her explanation of how Doug had also conned her with the aid of Lucy Weir, my belated drunken indignation, the episode at Doug's home and the horror of the crash and escape from the quarry near Broxburn. They both remained transfixed as I spoke.

When I concluded, Kostas spoke first. 'You are one *lucky bastard*. Are you sure that Doug didn't actually tell Lucy Weir who he had in the boot?'

'That's a good point,' Elise noted. 'I mean, if she had any inkling about this, and you then showed up in public anywhere, then she's going to *know*.'

I rubbed my face, the pain starting to increase again. 'I can't say for definite, but I don't think so. Doug appeared to be talking in code on the phone, hinting that someone was dead, as that's what he believed. Surely Lucy Weir's not connected to the Russian mafia too? I'm going to have to take the chance that if Doug or his car is *never* found, then Lucy Weir must assume he took off without her. If his body surfaces, though, which it might, then it still doesn't suggest that *I* have any money.'

'You'll need to get your car back. You can't leave it parked near a dead man's house,' Kostas warned.

'I'll get it, don't worry.'

'What about his body—it will resurface.'

'Not a nice thought, Elise, but the answer is that I don't know. He was using all kinds of aliases, it seems, so how would they know who he was? Unless he had a criminal record, of which I found no trace when I was looking, then it would be hard to identify him. He certainly made sure he was distanced from the bank, so he should be distanced from me.'

'What about Mandy, then?' she inquired. 'You might have died because of these Russians.' She folded her arms. 'Are you actually defending her after all she's done?'

'No. But she did give me a hint to get out of the house quickly, and no thugs have turned up here today, have they?' My words trailed off unconvincingly.

'But that might be because they think you're already dead,' Elise said.

'Let's change the subject, Elise. I don't feel that I'm at risk this instant. Honestly. I'm feeling like shit, but then we're *seven million* up.'

'We? So what's the plan?' Elise smiled.

'Plan!' Kostas grunted, grabbing bank notes from the cases and throwing them up in the air. 'If you want my help…*again*…you…can…have…it!' For the first time, he smiled.

It turned out to be a long evening. The principle of justice for charity, however, was maintained, and we agreed that, *if feasible*, the sums paid by the bank to Kid World Funds should be returned to the bank to distribute to worthy causes through the foundation. I had never intended to be a cheat at the level that Doug and the Weirs had created. I might have become a crook, but I wasn't Ronnie Biggs. And with the police now off my case about Leslie Weir, why be left looking over my shoulder for the rest of my life on a theft charge?

However, the obvious elephant in the room was how to convert the cash into an electronic payment that was untraceable to me. The foundation, technically, was owed over six million. Although Carole McLetchie had alluded to knowing about the Kid World Funds issue, she had not actually mentioned it directly. A smart, partially non-committal move on her part, yet enough to see me summarily dismissed. But in this case, the repayment of the money and a legal disclaimer against future claims would likely be received favourably. Globally, banks were extremely careful with their money these days and feared bad debt; so any unexpected repatriation of funds—even those marked for disbursement to others—would surely be a welcome boost.

My plan was to visit the Isle of Man personally and deposit the money in Doug's account—as if I were actually Doug. I knew that such a deposit would incur tax because the domestic authorities and the Manx government had agreed terms, but that wasn't the biggest obstacle. To prevent money laundering there were declaration forms for carrying cash overseas, which would open a can of worms for me if I was honest and filled them in. I also couldn't risk a search if I ignored the forms—how would I explain the money? I paced my flat, remembering that my uncle had told me how he'd once bribed a customs official when they had a bigger presence off the Scottish west coast. Elise was worried about this, but I insisted on phoning my uncle to surreptitiously pick his brains. It turned out that he knew a man who knew a man, so I wrote down a few details. I made a call and was given another name and a codeword, and we agreed the port of exit and ferry crossing.

The deal I struck with Kostas was that the instant I deposited the money in the Isle of Man, he would move it electronically to the nominated account that Elise's ex-husband had set up in Antigua. He'd figured a clever method of doing this after the first evening at Doug's house. Then, a loop could be created and the funds could be sent in an unconnected manner to Scottish Chartered. The payment would be accompanied by a legal disclaimer produced by an Antiguan lawyer hired to write the necessary legalese in the Caribbean.

Whoever else Doug had stolen from was anyone's guess, but I certainly wasn't going to pry further into his affairs for fear of opening a can of Russian worms. I did make a mental note to send something to Jennifer Sloan, the director of Gold Star whom Doug had cleaned out—without her help I wouldn't have been able to track his real identity. Elise and Kostas left after midnight, again sworn to secrecy.

The next morning, after taking painkillers I made a call to the customs name I'd been given and after providing the codeword I subtly agreed a sum and a time. Here I was, paying money back, yet I smiled to myself at how quickly the next guy just wanted to make a buck. I provisionally booked the ferry to the Isle of Man two days hence. The easiest crossing was from Heysham to Douglas, which I'd agreed with my contact. Heysham is a small ferry port in Lancashire, and I'd be able to drive there in around four hours then take the ferry. The medic at the hospital had advised against driving for at least a week, but I was anxious to complete the mission.

The next job was a little more awkward. I waited until lunchtime and called Elise's ex-husband. He might have been getting a bit pissed off with me by now, but I explained that I needed the electronic links to be untraceable back to the Isle of Man account. He sighed, and said that this was possible, and that he'd call back to agree details with me. I explained that the account was to be closed after the payment was made.

One light lunch later I then called Charles Henderson. He said he'd heard about my departure during a brief conversation with Carole McLetchie, and had been going to call me. He asked about my move. I hesitated before replying, but then he asked the pertinent question.

'Kid World Funds, per chance?'

'Charles, I can categorically assure you that I was *not* involved personally with Kid World Funds. However, as Leslie Weir attempted to implicate me, and I ended up ruining my career over the thing, I want to put matters right.'

'Fair enough. The fact that you were so closely identified with the project made no sense. Anyone involved would have tried to distance themselves. But that leaves us another question: who was the other conduit?'

I hesitated again, unsure of where he was going, yet also not wishing to talk about Doug, for obvious reasons. 'Charles, as I explained before, Leslie Weir seems to have been the protagonist.'

'But I don't think he was alone, Ally, do you?'

'Well…' Should I mention Lucy Weir? Oh, what the hell. 'Charles, look, I don't think that there's any point pursuing this at this stage, but I strongly suspect that his wife was involved.'

'What, Lucy Weir a crook?'

'It's not as ridiculous as you might think,' I said flatly.

'I don't think so, Ally. I met her at social occasions at the bank, and the Weirs seemed totally mismatched, but there are other reasons you're wrong.'

'What reasons?'

'Well, unlike Leslie, she seems to have had principles. She's joined a convent. Become a nun.'

I swallowed. 'What? When did this happen?'

'Last week. I was told at the bank that she apparently left her house, car, and everything else in the hands of her lawyer and headed south.' There was a brief gap as I processed this surprise. 'She decided to join a convent somewhere down there. One of these orders where they shut themselves away.'

'An excuse to hide?'

'Actually, no. The board wanted information on an unrelated matter involving Leslie, but her lawyer contacted us first. Apparently she was at the convent right enough. She decided to change her whole view of life after her husband's death.'

Suddenly I felt very guilty. Who the hell had been in the black SUV? Surely not Mandy? Was that possible? Had she duped me *again*? Had *she* been the person Doug had talked to on the phone?

'Now, do you recall our last conversation, Ally? You said you would try to locate a certain iPad? Well, assuming that you have some information, I'll trade you what you have for what I have? Maybe we can gain a mutually beneficial result.'

It was the time for blind trust, not negotiation. 'Charles, I have put my feelers out on the iPad front, and I have now located it. Don't ask how. Possession has not come easily, and you have my word that I have not accessed anything on it. I will send it to you regardless of what you tell me.'

'Good answer, Ally. And I will take your word. Now, I want you to consider something else. Who was most opposed to the re-organisation of the foundation?'

'Eh, that would be you, Charles.'

'Apart from me.'

'Let me think. It would have to be, um, Carole McLetchie.'

'Exactly.'

'What are you saying here?'

'I'll be specific. The very best way to self-protect is to distance yourself from possible disaster. She *officially* opposed the plan, but I think she did it because she *knew* it was going through anyway. She was probably the only person who could have smoothed through the changes to the whole foundation as she was the *Director of Compliance*. Think about it. Weir could only have really pushed this through with her help. She publically complained and made virtuous noises, asked questions, but she could have vetoed it if she'd wanted.'

This threw me. 'You think that this was a set up involving Carole McLetchie?' In league with Weir…and *Doug*.

The deceased.

'Are you still there, Ally?'

'Yes, I'm just…thinking.'

'You sound different. The thing is, young man, she said something to me that she shouldn't have. A mistake. Something she *could only have known* if she'd had inside information. I told her a week or so ago, as a bluff, that the splash on Kid World Funds you'd done was excellent. That this was exactly the sort of thing we should be highlighting. She replied that there might be more coverage of Kid World Funds coming out, proof of all the good work.'

'Right, but maybe she was just protecting the bank? I'm certainly not defending her—she just fired me—but this might just be PR manipulation on her side.'

'Ally, there's more. I managed to look at some of the Kid World Funds material. One of the IT guys at the bank accessed a whole lot of stuff that had been put on file by Leslie Weir. I couldn't believe it, but Carole's actually in a photo *herself*, involving some Kid World Funds project that apparently took place last year. You and I know that didn't happen. *There were no projects.* Leslie Weir had some kind of insurance on that woman, or they must have been connected and set out some fake PR stuff in advance, but changed their plan. The picture has not been faked by the way. I've had that checked.'

'Jesus...this is a shock.' Then I suddenly thought of something. 'She drives an MG, doesn't she?'

'Why do you ask?'

'It doesn't matter. She's got a bright red MG, right?'

'That was her last car. Apparently she had a bump. Now she drives a gas guzzler. Five-litre Range Rover. Black as the night.'

'Mmm.' I took this in before he continued.

'I'm taking her down, Ally. There's no way she's remaining at the bank. There's a board meeting coming up, and I want her gone by then. There are loose ends here, but with the permission of the board and the CEO I want to take executive control of the foundation until this thing is sorted out. Regain the moral high ground, with the aid of David Moritano. The only blemish is the funds that have been lost. If we could only...recover the money donated to Kid World Funds...it would make a huge difference.' His words conveyed an implicit expectation.

'It would be wonderful if that could happen,' I replied. 'If it did...it would be in the bank's interest to be *discreet*, wouldn't it? I mean, if *you* were overseeing the compliance issues? You'd find a way, if funds were repatriated, to smooth governance...and not wash dirty linen in public? Or chase *ghosts*?' I let my words trail off.

'I couldn't have put it better myself. And as soon as we have the money back, I want you and me to meet with *Ms* McLetchie.'

The tangy brine filled my nostrils as the ferry swept across the Irish Sea on my return to Heysham from the Manx capital. The forty-eight hour wait before the trip had witnessed a minor improvement in my health and facilitated some financial housekeeping prior to my drive south for the outward ferry journey. I'd been tempted to buy a new Ferrari in cash just for the hell of it, but common sense had converted my greed into a trip on the train to Glasgow to repatriate the Audi. The customs guy I'd arranged things with had barely given me a nod on the way over. The whole journey had proved positive, with apprehension about the huge cash deposit being replaced with relief at the smooth nature of the eventual task.

Clearly, money talks. But then I knew that, didn't I?

Having cleared the feasibility of the deposit into the account by phone, and by using the access codes that Kostas had helped attain on the first aborted visit to Doug's home, I simply faked Doug's signature—of which we also had a copy—to make the deposit. Because Doug had made his initial deposit electronically, that was enough. The bank in question was very used to such transactions. After all, they had paid a huge same sum *out* of the same account in largely the same large denominations very recently. I had arranged for a sum of four hundred thousand to remain in the account for future domestic or Manx tax liability, with a note in a sealed envelope to be retained by the bank should any enquiry arise. There were of course losses in conversion of high value foreign banknotes, but that had been expected and the bank simply pocketed the exchange differential. Perhaps out of superstition, I had adorned a short curly wig, and non-prescription glasses—purchased in a shop in Edinburgh—just in case one of the members of the bank staff had some sort of photographic recall of Doug from his recent visit, but the transaction appeared totally routine. After final currency conversion, fees, and some other promises, I figured that I would be left with a few thousand for myself and a couple of worthy helpers—ironically, not much more than I had 'invested' with Doug in the first instance.

On arrival back at Heysham, my phone buzzed. Elise.

'The albatross has landed,' she said, with a more than a hint of excitement. 'Thank you *so* much. Owe you big style.'

'I'll keep you to that.'

'See you soon.'

The 'Albatross' had been the code for the completion of the payment to Scottish Chartered via the complex electronic route set up by Elise's ex. Kostas had transferred the whole residual sum electronically, including an agreed fee for Alan, as soon as I had deposited the cash. I smiled without humour, gazing into the platinum sea off the coast. This should surely secure my safety, at last.

I called Charles Henderson to give him the news, and set up the last part of the plan. I'd already delivered the iPad to his home before I'd left for the Isle of Man, again in semi disguise, giving it to his wife in person, boxed up and marked 'confidential'. When I arrived home in Edinburgh after a tiring journey, I enjoyed one of my deepest night's rest in months.

On the second visit to Charles Henderson's club I was shown to a private meeting room on the third floor. When I opened the door, Charles was already present.

With Carole McLetchie.

'What's he doing here?' she barked, eyes darting back to Charles.

'I think you know the answer to that question,' he replied bluntly. 'But let's not flirt with semantics. *We* know, and you know we know, so we should begin on that premise.'

'I don't know what he's told you, but *he* knows nothing. I didn't agree to a meeting with a fraudster. I've a good mind to leave right now—'

'It's not in your interest to leave right now.' This time his tone was stern: it was amusing to see a Rottweiler bitch being tackled by a Bulldog. 'And I think we should lose the tag of fraudster all round, don't you think?'

The brief silence that ensued was interesting and we witnessed Carole McLetchie's mental gymnastics as she prepared her next line in the absence of all the facts.

'Get on with whatever you have to say, then.'

I broke the silence. 'The Kid World Funds are back with the bank. Sorted.' Her eyes leapt upwards this time as she absorbed this news. I could see her trying to figure how the hell this could have happened. Doug had disappeared with the money out of the blue, after all. Then she glared at me.

'What has this to do with me?'

Charles produced the photo. 'Oh, quite a lot. We know this picture's not doctored.' As she took in the scene of her smiling with a bunch of youthful African faces in a Kids World Funds leaflet, her mouth dropped.

I spoke next. 'No idea that photo was taken then, Carole? Or more significantly, that it was used in the Kid World Funds PR? I guess it was kept as insurance as *someone* we knew didn't trust you, eh?' I inquired. 'I know how that feels, *Carole*. When was the photo taken? Were you on holiday with Leslie, or was it…someone else?'

Charles glanced at me, wondering who else, but Carole simply stared.

'Do you mind if I have a minute with Carole alone, Charles?

He looked surprised, but shrugged. 'Be my guest.'

When he closed the door I sat in front of her. 'You couldn't wait to nobble me with that shit about the cops, but we both know that was bluster. So fuck you. Now you know how it feels to get screwed over. But I can also tell you something else. About Doug Mundel and Leslie Weir. It's taken me a while to figure it out, but I think you were having an affair with *both of them*.'

She looked away for a few seconds, a touch of vulnerability appearing for the first time. She then slowly swallowed, almost involuntarily. In that instant I knew I'd guessed right, eventually. And of course, she couldn't know for definite about Doug's demise. Her face then hardened once more.

Just as I was about to speak, I fleetingly considered an image of Doug kicking and clawing at me underwater, and wondered when he might surface. Elise had made that point. But then, he had no direct connection to me or the bank—*he'd* ensured that.

'Doug took off, Carole, as you know.' I stared directly at her to conceal my lies. 'And when I reasoned with him and convinced him to repatriate the money, he said that in order to protect you, I should offer you a way out. The question is, are you going to take it?'

'What do you want?'

'Charles will explain.'

I opened the door and found Charles along the corridor. I told him what she'd asked.

'Oh, I think you know what we want,' Charles said. 'A fresh start for the bank. Your immediate resignation. Ally here's fallen on his sword, so to speak, and you don't have a leg to stand on. *Director of Compliance*, indeed. The CEO is expecting some kind of news, eh, this afternoon. And when, not if, you comply, we will forget the whole matter.'

And with that she stood up and grabbed her bag, leaving without a goodbye.

The board meeting was due the following day at 11:00 am, and I awaited any news of Carole McLetchie with interest. By one o'clock a newsfeed on the *Financial Times* website confirmed that the Director of Compliance at Scottish Chartered had resigned. Bingo.

Apparently, she was 'leaving to pursue new opportunities'.

Elise, Kostas and I met at the *Bonkers* Champagne bar in Stockbridge for a well deserved celebration. The bar attracted a young, professional clientele, and easing into the Friday night party atmosphere proved more than an enjoyable exercise: a total release. To hell with tomorrow's hangover. I ordered two bottles of Krug, and quietly filled my co-conspirators in on the last piece of news.

Speculation over Carole McLetchie's resignation had swept the bank like wildfire. Kostas was chuffed, saying that we'd slain a dragon. He had also refused to be remunerated for his endeavour, telling me he was well enough off and didn't need my charity. I explained that given I'd budgeted to send money to both Mandy and the woman Doug had conned with Gold Star then on that basis he surely deserved something. However, he objected, and I made a note to give his kids something later on, in a manner that he couldn't refuse.

When the time came to order another bottle, Kostas made to leave, telling us that he was no gooseberry. Despite how much I owed him for his help, there was more than an element of truth to his observation. I was sure that Elise felt the same. There are times in life when you just *know.*

We arrived back at my flat in jubilant spirits; I'd said that I had a proposition for Elise. Actually, I had two propositions. The latter one would have to wait, however. And as we slid into each other's arms I considered how much I had wanted this moment, and when it boils down to it, how money means nothing.

Epilogue

Elise walked slowly out to the side garden, the summer bloom bursting over the slate dyke that bordered the garden. A single white sail graced the middle distance, turning northwards. She watched as the yacht meandered away from the Isle of Lismore entering the sparkling azure expanse of Loch Linnhie. She filled her lungs with sea air. A rare, perfect day in the Highlands; the sort of time that she had learned to cherish, knowing that her future in Port Appin could never match the climate of her native North Carolina. However, she was content, for she had become a mother exactly three weeks before.

What I couldn't get my mind around however, was that I had become a father exactly three weeks before.

Elise had unexpectedly benefitted from an inheritance bequeathed by an aunt in Tennessee, one just substantial enough for us to realise a dream. We'd bought a small hotel in the Highlands, and we were making a go of it. We'd had our ups and downs, and it was hard work, though so far we had not regretted leaving the banking industry behind. Let someone else worry about the spin, the greed.

Though if I was truthful, there had still been a modicum of fear in my life. A morsel of guilt, and a nagging sliver of fear.

I'd been recalled by the police in Edinburgh, who were re-interviewing everyone connected to Leslie Weir's unsolved death. Barker and Wilson had acted in character once again, haranguing me. This time I kept my mouth shut, just listening and giving the occasional yes, no or maybe.

Then, the following day delivered an unexpected admission by a conscience-burdened lorry driver that he'd accidentally killed Leslie Weir.

This left me gobsmacked, for there's something I haven't shared with you.

Until now.

On the night after I argued with Leslie Weir in the bank car park, I overdid the booze big style and took a run in the car to his house to have it out with him once and for all. As I approached his leafy Morningside home he'd suddenly appeared at the roadside, putting out his bin. No one else was in sight, and serendipity is a strange thing. Perhaps we all have it within ourselves to kill, who knows? What I did I am not proud of, but as he turned to face my headlights I mounted the pavement, accelerated and ran the bastard over. I watched his bin collapsing on top of him in my rear-view mirror as I sped away.

This, as you will appreciate, had left me with quite a problem, but also a potential solution. Naturally, I assumed that *I'd* killed Leslie Weir, but from the morning after, denial to everyone—including myself—proved to be the best medicine. If a lorry driver wanted to take the rap, fine with me. Maybe he did kill Weir after all. And like Doug Mundel, Weir was a menace and had left no fatherless children to worry about, so to hell with him.

The second surprise had been the gory appearance of Doug's body in the quarry in West Lothian some weeks after his death. The police were baffled, as the body had contained apparently genuine non-photographic ID for someone who was already deceased—the oldest trick in the book. His face had been chewed by fish so they'd produced an artist's impression of what they figured he looked like, which was completely different. So much for modern science. If Carole McLetchie had put two and two together at that point then she'd kept her trap shut, wherever she was. She may have lost a half share of seven million, but she still wasn't stupid.

But all this was history.

Since baby Samantha had arrived, our world had become an exciting, if exhausting synthesis of nocturnal manoeuvring and perpetual customer service. Running a hotel is a 24:7 job, and if the demands of parenthood exceeded those of the guests, then only I could fill that gap. I relished the challenge, and right now Samantha was asleep in her pram in the back garden.

A bell sounded inside. Someone was at reception.

When I popped my head round the corner, two men stood inside the front door, one older and one younger. Their expressions were serious.

'Can I help you?'

The younger man held up a black bag, unzipping it with the other hand. 'Are you Ally Forbes?' He spoke with an eastern European accent.

A Russian accent?

'Yes…I'm Ally Forbes. Are you looking for a room?'

'No. We have something for you. Something from…how can we say…the past.' The younger man moved towards me holding some kind of parcel. I stood back swiftly.

'Are you okay, Mr Forbes?' The older man spoke, and then smiled broadly. 'This…is a gift we have gift for you.' The younger man thrust the parcel at me, also now smiling.

'Please open it.'

I took the parcel tentatively, and they both gazed at me. Unsure what to do I hesitated momentarily, but then an older lady arrived at the front door, speaking in what also sounded like Russian to the older man. She smiled pleasantly too.

'Sorry, we don't speak much English,' the older man said. As I opened the parcel, a card fell onto the floor. I opened it up and scanned the words.

Ally

I hope that you are well in your new life. I tracked you down. I have a new life too, in Ireland. I am sorry that I may have placed you in danger shortly after we last spoke, but I had a critical decision to make. I chose to speak to the Russians. My price for giving them Doug was to free my parents and my brother from Chechnya. These are dangerous people, but there is some kind of honour and I knew that they would uphold their part of the bargain, strangely. I never thought that this would be possible previously, so I have you to thank for my family's freedom. I am sorry for what I helped put you through, but hopefully everything has worked out well for us both. Please accept a gift from Chechnya. This is a good luck totem. Place it on a on your wall, and it will bring you...good luck.

Mandy

I opened the parcel, revealing a painting of two small children playing on a beach. I thanked Mandy's people. They said that they couldn't stay, but that they knew that they had me to thank for their freedom. When they left I looked at the picture, and placed it on the wall. Elise came in from the garden, looking curiously at the picture.

'A gift from an old friend,' I said.

She stared at the picture of the children playing. 'Puts you in the mood to have another, don't you think?'

'We could have fun trying,' I replied, smiling.

After all, isn't life all about incentives?

THE END

Acknowledgements

I am very grateful to my family for the patience they have shown while this novel was concocted. Jean Campbell and Anne Campbell took time to suggest revisions, as did Ian Hopkins. I appreciate the advice from John Duignan and the enthusiasm from Campbell and Joy Cameron at the Bookends Festival. I would also like to thank you, the reader–without readers the author has nothing. Online reviews are much appreciated.

Made in the USA
Charleston, SC
17 September 2016